The Wraith's Return

The Wraith's Return

The Martha's Vineyard Murders

Raemi A. Ray

The Wraith's Return

Tule Publishing First Printing August 2024

The Tule Publishing, Inc.

First Publication by Tule Publishing 2024

Cover design by eBookLaunch.com

ISBN: 978-1-962707-56-5

Dedication

For everyone whose favorite place is
their reading chair with a cat.

Chapter One

"FLIGHT ATTENDANTS, PREPARE for landing."

Kyra Gibson jerked awake, startled by the pilot's staticky voice over the comms system. She hadn't meant to doze off on the short flight from New York's JFK Airport to Martha's Vineyard. She peeked out her window, hoping for a glimpse of the tiny New England island that would be her home for the next several months, but she could only see miles and miles of the Atlantic Ocean's white-capped waves.

A pathetic mew drew her attention to her travel companion, crammed into the largest cat carrier she could find. His bottle green eyes stared up at her. Kyra reached down to scratch his snowy ears through the carrier flap and was awarded a toothy yawn.

"We'll be there shortly, Cronkers," she crooned, trying to soothe the hell spawn she'd inherited from her father along with his island home.

The plane gave a shudder as the landing gear descended. Kyra straightened in her seat. She gathered up the items she'd pulled from her carry-on before stowing it in the overhead bin—a New York newspaper and a thick folder embossed with her law firm's name and logo.

Assaf Maloof, a managing partner at her law firm in

London, and Kyra's boss, had nearly had an aneurism when she told him she was taking a leave of absence. He'd been rendered speechless for so long Kyra had pulled out her phone to call 999. Despite his threats to sack her immediately, Assaf eventually agreed she could use her holiday time to take the rest of the summer "off," but only if she made herself available whenever needed. She knew she'd be working full days from the house, but summer on Martha's Vineyard, even working, was better than staying in London.

The plane dipped and banked. Kyra sucked in a breath and clutched the armrests. *Bloody hell, I hate flying.* In truth, flying didn't bother her much, but she found the taking off and landing parts ... unpleasant. Her stomach flip-flopped. She unfolded the paper and scanned the headlines in an attempt to distract herself from the turbulent descent. She'd purchased it at a stand in LaGuardia, an old habit. Even now, years after her father's retirement, and months after his death, she found herself looking for his byline.

No good news. *There never is.* Political disruption, Russia being Russia, stock market volatility, a violent environmental protest in Florida. A blurb caught her eye and her lips stretched into a soft smile. It was an article in the climate section about the return of a rare bird to Cape Cod and the Islands, and the influx of bird watchers. Her gaze fell on the article just below and her smile fell away.

Phil Hawthorn Senate Hearing Scheduled. She grimaced. Apparently, the newly reopened investigation wasn't going so well for the senator. It felt like a lifetime ago when she'd first come to the island and stumbled upon the mystery of her father's death, and deciphered the clues he'd left behind, exposing a corrupt senator, and a conspiracy to commit bribery.

"Are you here to see the petrels?"

Kyra's head jerked up. Her seatmate appraised her with curious brown eyes behind wireframed glasses. She'd barely registered his presence during the flight. She blinked, confused. The man gestured to the paper she was holding, her thumb next to the title of the birdwatching article.

"Ah, uh, no. Just a holiday," she said, a little unnerved. Americans loved chatting with strangers.

"Oh." The man adjusted his glasses. His watch face glinted in the sun, making her squint. "Well, if you get a chance, I recommend it. They're spectacular."

"Right, I will. Thank you for the tip," she said, at a loss for what else to say. She knew nothing of birds, American or otherwise. He closed the magazine he was reading and slid it into his bag. *Dive USA.*

Before she could ask him about it, the plane's wheels hit the tarmac. She stuffed the paper into the seat back's media pocket and switched her phone out of airplane mode. Immediately, it began vibrating, earning her an annoyed side eye from the birdwatcher.

The small screen filled with texts—from Assaf, her aunt Ali in England, and her friends from the island. Nothing from Tarek Collins. She wasn't surprised, but she was still disappointed.

The seatbelt sign rang off. Her seatmate gave her a curt nod goodbye and moved out of the way so she could access the overhead. She pocketed her phone, pulled her bag from the bin above and, with Cronkite's massive cat carrier slung over her shoulder, Kyra disembarked.

She followed the signs to the baggage claim area, barely a two-minute walk from the airport's two gates. With one eye on the world's laziest luggage conveyor, she scrolled through her texts and missed calls. After an endless train of golf bags, her battered suitcases finally appeared. Cronkite screeched his protest at being jostled as Kyra wrangled them through the automatic doors.

She wheeled her bags out onto the sidewalk and was assaulted by the steamy humidity of July on the island. She paused and took in a deep breath, the first taste of fresh air in nearly fourteen hours. The shrubs buzzed with the sound of the cicadas. Birds chirped and cawed from the trees. She stood on the sidewalk, a little overwhelmed by the sensory overload, so different from the eerie sound muffling mist of the island in April.

Kyra squinted against the late afternoon sun and rummaged in her bag for her sunglasses. She didn't notice the man barreling toward her. Her surprised squeak was stifled when a muscular chest smashed into her face. Strong arms wrapped around her shoulders, crushing her against him. He laughed into her hair. His T-shirt smelled like sunshine and hay. Kyra struggled halfheartedly against his hug.

He pushed her back, his hands still on her shoulders. "Kay!" Chase Hawthorn's grin reached from ear to ear.

"Ugh!" She batted him away, her own smile matching his. His striking blue-green eyes sparkled with amusement. "You scared Cronk." She feigned a chastising look, biting her lip to keep from laughing.

Somehow, Chase's grin widened. "Is this all your stuff?"

He turned to her bags, reaching for them. "Hey there, buddy." He took Cronkite from her shoulder and peered at the disgruntled fur ball. "How was the flight?"

"Are you asking me or the cat?"

"The cat. He says it was terrible. The car is over here."

"I thought Grace was coming to get me..." Kyra's voice trailed off, but she followed Chase as he led her to the parking lot.

"I volunteered. She's stressed herself out preparing for Charlie's birthday party tonight. Something about the caterer? Julia took another job at the last minute." Chase shrugged. "I told her Charlie would be happy with a cake and a bottle of wine. But you know Grace."

Kyra did. The *small gathering* she'd agreed to attend at her neighbors' house six weeks ago was shaping up to be quite an event. One she'd rather avoid, if she were honest, but she'd promised to be there for her neighbors-turned-friends. To be there for Charlie.

"How many people did she invite that Charlie actually likes?"

"There's you and me, so at least two."

"And your date?"

Chase always had someone, or he used to, before. She'd begun to think his debauchery was all part of the part he played for the public.

He shook his head. "No date." Chase stopped behind a new but very dirty Ford Bronco and opened the trunk. Making it look easy, he lifted Kyra's giant suitcases, sliding them in one after the other.

"New car?" She raised an eyebrow at the borderline practical vehicle.

"Yep." He popped his lips on the *p* and closed the trunk. He placed Cronk's carrier on the backseat. Chase slid on a pair of black wayfarers, making him look like a movie star in "incognito" mode. "I traded in the Porsche a few months ago."

"Traded in?" Kyra hopped into the passenger seat and looked around. The SUV was indeed new, but already bore the markings of hard use. Dirt and straw stuck to the crevices, and the floor was littered with paper napkins and crumpled coffee cups.

"This seemed more appropriate for the farm. Since I'll be staying year-round now, I needed something that can get around in the snow and mud."

Kyra looked over at her friend and studied him through her mirrored glasses. He'd gained some weight in the last few months, lost the gaunt, haunted look from when they first met. His dark blond hair was lighter, bleached by the sun, and longer, flopping stubbornly into his unique eyes. His previously pale skin was tan in that bronzy, healthy glow of someone who spent all their time outside. He looked really good, and she said as much with a big smile that grew bigger when Chase Hawthorn, notorious playboy, actually blushed, a soft pink creeping up his tan neck.

"Thanks, you don't look terrible, either."

"You flatter me," she deadpanned and resisted the urge to pinch him. "Thank you for picking me up."

"Of course." He glanced at her, his eyes moving behind his glasses. "I missed you."

"How?" she asked, laughing.

Kyra pushed her sunglasses into her hair and flipped down the sun visor to check her face in the mirror. Red-rimmed eyes looked back at her, made more obvious by the dark circles below. She sighed and snapped the visor back into place. Months of poor sleep had taken their toll. She had been functioning in a state of half exhaustion. Her skin had turned wan and dull. *A seaside holiday is just what I need.* It was what she'd been telling herself for weeks.

She pulled her glasses back down. "We talk every day."

They did. After she'd returned to London, she'd sent him a gift basket of English snacks as an inadequate but sincere thank you for saving her life. He'd called her appalled with the selection of potato crisps she'd included. They'd talked for hours. From there, they'd fallen into the easy habit of talking or texting every day and through many nights. He was the rode, connecting her to the island. It was Chase who ultimately convinced her to come back. She still wasn't certain whether she'd finally agreed for him or for her, perhaps both.

"I've missed you, too," she relented. "How's Mander Lane?"

"The farm is good. The restaurant is packed most days. According to Sara, it actually turns a profit." He sounded like it surprised him. "And with my parents staying in DC this year, the staff is much happier." A crease formed above the frames of his glasses.

She knew he struggled with the reality that everyone, including him, was much happier with Senator Hawthorn and his wife's extended absence. Thankfully, his parents, or their lawyers, had had the good sense to keep the farm in a trust, so despite his family's legal troubles, Chase's home was safe. In Kyra's opinion, the best thing to have happened to Chase was the complete implosion of his toxic family.

"And Adele?" Last Kyra had heard, Chase's half-sister had agreed to testify against her stepfather, in exchange for a sentence reduction, but she'd still be serving many decades in prison for the murders of Kyra's father and Chase's boyfriend.

Chase's smile melted away, and he shook his head. "The judge accepted the plea bargain just yesterday. She's being transported to a high security prison sometime this month."

"How's the halter training going?" Kyra asked steering the conversation toward less fraught territory.

"Barbossa is a horse prodigy." Chase's smile returned. He'd been helping train up the foal born on the farm last spring and had been sending Kyra nonstop photos and videos of the little horse, all tufty mane, and bobbin tail.

"Barbossa?"

"That's what I named him. He's a right wee bastard," he said in a terrible Brummie accent, eliciting another laugh from her. "You're going to love him."

"After the Disney movie?"

"The character was named after real pirates," he said dryly, lifting an eyebrow, and then under his breath, he muttered, "I think."

Kyra grinned and turned to look out the window.

The trees that had been bare in April were all filled out. Leaves danced in the gentle sea breeze. The hydrangea and rhododendron that seemed to grow wild on the island were in full bloom, splashing the landscape in paint splats of blues and pinks.

"It looks so different."

"Yeah, the island in the summer is a totally different vibe. And *crowded.*"

Now that he mentioned it, she noticed that there were more cars on the road. As they made their way closer to South Beach, and Kyra's house, the congestion increased, and not just on the road, but on the bike paths that ran alongside the roads, too. The traffic flowed in the opposite direction, visitors returning home from the beach in the late afternoon. Chase turned off the street, and the tires crunched on the gravel of her driveway.

Kyra peered through the windshield and took in Ed's—her—house. The white colonial with black accents was a stark contrast to the lush greenery and bright blue sky. Chase was watching her, and with a steadying breath, she stepped out of the car.

Kyra worried her bottom lip. A million emotions ran through her—anxiety for what the next few months would bring, grief for her dead parents who'd loved it here, joy and trepidation to be back on the island, to be here in front of her house once again. It was all too much to process, leaving her mouth feeling dry and her palms damp. She tried to swallow, but her tongue felt too big.

She had never had a real home before, not really. The apartment her parents rented in New York was a postal address, a place to stay between her father's assignments. Then, after her mother passed from breast cancer, Kyra was sent to live with her aunt in London. From there, she hopped from her aunt's rowhouse, to her college dorm, to law school and her associateship, and then finally her drab flat in London. Each place was meant to be temporary, until she finally found what she wanted with more permanence. At some point, she'd stopped looking. This house was the first thing that could be entirely and truly hers. If she wanted it, for as long as she wanted it.

Using the keypad Detective Tarek Collins had insisted she install; she unlocked the front door and pushed it open. Kyra held her breath, uncertain what she'd find in the house she'd left three months ago. The tingly feeling that settled in her chest, though, when her gaze swept the room, was the comfortable, relieved feeling of finally coming *home*. Her body felt lighter. The stress and uncertainty about returning that had plagued her over the last few months sloughed off, as she stepped into her foyer.

It was the same.

The back wall was entirely made of glass. The furnishings were contemporary and minimalist, highlighting the view of the sloping backyard and Crackatuxet Cove below. Only now, she could barely see the water through the thick vegetation surrounding it.

Something beeped. It beeped again. Kyra spun around.

"The security system," Chase said, dropping her bags on the floor. "Charlie showed me." He pressed in the code, showing her how to enable and disable the alarms.

They had been installed after she left, again at the detective's insistence. Chase went back to the car and returned with the cat carrier. He set it down and opened it. "Freedom, buddy!"

Cronk took a few tentative steps into the room, gave the

humans a withering glare, and with his signature tail flick, trotted away.

"Nice cat."

Kyra watched her pet saunter off to become reacquainted with his favorite spots.

"Charlie had the place cleaned and made ready for you."

"Of course she did." Kyra made a note to thank her.

"Where do you want your bags?" Chase asked, pulling on one of her rolling suitcases.

"Oh, I can take care of it."

Chase looked down his nose at her, peering over his sunglasses.

"Fine." She grabbed her carry-on from the floor. "I'll take the primary bedroom. It's upstairs at the back of the house. I'll show you." She led Chase up the stairs and into the largest bedroom that had once been her father's.

Detective Collins had moved her into this room after rescuing her and Charlie from the Hawthorns' sailboat last spring. Now that she'd sort of decided to not sell the house, at least not right away, it made more sense to stay in the primary suite with the view *and the walk-in closet.*

"The bags can go in here." She opened the doors to the walk-in, not much smaller than her old bedroom in London. Chase dropped off her suitcase, then ran downstairs for the second one. He deposited it next to the other before flopping down lengthwise on one of the two sofas making up the bedroom's sitting area.

"Get cleaned up. Then we'll walk over to Charlie and Grace's." He waved toward the en suite bathroom and folded his hands behind his head.

"What?" She looked up from her bags, her hands on her hips.

"Don't unpack now. Grace said that unless I walked you over there myself, you'd probably just ignore us and stay inside all night."

Kyra frowned. *I do want to do that.* Again, her emotions bubbled uncomfortably, simultaneously annoyed Grace interfered, and a little pleased she knew her well enough to know to.

"It's Charlie's birthday party. Of course, I wouldn't miss it."

Chase made a coughing noise that sounded an awful lot like *bullshit.* "If you don't show up, you know Charlie will leave her own party to hide away here with you." The way he said it, Kyra suspected he found the idea appealing, too.

"She would. She hates these things. Why does she let Grace talk her into them?" Kyra opened her bags. "What do I wear?" She sighed.

"I don't know. Clothes?" he said and waved to his own T-shirt and shorts.

Kyra glared in his direction. To be fair to him, Chase didn't need to worry about improving his appearance. He could wear a trash bag and still turn heads.

"Charlie was trying to get out of it this morning. Said she was sick." Chase mimed coughing and put the back of his hand to his forehead with an over dramatic sigh.

"Grace didn't fall for it, I take it?" Kyra unearthed her toiletries bag and headed to the bathroom. "Telly remote should be on the table. If you can't find it, call Grace," she called over her shoulder and stepped into the bright white bathroom.

She turned on the shower, but her gaze fell to the oversized soaking tub. Embarrassment heated her cheeks at the memory of the last and only time she'd used it. She'd had two broken ribs, and a torn shoulder. Tarek, *Detective Collins*, had to help her take a bath and get dressed. It had been mortifying. That he'd stayed with her to help her when she was injured made his sustained silence sting that much more. Turning her back on the tub, she stepped into the shower.

The water cleansed her of the grime of travel. She took her time scrubbing away at her airplane-dry skin. The door cracked open, and she let out a little squeal.

"Kay, hurry up. I'm *staarrving*," Chase whined from the other side of the door and slammed it shut.

Grumbling, she turned off the water and grabbed one of the plush towels. She emerged from the bathroom and squatted down in front of her bags. She chose a minimally wrinkled white sundress and slid on a pair of sandals. Her still-damp dark hair fell down her back in tousled waves and Kyra prayed her anti-frizz hair product worked miracles. She checked herself in the mirror, smoothing her dress.

"You look great. Let's go. I'm *soooo* hungry!" Chase called from the couch; his eyes glued to the sports news broadcast on the television.

Wanker. Kyra pressed her lips together and gave him an epic side-eye he couldn't see.

"I'm ready." She yanked her denim jacket from the bottom of one of her suitcases, spilling all its contents on the floor. "Fucking hell," she mumbled.

She tried to stuff it back in, but gave up, leaving it where it fell, a future nest for the white house demon who'd assuredly find it.

Chase jumped up and spun around with a flourish. He moved with surprising grace for someone so tall and lanky.

"Will we know anyone there besides Charlie?"

"Umm." Chase rubbed his jaw. "Grace?" He shrugged and gave her a look that said he knew exactly what she was thinking. *Who* she was really asking about. Kyra's heart sank, but she wasn't sure what she'd expected.

When Grace had called a few weeks ago about the party, Kyra had wanted to ask whether Grace was inviting the detective. She knew he talked to the Chamberses in her absence. Chase had told her that when he was on the island, Tarek made a point of checking in on Charlie, and the two had struck up an easy friendship over their shared enthusiasm for Boston sports. Only two weeks ago, Chase had watched a baseball game with them at the Chamberses' house. But, she reasoned, if he was planning on attending, someone would have mentioned it to her. It was also possible he wasn't invited or available. Tarek lived on the mainland, and his work with the state police investigatory unit required him to travel all over the state.

When she'd last been on the island, she'd thought she and the detective had become friends. With the perspective of hindsight, she realized she'd had bouts of madness thinking they'd formed a team of sorts when they'd uncovered the conspiracy her father had been investigating before his death and then solved the murders. She'd even thought something more was growing between them. He'd driven her all the way to Boston for her flight back to London because he knew how much she hated the tiny propeller planes that serviced the island in the off season.

When she returned to England, they'd spoken a few times, mostly about the case and her answers to the prosecution's interrogatories. Then, when the case was turned over to the Department of Justice, Tarek had gone silent. She'd texted at the end of June about her plan to return in July, but it had gone unanswered. Whatever she'd thought they had started last spring, she'd been mistaken.

Kyra followed Chase outside and across the yard. They slipped through the brambly hedgerow, taking her father's old shortcut. While both her and the Chambers' properties backed up to Crackatuxet Cove, their addresses were on different dead-end streets. The fastest route between the houses was a trampled down path through a narrow no-man's-land.

Grace and Charlie's house was like the older sibling to hers, nearly identical, but grander. Kyra's house was charming and quaint by comparison.

A Jimmy Buffett song was playing from a speaker in the backyard and Chase chuckled, his eyes sparkling.

"Charlie's deejaying. Want to take bets on how often Grace clutches her pearls tonight?" Chase mimed grabbing at his neck, his eyes going to the sky.

"No bet. Grace doesn't wear pearls." Kyra grinned, picturing Grace's frustrated face, her lips pursed, and those perfectly penciled eyebrows furrowed.

They rounded the house into the backyard, where the party was already in full swing. Buffet tables had been set up along the perimeter of the patio, decorated like a tablescape-spread in a hosting magazine. Pillar candles and flower arrangements had been set at varying heights for visual interest. Strategically placed garlands surrounded platters overflowing with food. A temporary bar had been set up on the far side of the patio where a young woman wearing a tie was vigorously shaking a cocktail shaker. Despite the summery warmth, a low fire burned in the giant bluestone hearth, adding to the casual, elegant ambiance.

"She doesn't do anything by half, does she?" Chase murmured in her ear.

No, Grace certainly doesn't. Kyra hummed her agreement. A server walked in front of them with a tray of hors d'oeuvres. Chase let out a noise that sounded a lot like a whimper and her mouth tugged into an amused smirk. Charlie was standing in front of a table staring at a Bluetooth speaker, phone in hand, a wicked gleam in her eye. From a few feet away, Grace glared at her wife, her painted pink lips pursed just so. Chase saw them at the same time and raised his eyebrows in delight.

"Look who I found!" Chase shouted above the blaring music. Kyra bit back her giggle when she recognized the song. Nineties novelty rap. *Grace is going to strangle her.* Grace spun around. Her grimace smoothed out and she opened her arms welcoming them. The music volume plummeted.

"Kyra!" Grace grabbed Charlie's arm and yanked her toward Kyra and Chase. "Char, look!" Grace beamed. "Our dear girl is home!"

"It's so good to see you." Kyra hugged her friend, careful

not to rumple Grace's linen pantsuit. "Happy birthday, Charlie." She met Charlie's warm brown eyes.

"Welcome back!" Charlie gave Kyra a kiss on the cheek. "How was the flight?"

"It was fine. Just long." She made a show of looking around at the well-dressed guests. "How's the party?"

"Wonderful!" Grace singsonged at the same time Charlie barked, "Boring."

"Char," Grace admonished. "It's *your birthday*. You're having a lovely time."

"I will now. Drinks?" Charlie rubbed her hands together.

"Chase, how are you, dear?" Grace asked, turning her back on Charlie.

"Very well, thank you. And you?" He dropped a kiss on her cheek and winked at Charlie over Grace's shoulder.

Kyra caught Charlie's mischievous grin. She shifted her gaze between them. Charlie looked too pleased; Chase's smile too smarmy. *They're up to something.* Kyra felt a pang of sympathy for Grace. Chase pulled a pristine envelope from his pocket.

"Happy birthday, Charlie. From Kay and I." Kyra read the logo and pressed her lips together to keep from laughing. International Beer of the Month Club.

"What? For me?" Charlie tore the envelope open with a screech. "Beer from every nation?! Look, Grace! We can have lager from Lichtenstein, pilsners from Palau!" Charlie hopped up and down, her wild curls bouncing.

"Lovely. I can hardly wait." Grace frowned, her eyes narrowing on Chase. She took the envelope between her thumb and pointer finger and passed it to a server. "Michelle, can you put this in the kitchen, please?"

"Thanks, guys! I can't wait until the first shipment comes. Grace, what do you think it'll be?" Charlie beamed and hugged them both.

Chase nudged Kyra with his elbow and shut his left eye in an exaggerated wink. She let out a breath. *This is going to be a long night.*

"Come, dear. I'll introduce you to the other guests." Charlie rolled her eyes as Grace linked her arm through Kyra's and steered her toward the party. Chase disappeared into the crowd, reappearing a moment later to press a champagne glass into her hand. He gave her a jaunty salute before disappearing again.

The sun inched closer to the horizon, stretching the shadows on the lawn, and the guests shifted closer to the hearth as much for light as warmth. Kyra was glad for her jacket and pulled the sleeves down over her palms.

"Excuse me, I think I need a refill." She raised her empty champagne flute and excused herself from the dullest debate over the proposed renovations to Fenway stadium between two gentlemen from Grace's pickleball club. *Where has Chase gone?* She scanned the crowd. A server walked by with a tray of fancy-looking chicken wings, and she pounced on him when he paused. She heaped a pile onto a napkin and received a judgmental frown that would have rankled her if she wasn't so hungry.

She was just biting into one of the saucy drumettes when someone tapped her shoulder.

"Kyra, I want you to meet my childhood BFF Lisa," Charlie said, her hand on the arm of a blonde woman. "Lisa, this is Kyra Gibson, our new neighbor. Kyra, Lisa Mackey."

"Oh, hello." Kyra hastily dropped her snack on a table and wiped the sauce from her lips and fingers.

"It's so nice to finally meet you," Lisa said and gave Charlie a one-armed hug. "Charlie's told me so much about you."

"Nice to meet you, too." Kyra watched with dismay as a server picked up and disposed of her snack. "Childhood friends? You must have grown up on the island, then?"

"I did. Charlie and I met in grade school and quickly became best friends over cats' cradle, I think."

"Wasn't it that ball and chain toy? The one that wrapped around your ankle, and you had to skip around?" Charlie tilted her head and pressed her lips together. "I'm pretty sure we met because I had the pink one and you had blue, and I wanted blue."

"Oh, you may be right. I can't remember." Lisa laughed. "We couldn't have been more than seven or eight."

Lisa wore pressed green cotton shorts and a complementary short sleeve pale blue blouse with mother-of-pearl buttons. She'd thrown a lightweight cream sweater over her shoulders, tied at the neck. With her neat platinum bob and bright blue eyes, she looked like she'd stepped out of a Vineyard Vines catalog. Standing next to Charlie, who was dressed in a faded Red Sox sweatshirt and utility shorts, Kyra couldn't help but think the two an unlikely pair.

"What were those things called again? A hopper?" Charlie frowned. "No, that's not it. Whatever. Anyway, Lisa, Kyra is spending the summer on the island, and, Kay, Lisa teaches seventh grade in West Tisbury." Charlie beamed at her friend, like teaching preteens made her a superhero.

I suppose it does.

"West Tisbury? Is that where you live?"

"No." Lisa shook her head. "My husband and I live in Chilmark, but I grew up in Tisbury, same as Charlie. I moved up island when I got married."

"We all went to high school together. Her husband and his family run a fishing company, Mackey Fishing, Co. Speaking of, where is your other half tonight? I haven't seen him." Charlie swiveled her head, looking around the crowd.

"Oh, he's at the Raven's Nest or at home in front of the television. Sox game." Lisa lifted her hand and let it drop. "What can you do, right? He said if we're still up, he'd stop by after the game."

Kyra shook off Lisa's apology. The New Englander's love for their local teams bordered on the fanatical.

"Oh, we'll be up. Won't we, Kyra?" Charlie asked, finishing whatever cocktail had been in her glass.

"We'll see." Kyra forced a yawn behind her hand.

It wasn't a total lie. The long day of travel was catching up with her. Charlie looked like she was going to argue when Grace's voice pierced the din from behind them.

"Ida! There you are. You made it. I've been dying to ask. Do you have news about the discovery?"

Kyra turned around. Grace was on the couch, next to a Black woman with close-cropped hair. Colorful chandelier earrings accentuated her long neck. Kyra caught Charlie's eye and nodded toward the woman.

"That's Ida Ames," Charlie whispered in Kyra's ear. "She's head of the Martha's Vineyard Community Council, a quasi-political organization. She knows everything worth knowing."

Kyra could almost hear Charlie's eyes rolling.

"What discovery?" Kyra whispered back.

"Oh, yeah." Chase appeared as if out of nowhere.

He handed Kyra a glass of champagne and reached over Grace's shoulder to grab two mini lobster rolls from the platter sitting on the table.

He handed one to Kyra and shoved the other into his mouth. "I heard something about that. That storm that hit Gay Head a few nights ago. It caused a microburst," he said around chews. "Disrupted the seabed of the ravine next to the Devil's Bridge shoal. Uncovered something. Jimmy said they thought it looked like a wreck."

"Devil's Bridge shoal?" Kyra repeated.

"Mmhmm. It's a shallows bordering a deep ravine in the Vineyard Sound. The lighthouse up at Gay Head warns boats away from it."

"A wreck? Like a boat crashed? Was anyone hurt?" The pitch of Charlie's voice rose.

Kyra wondered if she was thinking of their own narrow escape from a boat lost in a storm.

"No, Charlene." Ida shook her head. "The council received the preliminary images earlier this morning. It looks like whatever is down there is old." Ida waved her hand. Her rings glinted in the firelight. "There have been no unrecovered salvage contracts in the Vineyard Sound for over fifty years. So, the Coast Guard estimates it's at least that old. Likely just flotsam or jetsam, or something from World War II. We're waiting on the experts. Mr. Hawthorn, that

Jimmy knows better than to spread rumors." Ida pressed her lips together and gave Chase a stern look that wavered somewhere between annoyance and affection.

He flashed his paparazzi smile, all white teeth and playboy charm. Ida huffed and turned back to Grace. Kyra raised an eyebrow at him. Chase's lips dipped into a smirk, and he hopped over the couch back, sliding into the seat next to Ida. He slung his arm around her shoulder. Ida went rigid. Then she let out a honking guffaw.

Soft coral spots bloomed on her cheeks. "Oh, you're still trouble, Chase Hawthorn." Ida shook her head, her heavy earrings swaying.

Chase grabbed another mini lobster roll from the table, looking very pleased with himself. "I'm thinking of sailing out sometime this week for a closer look. Any interest?" Chase glanced around at the crowd. "Charlie?"

"Absolutely fucking not," Charlie spat.

The vehemence in her tone shocked Kyra, and the rest of the surrounding group fell quiet. The music from the speaker blared loud in the sudden silence. Someone cleared their throat.

"I've had enough *sailing* for a lifetime after the *Neamhnaid*." Charlie glared at him.

Chase froze, his hand halfway to his mouth. Even in the shadows, Kyra noticed the anguish flicker behind his eyes. Despite the many times she'd told him that it wasn't his fault, that neither she nor Charlie blamed him, she knew he felt responsible for what had happened to them on his mother's sailboat. As quick as it appeared, he shuttered it away, settling his features into a mask of boredom. He raised one shoulder in a lazy shrug and stuffed the lobster roll into his mouth.

"Anyone else? Ida?" His smile was all teeth this time. "What do you say?"

"Hell will freeze over before you get me on that death trap you've got anchored in Menemsha."

"Suit yourself." Chase huffed.

Kyra thought he almost sounded hurt. She moved closer to the fire and sat down in the empty seat next to him.

"Hold my seat. I'll get us more drinks." Chase stomped off.

She pulled her jacket tighter and shivered. She was only half-listening to Ida explain in tedious detail the plans for a new hotel that was to be developed in the fall. Weariness settled on her shoulders. She yawned for real this time. *I'm ready to go home*, she thought and her chest warmed when she realized she meant the house just a few yards away. She didn't want another drink, just her bed.

Where is Chase?

As if hearing her thoughts, "Kay!" he hollered from in front of the speaker.

He was holding a mic. Charlie was standing next to him. She was holding one, too. Kyra froze. *Oh, no. No.* He motioned for her to join them while Charlie scrolled through her phone. Music started playing.

"Happy birthday, Charlie Chambers!" Chase crowed, swaying to the music.

"Thank you, Chase Hawthorn." Charlie bowed and started singing, "*They say we're young and we don't know...*"

Kyra slipped off the couch and strode for the house as

fast as she could without breaking into a run. She glanced over her shoulder at Chase's mock disappointed pout. Without missing a beat, he turned to Charlie and sang, "*Well, I don't know if all that's true...*"

Sonny and Cher? Kyra couldn't suppress her chuckle as she slipped inside. *They're children.* Charlie's voice was getting louder and more off key. Chase was laughing so hard his own lyrics were unintelligible. Shaking her head, Kyra stepped into the Chamberses' kitchen.

Two people were standing close together in front of the sink. Kyra's sandals *clicked* on the hardwood floor, and they sprang apart.

"Oh. Pardon me," Kyra mumbled, hovering in the doorway.

The man stepped back as if to put distance between himself and the woman.

Oh, that's Charlie's friend... Lisa, was it?

Kyra glanced between them. The man cleared his throat.

"I was just looking for the loo? Sorry, restroom?" Heat creeped up her neck, and she made to step around them.

The man rubbed the back of his neck and peered at her from under his lashes before stuffing his hands into his pockets. "I'm Andrew. Andrew Mackey." Kyra glanced at Lisa, who also looked embarrassed. "This is Lisa."

Lisa attempted a weak smile.

Oh, the husband.

"Nice to meet you. I'm Kyra, Grace and Charlie's neighbor." She waved in the general direction of her house.

"The restroom is through there." Lisa pointed and raised an empty glass to her lips.

"Right, thank you." Kyra ducked into the powder room.

She leaned against the sink and peered at her face in the mirror. Her eyes were bloodshot, and her dark circles had become more pronounced. She checked her phone. The battery was barely hanging on. *It's gone 3 a.m. in London.*

She rubbed her forehead and splashed cool water on her face, trying to wake herself up.

Kyra returned to the backyard, taking care to avoid the kitchen and Lisa and Andrew Mackey. She found Grace and Charlie sitting next to the fire, talking, their hands entwined.

"I'm going to head home. It was a lovely party, Grace. Happy birthday." She pressed her cheek against Charlie's. "I'll talk to you ladies tomorrow?"

"Go on, dear. Get some rest. We'll see you tomorrow."

"Thank you for the present. I love it."

Grace rolled her eyes in a perfect imitation of her wife.

Kyra snuck away, avoiding drawn-out goodbyes with Grace's friends and headed toward the path. She had just stepped through the break in the hedgerow when she heard a noise behind her and whirled around, her heart in the throat.

"Leaving without me?" Chase put a hand to his heart.

"Do *not* sneak up on me! Jesus!" Her hands fisted at her sides.

"Calm down. I'm ready to go, too." He grinned and pushed his long blonde hair out of his eyes. "How can you see out here?"

"I barely can, but my phone is dead."

Chase pulled his phone from his pocket and shined the light on the ground, so they could walk back.

Kyra stepped on the first tread of her front porch and

turned around to say goodbye, but Chase pulled her into a hug, flattening her against him.

"I'm glad you're back," he whispered into her hair.

"I'm glad to be back." It was the truth. She pressed her cheek against his warm chest and wrapped her arms around his waist. Chase rested his chin on her head and gave her a gentle squeeze. Kyra let herself lean into him.

She remembered a late-night phone call weeks ago when he boasted about giving the best hugs. She'd assumed he was full of shit, but no, Chase Hawthorn gave excellent hugs.

"I'll see you tomorrow," she said, pulling away.

"Count on it. G'night." Chase waved and climbed into his car.

Kyra dragged herself through the front door. She barely made it up the stairs and into the bathroom to brush her teeth. Dropping her dress on the floor, she didn't bother searching for pajamas before sliding into bed. Her eyes were closed before her head even touched the pillow.

Chapter Two

THE GREEN AND gold Mander Lane Farm arbor came into view and Kyra navigated her SUV down the gravel drive to the public parking area. Since she'd been here last, the farm had bloomed. The fields were green and lush with whatever crops Sara, the farm manager, was growing, and the air was thick with the rich scents of earth, grass, and wild-flowers. Cars filled the public parking area. The deck of the farm's restaurant, L'Huitre, was full. People bustled in and out of the farm stand carrying Mander Lane Farm branded tote bags.

When she'd visited in the spring, the farm's pickings had been limited, contained to a small shed. Now in the season's peak, the shed's goods overflowed into the surrounding yard. Wood crates containing fresh produce, fruit, bouquets of flowers, and loaves of bread sat on folding tables shaded by canopies. It all looked delicious, and Kyra made a note to grab a few things for home before she left.

"Kyra!" Sara waved from the shop doorway. Her entire body shook with the effort.

"Hi, Sara." She returned Sara's wave, but with less enthusiasm. Still, two shoppers cast her a wary glance and gave her a wide berth.

"You're here. Staying for the summer," Sara said, not bothering with unnecessary pleasantries.

"Yes. Got in yesterday. I'm staying for as long as I can. How are you?" Floor fans whirred, keeping the heat inside the shed barely tolerable. Sara opened a box and began stacking bottles of jams and jellies on a shelf.

"Fantastic, actually." Sara's tone bordered on cheerful, and Kyra glanced around the room to see if anyone else noticed. They didn't. Cheerful was a new look on the stern woman she'd met months ago and apparently the new norm. "We're partnering with local businesses, which means we've been able to reduce our production and still diversify our offerings." Sara held up one of the jams. "With Margot gone, Chase has given me free rein. We're running it just the way we want."

"That's great news. I'm glad it's working out with Chase." Kyra had no doubt Sara would make a success of it.

"Me, too." Sara stepped down from the stool she'd been standing on. "He told me to tell you to meet him. He's down in the west field." Sara briefly described the best route and made Kyra promise to stop by before she left.

With a subdued wave goodbye, Kyra walked down the path. She checked her phone and bit back an annoyed grumble. She had at least a half dozen texts from Assaf. Too many. She'd already spent two hours going over a contract with him and her clients this morning. Now he was checking in on other clients. Kyra gritted her teeth. *I delegated all of this to the associates.* She ignored her boss, knowing she'd pay for it later, and scrolled through to the earliest text. It was from her aunt Ali.

Ali asked after her flight, the house, and, of course, Cronkite the cat. She'd also sent photos of her seven-month-old son, Iggy. She'd dressed him like a sailor with a tiny BON VOYAGE sign. Kyra swiped through the photos of her increasingly unhappy little cousin and she couldn't help the pinch of disappointment.

Ali and her husband Cam had been planning to join Kyra for a week or two this summer, but Iggy came down with a serious ear infection and his doctor recommended they postpone flying. They still planned on visiting before Ali's parental leave ended, and when Cam could get away from work.

She turned a corner, and the site of the old barn came into view. Kyra took in the bald landscape. Gone were the skeletal burnt-out remnants of the barn destroyed by a fire set by Chase's sister after she murdered his boyfriend. Nothing replaced it, not even grass. There was just a dirty muddy hole where it had stood, as if the earth itself still grieved.

Just beyond the demolition site, spread out over the west field, was a cluster of small temporary structures that housed the animals until the new barn was complete. She entered the second one, the one Sara designated for the horses. Chase was standing in the largest stall, with a big bay mare and a gangly foal.

He must have heard her, because he turned as she stepped inside.

His face lit up with a genuine boyish grin few people saw. "You made it." He opened the gate so Kyra could see inside. He spread his hand to introduce the little foal. "This is Barbossa." Barbossa peeked out from under his mother's belly, his too big ears twirling in all directions.

"You can pet him." Chase said.

Kyra murmured soft sounds to the little colt as she approached him. She rubbed his silky ears and muzzle. His big momma eyed her and with a snuff, turned her attention to the hay Chase was piling into her feed tray.

"He's precious, Chase." She squatted down for better access. The noises she made could only be described as coos. Barbossa pressed into her, moving his rump to get prime scratches.

"The training is going really well. He's learning to be led." Chase was beaming, his chest puffed out. "Wanna see? We can take them for a walk."

"Yes, please." She'd never wanted anything more.

Chase showed her how to halter and lead Goldie, then handed her the rope. The gritty nylon was rough and foreign between her fingers. Chase buckled the tiny halter and lead on Barbossa. Kyra had loved horses since she was a little girl, but growing up moving around with her parents, then living in London, she hadn't had many opportunities to see them up close. She was grinning like an idiot as they led the horses out of the barn.

Goldie plodded along, stopping to snag grass alongside the path. Barbossa skipped and hopped around Chase, tangling him up in the lead. Chase told her about the summer crops, the new planting and harvesting schedule, his frustration with a change in feed supplier. Kyra half-listened, less interested in what he was saying but engrossed in his enthusiasm for the farm. He fell quiet when they walked by the site of the old barn and Kyra peeked at him through the side of her eye.

"Chase?"

His gaze met hers, and his mouth tugged into a quivery smile. "I feel like it's bad luck to walk by it, you know?" She did. "It's weird because Brendan and I, we weren't that close. We'd only started seeing each other, but I'd liked him. He was a good person. He didn't deserve what happened to him." His pace slowed to a stop, and he stared at the ground. When he spoke, his voice was barely a whisper. "I feel like I should feel worse than I do, and that's what keeps me up at night."

Kyra reached out and squeezed his forearm. She understood. It wasn't so different for her. She struggled with coming to terms with her father's death. The man had abandoned her when she was twelve. She'd barely known him as an adult. His death asked her to mourn his loss all over again.

"You don't have to feel guilty for surviving, Chase."

He held her gaze and his eyes glistened with gratitude. He pushed his hair off his forehead, clicked his tongue, and urged the horses forward.

Chase was telling her about the agriculture fair later that summer and his intent to enter Titus, their award-winning silkie chicken and reigning champion, when his phone buzzed. He pulled it from his pocket and his eyebrows shot over the rims of his sunglasses. He made a motion for her to wait.

"Hey," he answered, and stepped a little away. "Yeah."

Kyra wasn't trying to listen to Chase's one-sided conversation, but Goldie wouldn't move more than a few feet from her baby. She was stuck, awkwardly stroking Goldie's neck, pretending she couldn't hear.

"Yeah, maybe," Chase said into his phone. "She's here now."

Kyra's hand froze, and she dropped all pretense of not listening.

Chase turned to face her and scraped his hand across his jaw. "Fine. I'll ask." Chase made an annoyed face. "I don't know. I'll see you soon." He hung up and slid the phone back into his pocket.

Kyra clicked her tongue, coaxing Goldie forward. They walked in silence for a very long thirty seconds before she broke down.

"Who was that?" she asked, trying to sound casual.

"Tarek."

"Mmhhmm," Kyra hummed. It seemed like the safest response. That and not acknowledging the uncomfortable way, her stomach dropped.

"He just arrived on the island and is meeting Gully at the pub. He asked if we'd like to join them. Gully has some big news."

Kyra thought it over. She felt like she wasn't really wanted, that if she hadn't been with Chase just now, the invitation wouldn't have been extended.

"No, I don't think so."

Chase made a frustrated noise in the back of his throat. "Just come. You don't have anything else to do, do you?"

Kyra shook her head. She could work, she supposed.

"Good. Now you have something to do. We're going."

Kyra narrowed her eyes at him, but didn't argue.

"I'll take the horses back." He took Goldie's lead from her hand. "We're meeting there at three." Chase led mom and baby away. He stopped, turned back and said, his voice mock stern, "Don't be late."

Kyra showed him her favorite finger.

Chapter Three

DESPITE THE HEAVY traffic and crowded streets, Kyra made decent time returning home. She'd had plenty of time to put away the groceries she'd purchased at the farm stand and take a quick shower before driving into Edgartown. Kyra found parking a few blocks away and walked up Water Street, taking in the shops' festive window displays. She paused outside a window where a man in an old-fashioned paper hat folded fudge on a marble slab. He raised a dish through the window, offering her a sample. Kyra declined with a wave and turned right down Kelly Street.

When Gully's pub came into view, she stopped on the sidewalk. The ivy clinging to the building was a rich dark green. Someone had cut it back around the pub's ancient oak door. Hydrangea bloomed in boxes separating the sidewalk from an outside eating area. She pulled her phone from her purse and shifted her weight. She debated whether to beg off, go home. *Chase would probably come get me, or worse, convince them to come to mine.* She let loose a defeated sigh, smoothed the front of her saffron-colored sundress, and slipped inside.

Gully's pub was cool. The fieldstone walls insulated the dank bar from the oppressive July heat. It looked much the same as she remembered, with minor changes for the summer season. There were more tables. They'd been crammed into every available space, pushed against the walls and even the fireplace. Extra high-top tables stood in front of the bar to accommodate standing patrons. Ceiling fans spun lazily, barely stirring the thick air, heavy with the too sweet scents of varnish and beer.

Kyra scanned the cozy restaurant, searching for Chase, but her gaze alighted on Gully, instead. The massive pub master was wiping down a table. He noticed her a half a beat after she saw him, and his bushy eyebrows rose in surprise.

His beard split in half, and she caught a white flash of teeth. "London!" His voice boomed across the room, and he waved a paw at her.

Kyra scowled at the nickname, and Gully let out a barking sound that could have been a laugh.

"Hi, Gully, how've you been?" She looked up at the mountain of a man.

His giant hand engulfed hers. "The AC is on the fritz, and it's hotter than Satan's balls out there, but can't complain … much." He barked again. *Definitively a laugh.* Kyra attempted an uneasy smile and dropped his hand, stepping away. If Gully noticed her discomfort, he didn't let on. "Need a table?"

"Umm, sure. I'm meeting Chase and Tar—Er, Detective Collins."

Gully's eyebrows pulled together, and a crease formed on his forehead.

She guessed he was frowning, but couldn't tell for certain behind all his facial hair.

"They're not here yet, but I have a table set up. It's this way." Gully led her to one of the larger tables and gave it a wipe down. "Take a seat. I'll grab us some menus and drinks. Sav blanc, right?"

Kyra nodded, surprised he'd remembered her drink order. She took the seat tucked into the corner and looked around the restaurant. It was mostly empty, only a few afternoon patrons sipped drinks and snacked on icy plates of oysters. Kyra adjusted herself in her chair, conscious of the backs of her thighs sticking to the wooden seat. She tried, unsuccessfully, to smooth her skirt down to create a cotton barrier, wishing she'd chosen something more casual than the sundress. She gave up, resigned to the peel-and-stick sensation of hot skin on varnish.

Gully returned with their drinks and took the seat at the other end of the table, farthest from her. "How was your flight in?" he asked and took a long swig of his beer.

His tone was polite, formal, adding to Kyra's discomposure.

"Oh, fine." She lifted one shoulder and pushed her long hair behind an ear. "Long. How's the summer been?" she said, matching his bored small-talk tone.

She knew he was watching her and saw her too frequent glances at the door. He probably thought he made her nervous. He did, but only because he was Tarek's closest friend. And the thought of speaking to the detective after months of silence? That had the back of her neck feeling prickly, her palms sweaty. She tried smoothing her skirt again.

"Business has been good, although I guess you wouldn't

be able to tell right now." He gestured to the empty tables.

Kyra sipped her drink and held it to her lips, scrambling for a response, but was saved when the door swung open and Chase stepped in.

"Hey, guys!" he said brightly, taking off his sunglasses and shaking out his hair. "Look who I found." Detective Tarek Collins stepped from behind him into the gloom of the pub.

Kyra's eyes met his, and she thought he stiffened.

"I was waiting for you, asshole," Tarek muttered and averted his gaze from Kyra's.

Gully sprung up to greet his friend. He was surprisingly light on his feet for a man of his size. Tarek's lips pulled into his signature half smile, like he couldn't be bothered to commit to a full one. Gully yanked Tarek into a hug and thumped him on the back hard enough Tarek's half-smile pulled into a grimace.

"You made it!" Gully stepped back and motioned to one of his staff members.

Chase slid into the seat next to Kyra. He dropped a kiss on her cheek and slung his arm over the back of her chair. He matched her chastising frown with an exaggerated wink, and she couldn't help but laugh. She'd assumed incorrigible was a word reserved for fictional characters, but it fit Chase Hawthorn to a tee.

Gully and Tarek sat down, and a waitress took their drink order. Another staff member set down a platter of raw oysters on the half shell.

"Fresh from Menemsha." Gully pointed to the plate. "Mackey's is serving the best this season."

Kyra eyed the plate of crushed ice and shells doubtfully. *Charlie's friends?* Kyra vaguely remembered Charlie saying Lisa's husband did something in the fishing industry.

"I got a boat as soon as I could when I heard about the wreck. Do you think it's the *Keres*?" Tarek asked as a waitress set their drinks down.

"Could be." Gully's beard moved and his eyes glittered. He reached for an oyster, spooning stuff from the little metal tubs onto it. "I've gotta get eyes on it." His beard cracked open, and he tipped the shell back, swallowing the oyster whole, then chased it with his beer.

It wasn't the first time she'd witnessed people eating oysters, but something about the slimy gelatinous blobs turned her stomach. *They look like snot.* Chase caught Kyra's eye; one eyebrow cocked. She shifted in her seat and immediately regretted moving. The experience was akin to peeling off a band-aid.

"What's the *Keres*?" Chase asked, for both of them.

"The short version." Tarek's tone held a warning.

Gully's eyebrows moved close together in a scowl, then separated when he looked over at Kyra. "It's a ship," he said finally. He tipped back in his chair, the front legs leaving the floor, and looked up at the ceiling. "A pirate ship." The legs came down with a thud.

"A pirate ship?" *Seriously? Is he teasing us?* "Like yo-ho me mateys? Eye patches and parrots?"

Chase bumped her leg with his under the table.

"Yes, seriously, a pirate ship." Gully gave her a pointed look. "It was called the *Keres*. It's rumored to have wrecked during a hurricane in 1712, run aground on Devil's Bridge."

"This far north?" Chase's nostrils were flared like he was ready to laugh but was waiting for the punch line.

"Do you want to hear the story or not?"

"No." Tarek said as both Chase and Kyra nodded.

"Shut it, Collins."

A waitress brought another round of drinks, and a tray of fried food—clams, calamari, what Kyra surmised were hushpuppies. Gully took a big breath. Kyra caught Tarek rub his eyes and settle back in his own chair. His expression was one of tortured resignation. He looked miserable. *Too bad.* She raised her drink to her lips to hide her smirk.

"William Roberts was a sailor from the Isle of Man." Gully began speaking. His normally gruff voice softened to a deep timbre, like a tale spinner of yore. Surprised, Kyra chanced a glance at Chase, but he was leaning forward, his chin in his hand, his attention on Gully.

"He was a crew member on the merchant ship the *Patience.* A favorite of the captain, Roberts, quickly rose through the ranks. The legend goes that it was during a crossing, from Man to Caracas, that the *Patience* was besieged by pirates and sent to the depths. The crew was conscripted. For years, Roberts sailed under the banner of the pirate ship *Dread*, and by his own account became first mate. Eventually, he took his own ship.

"His ship he named the *Keres* after the Greek death spirits, and he became known as the *Wraith.* He and his crew haunted the Spanish Main, only ever attacking at night under the cover of mist and fog. His presence and that of his men, always dressed in black, their eyes blackened with kohl, meant death." Gully paused, his sparkling eyes flicked between Kyra and Chase.

She hadn't realized she'd scooted to the edge of her seat.

"In the spring of 1712, the *Wraith* attacked the *Corozon de Maria*, a Spanish treasure ship returning from Veracruz. Roberts filled the hull of the *Keres* with the spoils—silver, gold, spices, and molasses—then turned north to the Colonies." He took a breath and a gulp of beer. He leaned forward. His voice dropped to just above a whisper. "It's said he had a sweetheart; you know." Gully's eyes rested on Kyra for half a second before focusing again on the wall behind her. "She was rumored to be a woman of unrivaled beauty, and he sought to return to her. But she was from a wealthy family who did not approve of their union, and while he sailed for his fortune, she was married to another. With the hold full, Roberts set sail for Gloucester to collect his love and return home to the British Isles. But he never made it." Gully paused and clasped his hands together on the table. "There was a storm. A hurricane. And the *Keres*, riding low in the water, overburdened by Spanish treasure, was torn apart on the Devil's Bridge, her crew, even the *Wraith* himself, lost to the sea."

Kyra blinked. *That's it?* Chase also looked troubled, the two lines between his eyes more pronounced. Tarek's face was blank, his attention on the glass in front of him. She narrowed her eyes, trying to read his expression. He looked bored, like he'd heard the story hundreds of times.

"You're saying that the wreck is a three-hundred-year-old pirate ship, full of treasure," Chase said, his words measured but his tone skeptical.

"Aye," Gully growled and waggled his eyebrows.

Tarek made an exasperated noise in the back of his throat and mumbled something about talking like a pirate and he'd leave.

Chase frowned. "And you're some sort of part-time treasure hunter, like Indiana Jones?" Chase's eyes swept over Gully's bulky form.

Gully slid one of the pub's cocktail napkins over to Chase and Kyra. He tapped the image stamped on the front. She hadn't taken notice before. Now she studied it. It was a drawing of a ship's masthead. A winged woman with flowing hair. Her mouth, full of pointed teeth, was stretched open in a battle cry. The name of the pub was written below in old-timey script, *Wraith & Bone*.

"I'm … committed," Gully said, and Kyra could have sworn the skin above his shaggy beard turned pink. He shrugged. "I've been researching the *Keres* since I first learned about her. When I bought the pub, I changed the name, but everyone calls it Gully's." His beard twitched to the side.

"Is that a Keres then?" Chase pointed to the masthead.

"A Ker. Probably what Roberts thought one would look like, anyway. According to the accounts I've found, this is what his masthead was reported to look like."

"And you've been researching this your entire life?" Kyra was having a difficult time picturing the gruff pub master as a clandestine academic.

"Nearly twenty years?"

"It feels like forever," Tarek grumbled.

"Since high school. One summer we were working on the island, and while Tarek was learning to drive a bus, I took a painting job at the library for extra cash. I found a box full of research on the *Keres* in the basement." Gully pulled the napkin back and looked down at the drawing. He ran his finger along the pub's name. "A man with a place on Tashmoo. If I remember correctly, he was a retired history professor. He donated a bunch of boxes to the library. He was convinced the ship was in the ravine. It looks like he may have been right."

Something tugged at Kyra's memory. *Tashmoo? Where have I heard that before?* She bit into a hushpuppy and chewed thoughtfully.

Gully turned to Chase. "Do you think the storm we had the other day would have been strong enough to uncover something like that?" He tapped the napkin again.

Chase had grown up sailing the waters around the island and knew them better than most. He pursed his lips and tilted his chin, thinking, before slowly nodding. "If the tide was right, and the wind came in at the right angle, sure. A storm surge can alter the seabed and cover or uncover things. Big things."

"What's the next step? How will you identify the wreck?" Tarek asked.

Kyra caught the edge to his voice and looked at him, but he was focused on Gully.

"Terry Rose is coming in today." Gully pulled his phone from his pocket and looked at the screen. "Actually, he should be here any minute." Tarek frowned and opened his mouth, but Gully cut him off. "Before you say anything, I trust him, Tar." Gully's voice was stern. Tarek's scowl deepened, but he inclined his chin in a curt nod. The waitress checked in on them. Gully spoke to her quietly.

"Did you decide to do the regatta?" Kyra asked Chase to fill the silence.

He held a cluster of deep-fried calamari tentacles between his fingers. "Think so." He popped it into his mouth. "I registered with the *Elpis*. I can sail it by myself, but it'd be more fun to have company. Interested?"

Kyra stilled. Chase and Tarek were both watching her.

The *Elpis* was Chase's new-to-him sailboat. He'd proudly sailed it up from Baltimore last month, sending her an unending photo montage of his trip.

"Umm." Kyra bit her lower lip, stalling.

The last time she'd been on a sailboat, she'd almost died.

"It'll be fun." Chase nudged her shoulder with his. "I entered in the pleasure boat category. The *Elpis* can't compete against the racing boats or the cats. It'll be a leisurely sail around the island. I'll be bored by myself. Please?" He looked up at her from under his eyelashes and pushed out his bottom lip.

She knew Chase could easily fill a hundred boats with young people who wanted to spend time with him. He was trying to help her. She gave him a flat look and reached for her wineglass, annoyed with herself for bringing up the subject.

"When is it?" Tarek asked.

"A week from Saturday." Chase pushed his hair off his forehead and glanced at Tarek across the table. "Wanna come?"

"Yeah, I'd go. You're here for the summer, right?" Tarek spoke to her, directly acknowledging her for the first time since he stepped inside the pub. She dipped her chin. *Yes.*

"Will you come?"

"I don't know," she hedged, and gripped her seat.

The pads of her fingers pressed against the rough unfinished wood underneath. Her memories, and frequently her nightmares, of her time on the *Neamhnaid* were still vivid and front of mind. The idea of being back on the water, of being thrown around by the waves … Kyra swallowed, trying to calm the churning in her stomach.

"Just see it before the race, and then you can decide, Kay. No pressure." Chase's voice was soft, cajoling.

"Gully!" A rich baritone boomed from the front of the pub, saving Kyra from having to answer.

Gully jumped from his seat. His chair skidded back and toppled over. Tarek retrieved and righted it. A man, perhaps ten or fifteen years older than Gully, had entered the pub, followed by two companions, a trim, muscular man, who looked to be about Kyra's age, wearing cargo shorts and a Baltimore Orioles T-shirt and a woman at least ten years his junior with shoulder length strawberry blonde hair. Her turquoise sundress highlighted her athletic curves and long, tan legs. Gully clapped the T-shirt guy on the shoulder, and his beard split in a wide grin. T-shirt guy embraced the larger man like they were old friends. He said something to Gully, but they were too far away for Kyra to hear. The man stepped aside, and Gully turned to the woman. He shook her hand, his head inclined in a polite, more reserved greeting.

"We're over here." He led the trio to their table and motioned to someone at the back of the restaurant. "Terry, you know Tarek."

Tarek glared at the older man. Kyra's eyes shifted between them, surprised at Tarek's outright hostility.

"Nice to see you again, Rose," he said, his expression flat.

Terry Rose took a seat. "Always a pleasure, Collins." He matched Tarek's dry tone.

"Terry, this is Chase Hawthorn," Gully continued, ignoring the iciness between the two men. "And Kyra Gibson. Chase, Kyra, this is my old friend Terry Rose. We were in the Marines together." Terry inclined his head. "And this," he pointed to the T-shirt guy, "is Matty Gray. He served with us. And Jaycee." Gully looked at the woman and blinked. "Jace, how do we know you again?"

"I found her in a dive shop outside Sydney. When was it? Three years ago, now?"

Jaycee tilted her chin. "Sounds 'bout right. Nice to meet you lot," she said in a thick Australian accent.

"Can't remember how we managed before we found her," Terry said, his eyes gleaming with paternal affection. "Nice meeting you folks." He reached for the large beer stein a server had placed in front of him. "Is his beer still piss?" he asked Tarek, who gave a noncommittal shrug and finished his own drink. "Still a man of few words, I see." Terry raised his glass to his companions and took a long swig of his beer. He feigned an exaggerated shudder and swallowed. "Yeah, still piss."

Gully let out a big belly laugh and clasped him on the shoulder. "It's good to see you, Rose. Where did you come in from?" Gully glanced at Chase and Kyra. "Rose runs a marine salvage company."

Kyra straightened. *Ah.* Terry and his friends' presence made much more sense.

Terry nodded. "We were in Stonington, Maine, two

weeks ago. Carted back over five hundred pounds of live, uncrated lobsters."

"It was a fucking disaster," Matty Gray snapped, and Jaycee's mischievous smirk deepened. "I found one in the berth two days after we unloaded." His shoulders shook with a shiver. "Sea bugs. Disgusting things."

Jaycee clapped her hands and let out a chuffed squeak.

"Quit your grousing, you big baby," Terry chided.

"Says you! It could have *got* me!"

"Calm down, Jace kept you safe."

Jaycee snickered. Matty Gray shot her a withering look and crossed his arms over his chest.

Ignoring him, Terry continued, "After Maine, we were on site at Newport. We'd just finished there when I got your call."

"You were at Newport?" Chase asked, suddenly much more interested in Gully's guests.

At Kyra's confusion, he leaned down and said, "It's a regatta. One of the biggest ones in the country."

"We were." Terry nodded.

"Did you see the accident?"

"You mean the drunk socialite and her frat-boy boyfriend who crashed daddy's toy?" Matty Gray scoffed and slurped an oyster.

Chase stiffened. "I went to school with them." Chase slung back the rest of his beer, and something dark passed over his features. "It's not the first time they crashed a boat," he muttered into his empty glass.

Kyra gaped at him. Chase just shrugged. His words from last spring floated back to her. *It's something I'd do. Get wasted and do something destructive and stupid.* She wondered what the destructive thing he'd done was—crashed the boat or taken the blame.

"Was anyone hurt?" Kyra asked.

"No." Jaycee shook her head. "The harbor police pulled them out of the water. The girl was spitting mad. She was screaming after they hauled them up."

"They lost a few cases of Cristal, Jace." Matty Gray said solemnly and placed his hand over his heart. "It was a tragedy."

"Some tragedy," she mocked. "As soon as harbor police pulled them out, you skipped over and yanked the cases out of the water."

"Did you drink two bottles and eat two hotdogs that night?" Matty Gray pointed a finger at her.

Jaycee made a huffing noise. She raised her hand to cup the side of her mouth, and whispered to Kyra and Chase loud enough so the rest of the table could hear, "Three hotdogs and I stashed a case for later." Jaycee gave Matty Gray a triumphant grin and flipped him a two-fingered salute.

Kyra couldn't help but laugh alongside the rest of the table. Terry and his crew were fun.

"Are you here about the wreck?" Chase asked.

The table got quiet for a moment and the salvagers shared a silent communication. Terry raised his eyebrows.

"They're fine. I told them."

"I guess the cat's out of the bag, then," Terry grumbled and let out a breath. "Yeah, although we don't know what it is yet, despite what Gully's probably told you. We need to get eyes on it."

Jaycee looked at Matty Gray and he gave a slight shake of

his head like he was warning her off.

"The environmentalists are already here objecting to whatever they think we're planning on doing," Matty Gray said and made an irritated face.

"Environmentalists?" Kyra asked. "Why?"

"Whenever they think we plan to disturb the sea floor, they show up with their injunctions and signs." Terry frowned. "It's a headache, but part of the gig."

"It's premature since we don't know if anything's down there, much less salvageable," Matty Gray broke in. "It's just as likely to be refuse or jetsam as something worth hauling."

"You'd think before they started complaining they'd want to know what to complain about." Terry rubbed his jaw with his palm.

"What groups are here?" Gully asked.

"The Environmental League, Clean Water, and I think my assistant said the Oceanic Conservation posted their opposition to any salvage efforts on their socials. If the OC isn't here yet, they're on their way."

Gully's caterpillar eyebrow shifted, and he gave Tarek a look Kyra couldn't interpret. Tarek shook his head, but Kyra caught that tick in his jaw.

"Are you worried?" Chase asked.

"Nah," Jaycee said. "It's just a bunch of posturing. Like Matty Gray said, we don't know what's down there yet."

"No," Terry agreed. "The real headaches start once we know what we're dealing with." He leaned back. "Remember that fiasco in Turku?"

"With the walrus?" When Terry nodded, Jaycee relayed a story about a walrus who'd taken to sunbathing on people's boats that had the table in stitches. Matty Gray seemed to take it as a challenge and recounted a tale of his own about a pair of octogenarian sisters feuding over their father's Riva, that ended up at the bottom of Lake Como.

Kyra brushed tears from her eyes and glanced at her phone. *Shite.* They'd been sitting there for hours, listening to Matty Gray and Jaycee's stories. Even Terry had told a few. Her sides hurt from laughing … and drinking. She eyed the table littered with platters of picked over food and glasses.

She pushed her seat back. "Thank you. I've got to get home." Kyra stood, wincing as her skin peeled off the seat.

She had to set her hand on the table to steady herself. She told herself it had nothing to do with the four or more drinks she'd had. Kyra pulled her purse from the back of the chair.

"It's been lovely meeting all of you. Thank you, Gully. Good luck with the *Keres*. Jaycee, I'll text you tomorrow."

Jaycee raised her still full beer and set it down without drinking. They had made plans to go shopping and Jaycee was going to teach her to paddleboard.

"I'll give you a lift," Tarek said quietly and stood up.

Chase sucked in a breath. He turned his alpine eyes on her, his eyebrows raised in a silent question.

"Oh. I…" She shook her head, ready to decline his offer, but Tarek pointed to the wineglasses sitting in front of her empty seat. Her eyes slid closed, and she let loose a breath. *Shit. I can't drive.* Her eyes opened, and she nodded. "Okay. Thank you."

"We should check in to our hotel and get settled." Terry looked at his team. Matty Gray shared a look with Jaycee, then glanced at Gully.

"We'll talk tomorrow?" Gully asked, clasping Terry's

hand in his giant one. Matty Gray leaned over to say something to Jaycee. She tilted her head slightly and stood up. Kyra frowned. Everything was moving like it was underwater, slow with blurry edges. She pressed a hand to her forehead. *I've had way too much to drink.*

"You'll be okay?" Chase whispered in her ear.

"Mmhhmm."

He gave her a one-armed hug and pressed a kiss to her temple. "Talk to you tomorrow. Don't do anything I wouldn't do."

"Is there anything you wouldn't do?" she grumbled under her breath.

"Probably not."

Kyra tried to glare at him and had to bite her lip to keep from smiling.

Outside, a gentle sea breeze tempered the evening's brutal heat. People crowded the sidewalks and the streets. Suddenly, Kyra was exhausted. The thought of sitting next to Tarek, of making awkward, stilted small talk, pretending she wasn't still hurt, was just too much to bear.

"Thanks for the offer, but I'm just going to grab a rideshare." She stepped away.

His hand wrapped around her elbow, halting her. "Kyra, wait." His voice was soft.

She met his eyes. She'd forgotten how green they were. Part of her wanted to stay, to hear what he had to say. Let him explain why he ghosted her, but her thoughts sloshed around in her skull. *No.* She shook her head. Tarek's hand dropped from her arm.

"Goodnight, Detective." Kyra walked away.

Chapter Four

A FURRY SKULL bumped against Kyra's chin. "Ugh, no. Go away! Too early." Her voice was gritty and dry. Cronkite responded with a deep purr and another bump, more insistent this time. "Fine. *Fine.* I get it. You're hungry."

Kyra rolled out of bed, cursing the sharp thrumming that had taken up residence behind her eyes. *How much did I drink?* Kyra rubbed her face, trying to remember. She'd had too much wine, and she hadn't eaten enough. The alcohol had hit her hard. When she'd arrived home from the Wraith & Bone, she'd gone straight to bed, despite the early hour.

The Wraith & Bone. Gully's story. She had to admit the tragic story about the lovers trying to find their way to each other was compelling, romantic, even.

Cronkite gave her another insistent yowl, demanding her immediate attention. "Breakfast, I know. I know," she muttered. The white gremlin herded her downstairs, pausing on each tread to look back, confirming she was following. "Move faster, you monster." She toed him.

He scampered to the kitchen and sat next to his empty bowl. Cronk looked up; his poisoned apple eyes rounded in a plea. Kyra fed him and placed a pod into the coffeemaker. While the machine whirred, she toasted a few slices of the fresh bread she'd bought at Mander Lane and retrieved her phone from her purse.

She checked her messages.

Chase had texted to make sure she'd gotten in, but nothing from Tarek. Her stomach sank. *But what did I expect? I left him standing on the side of the road.*

Kyra poured vanilla almond milk into her coffee and carried her breakfast to the living room. She settled on the couch and flicked on the morning news. The calories and caffeine eased her headache. Sipping on her coffee, she scrolled through her social media, half listening to the reporter. She texted Ali about Gully's pirate and his ship, the *Keres*.

The first time she heard it, it didn't quite register, but the second time she heard the name, her eyes traveled to the television almost without volition. She squinted at the screen. A broadcaster dressed in an appalling Hawaiian shirt stood in front of grayed-out weather-beaten buildings. Cormorants stood on seaweed covered pilings along a long dock. Her arms and shoulders broke out in a cold sweat. Her vision darkened at the edges, focusing on the docks. *Menemsha.*

"The two victims have been identified as employees of Rose Marine Salvage. The police have detained two men for questioning: Terry Rose of San Jose, California and owner of Rose Marine Salvage and local businessman Andre Gould, III, proprietor of the Wraith & Bone restaurant in Edgartown here on Martha's Vineyard. Investigators have declined to provide a cause of death but have released the images from the illegal night dive. Please use discretion in watching the video. It contains graphic material."

Kyra stood. The blanket she'd wrapped around her legs fell to the floor. She stepped closer to the TV. The footage was grainy. In the beam of the camera's spotlight, Kyra made out seaweed swaying in the current, a sandy seabed. She sucked in a sharp breath, dreading what she knew was coming.

The diver controlling the camera panned up and over. Another diver swam into the beam of light, strands of hair floating around her goggles. Delicate hands made motions, communicating something to her partner. Kyra had little doubt who those hands belonged to. Her own hands fisted the bottom of her shirt.

Jaycee dug around in the sand, shining a light on the ocean floor. She brushed the sand aside, revealing what looked like a rough wooden beam. Kyra's mouth fell open. She stepped closer to the screen. Despite the poor video quality, she could see a woman's face emerge from the sand. Her carved hair was swept back from her forehead, her mouth agape in a frozen scream.

"The *Keres*."

Kyra swiped her phone from the couch where she'd dropped it. Her fingers flew over the screen. She texted Chase, telling him to check the news.

Then she called Tarek.

"Hello?" He answered after the second ring.

"Tarek, it's Kyra. I just saw the news. Are they okay? Is Gully okay? What happened?" Her questions tumbled out. Tarek was quiet and she could hear her breath back through the line. "Tarek?"

"No," he said roughly. "Jaycee is dead." She heard a waver in his voice. "Matty Gray has been airlifted to Mass General … in Boston. He's in critical condition. They're not sure he'll wake up. Gully's been detained for questioning."

Kyra's hand flew to her mouth. She fell onto the couch. Stunned. *Jaycee? Dead?*

"Do you … do you know what happened?"

"No," he ground out, like he was talking through clenched teeth. "I've been here at the station in Menemsha all morning, but I haven't been able to speak to him."

They're not letting him see Gully? Kyra frowned.

"Because you have a conflict of interest? As his friend?"

"Something like that. I'm on PTO. I'm not here in any professional capacity, and unless the state police assume jurisdiction and I'm assigned to the case, the local forces won't share information with me." His words came out in a staccato.

Kyra could picture him pacing, running his hand through his hair.

"Hold on." The phone muffled like he'd covered the microphone. She heard voices. Tarek barked out a string of curses.

"Hello? Tarek?"

"Yeah, sorry about that. I gotta go. They're going to hold Gully for a while. I have to get to the pub."

"You're opening his bar?"

"No, he has deliveries this morning, and I don't know how to get in touch with his staff. And no one will ask him for me." He snapped the last words, likely targeted at whomever was behind the desk at the station. "I'm heading there now."

"I can help." She offered without thinking.

"You don't mind?" Tarek sounded surprised. "I need to unload the deliveries before eleven, when the pub opens, or the trucks have to leave."

"I'll head right over."

There was a beat of silence before he said, "I'll meet you there." Tarek hung up.

Kyra stared at the phone. Her eyes drifted to Cronkite, sitting on the couch, his fluffy tail swishing in long languid sweeps.

"How hard can it be?"

Cronkite's pink tongue slid across his muzzle, and he laid his head back down.

FORTY MINUTES LATER, Kyra walked up to the Wraith & Bone. She'd had to call the Chamberses for a ride, since her car was still parked in town. Thankfully, Grace had been on her way to an emergency council meeting and was able to drop Kyra off. She'd told Grace about Gully in the car. Grace had been horrified and promised to learn as much as she could about the wreck and the accident at the meeting and report back.

"Call us later, dear," Grace said, pulling up to the curb. "If you and the detective need anything, let us know."

"Thank you for the ride. I will."

Kyra watched Grace's car disappear before stepping up to the front door of the pub. She pushed her hair away from her face and pulled it into a messy bun. Sweat already clung to the nape of her neck and her lower back. She wasn't used to this weather, steamy and salty, so different from the hot dry Mediterranean, or the cool damp of Britain. She looked up, turned her face into the sun. There wasn't a cloud in the sky. She groaned inwardly and said a silent prayer for the staff to arrive before any customers.

She stared at the door, regretting her impulsive offer to help. Doing manual labor with Tarek Collins wasn't how she thought she'd be spending her morning. She probably wouldn't have been so dismissive last night had she known she'd be seeing him again so soon. *No, I would have.* Kyra sighed and tried the door. It swung open, and she slipped inside Gully's pub.

Cool air enveloped her. The pub was empty. And dark. Scant milky light came from a few wavy glass windows. The scent of disinfectant lingered and mixed with the tangy, cold smell of artificially cooled air. The Wraith & Bone felt like a tomb.

"Tarek?" Her voice came out softer than she intended. She peered through a doorway off the dining room. "Tarek? Are you back there?"

"Kyra?" a voice came from behind her.

"Gah!" She whirled around, her hand to her chest.

Tarek's eyebrow hitched, and he rolled his lips like he was trying not to laugh.

"Where did you come from?" she hissed, her heart banging against her ribs.

"The office." He pointed to another doorway she hadn't noticed. "I was calling the staff. The cook gets here in a half hour, the rest around eleven." The corner of his mouth tipped upward a fraction. He waved to the purse and unnecessary sweatshirt clasped in her hand. "You can put your stuff in there. It's open. I made coffee. It's in the kitchen."

Kyra dropped her things on a metal desk, buried under piles of papers and mail. She pulled a pair of garden gloves she'd found in the garage from her bag, stuffed them in her back pocket, and followed Tarek to the kitchen. She poured a cup of coffee, while listening to Tarek explain they needed to unload food, linens, and alcohol deliveries.

"Ready?"

"As I'll ever be." She set down her mug and pulled on her gloves.

She followed Tarek to the back delivery entrance. Plastic bags of towels, tablecloths, and napkins had been tossed on the pavement. Tarek picked two up by the plastic strap, and Kyra grabbed one. She followed him back into the restaurant to a supply closet near the kitchen.

"Can you put this stuff away? I'll get the rest."

Kyra nodded and tore open the bags. She stowed the linens on the labeled shelves, stacking the folded items as neatly as possible. Tarek brought in bag after bag until he finally stooped and tore one open to help. He'd turned on a radio, and the voices of the broadcasters reporting on the local Boston news between classic rock songs filled the near silence.

Tarek's phone buzzed. "That's the food delivery."

Kyra motioned that she'd follow and stuffed the towel she was holding on the shelf.

A truck had pulled up to the curb, and a man jumped

down to unlatch the swing doors. "Gould?" he asked, looking at Tarek.

"I can sign for him." The man handed Tarek a clipboard, and he signed off on the delivery.

"Those cartons—there—are all yours. I'll hand them down." He ran a skeptical eye over Kyra before climbing inside the truck and grabbing a carton. He handed it down to Tarek, and another to Kyra.

She walked back and forth from the alley to the kitchen over and over. Crate after crate. Cartons of eggs, produce, meats, fish, dairy, spices, and whatever else Gully had ordered. She stacked the boxes in the walk-in refrigerator, each time gooseflesh erupting over her sweat slicked skin.

"That's it." Tarek said as he walked into the fridge. He wiped his face with the hem of his T-shirt. He opened a box on the top of the stack and inspected its contents. "I don't know how he organizes in here, so I think we can just leave it for the kitchen staff."

"I can take care of it."

An accented voice came from behind them, and Kyra turned with a start. She hadn't noticed someone enter the kitchen.

A young man wearing a green bandana tied around his head, holding back his thick golden curls, was standing in the doorway. "Hi." He raised his hand in a wave.

"Mikael." Tarek sighed. "Finally. Gully had an emergency and asked us to accept deliveries."

"He called me on my drive here. Said he was heading home, and you were here."

Relief slackened Tarek's features and he let loose a

breath. "Thank you. I'll call him."

Kyra followed Tarek out of the fridge. Her sneakers made a squeaking sound on the metal floor.

Tarek looked over his shoulder at her. His eyes widened, like he'd forgotten she was there. "Oh, Mikael, this is Kyra, our um … friend. Kyra, Mikael. Mikael is Gully's cook."

"Nice to meet you," he said with a nod as he tied on an apron. He spoke with an accent, but not one she could place, possibly Eastern European. *Ukraine? Or Belarus?* "I can take care of this and the rest of the deliveries."

"Do you need anything else?" Kyra asked, rubbing the chill of the walk-in from her arms.

"If you don't mind. Can you take the chairs down in the dining room?" Mikael called over his shoulder as he headed inside the cold room. Kyra gave him a weary nod and followed Tarek to the front of the pub.

The chairs were stacked on the tables in the dining room. One-by-one, they took them down, wiping the tables as they went. They were heavier than they looked, and Kyra's fatigued arms ached with the effort. More than one chair fell to the floor with a thud.

She finished the last table, pulled down the last chair, focusing on not dropping it. She barely noticed the three people walk through the door, dressed in matching black T-shirts.

"Who are you?" demanded the tallest one from the doorway.

Kyra's balance shifted, and the chair slipped from her sweaty hands, landing with a crash.

He narrowed his eyes at her. "Where's Gully and Mikael?" The others craned their necks, looking around the room.

"She's with me. I asked her to help with the deliveries." Tarek appeared behind her, holding her things. She hadn't even noticed he'd disappeared. "Mikael's in the kitchen. Gully had an emergency. He'll be back tomorrow."

"Is he okay?" the blond one asked, his suspicion replaced with concern.

"Oh, yeah. Nothing to worry about."

Nothing but his friend dying and the other in hospital, and he's being held by the police. Tarek caught her eye and subtly shook his head, a silent request to play along.

"You guys can take it from here?"

"For sure." The tall one nodded. "Uh, thanks for covering."

"No problem," Kyra said, her throat dry.

"Ready?" Tarek asked, handing over her things. She dipped her chin in a weary nod.

Outside Gully's pub, the heat was oppressive. She was keenly aware of how her shirt stuck to her body and loose strands of hair clung to her neck.

Tarek slipped on his sunglasses. "Thank you. For your help. You have no idea. I'd still be unloading all that stuff." Kyra waved off his thanks. "No, really, Kyra. Gully has a contract with the hotel for his summer business hours. He … *I* really appreciate it."

"Don't mention it, really." She pulled her phone from her purse. "Sounds like the police let Gully go?"

"It does."

Kyra waited for him to say more, but the moment stretched on, and her patience waned. *Why do I even care?*

"Okay. Well, tell him I'm glad he's home. I'll see you later, then." She stepped off the curb.

"Wait, Kyra?"

She paused.

"Can I buy you lunch?"

Kyra turned to him and faced her reflection in his glasses, uncertainty flashing over her features.

"Please, it's the least I can do after you gave up your morning off."

She looked down at her grimy shirt.

"I'll grab us something to go. Bring it back to your place?" He pulled his keys from his pocket and he waited.

"Okay," she said, giving in. She heard the waver in her voice and knew Tarek would have caught it, too. "Thank you. I'll see you in a bit."

The inside of her car was like the surface of the sun, and Kyra opened all the windows and blasted the AC to bring the temperature down below face-melting. She bit her lip. Part of her wished she'd declined Tarek's offer. That she'd come up with some excuse. But she was curious about what happened on the dive the night before, why the police had questioned Gully. And if she gave herself permission to be honest, she could admit she enjoyed spending time with Tarek, even if it was spent doing manual labor.

Chapter Five

KYRA LINGERED UNDER the shower. She let the water pressure drum her weary shoulders, her back. She turned and forced her face into the spray. Her shoulder muscles protested when she raised her arms to wash her hair. She stepped out of the shower and toweled off. The air conditioning was running in the house, and even though her skin pebbled, she relished the respite from the heat outside.

She threw on cutoffs and her favorite T-shirt, softened and thin from years of wear. She wrung the moisture from her hair and let it air dry, knowing she'd regret it later but not having the energy to do more.

Cronk was curled up on the living room sofa, his tail twitching as he watched birds hop around on the patio through one half-open eye. Someone, Charlie's company probably, had set up the outdoor furniture under the pergola.

"Do you think we have cushions?" she asked the cat, who answered by stretching a paw, and shutting his eye.

She found a plastic storage trunk outside, tucked under a window. It contained the cushions for the chairs and sun loungers. She yanked on the top one stumbling back as it fell to the ground. She stared at it, debating whether sitting outside was worth the effort of getting hot and sweaty again.

There was a knock on the front door and she abandoned the cushion where it lay.

"Hey," Tarek said when she opened it. Kyra waved him in. "How are the arms?"

"Painful." She feigned a grimace. "I tried to set us up outside." She pointed to the cushion she'd dropped. "But if it's too hot, we can be in the kitchen."

"No, I like outside." Tarek followed her through the house and out to the patio.

He placed a paper bag and a beverage tray on the table. Kyra recognized the packaging and the logo. *Café Joy.*

Last spring, she'd fallen a little in love with the café and its owner, Nina, who was a magician when it came to the perfect cup of coffee.

"Unpack the food. I'll set up the cushions." Tarek had changed his clothes. Like her, he'd dressed in shorts and a faded T-shirt. Casual clothes suited him, made him appear less severe, younger, more boyish. His hair was damp and pushed back off his forehead. He'd clearly stopped off first, and she wondered where he was staying. Last spring, the department had set him up in a hotel, but he wasn't here with the police this time. She imagined it'd be difficult, and expensive, to get a last-minute hotel reservation during the high season.

Tarek sat across from her. He pulled one of the plastic cups from the tray and handed it to her. "Iced Americano, vanilla almond milk."

He'd remembered her coffee order. Kyra's fingers wrapped around the cup. It was such a small thing. She bit down on her lip, swallowing back a swell of emotion. She hadn't realized he'd been paying attention.

"Thank you." She angled her chair toward the cove, propping her bare feet on the chair next to her. She concentrated on unwrapping her straw and threading it through the opening in the plastic cup.

Tarek tore open the bag and pulled out the contents. He passed her a sandwich wrapped in paper.

"BLT with avocado. No mayo. I guessed. I hope it's okay."

"It's brilliant. Thank you."

"No, thank you. For helping me this morning. Gully also wanted me to tell you."

"You spoke to him, then? He's home?"

"Mmhhmm. I just came from his place. He's fine. Physically, anyway. He's resting now." Kyra's eyebrows hitched together. "I'm staying with him."

Ah.

Kyra picked at a pickle spear. "Have you heard anything more about Matty Gray?"

"I called Terry on my way." Tarek removed his sunglasses and rubbed his eyes. "He was deprived of oxygen for too long. He has no brain function." Tarek's throat bobbed, and he looked away. "Gray's family will be signing the papers to remove him from life support sometime today."

Kyra blew out a long breath and her throat tightened. "I'm so sorry." She'd only just met Matty Gray and Jaycee, but she'd liked them, especially the girl. Their deaths were triggering her own memories—losing her mother after a long illness, her father's murder.

She looked up at Tarek. His eyes were red, tired.

"Were you friends with him? Jaycee?"

Tarek slipped his glasses back on and she caught her own wretchedness reflected back at her.

"No, not really. I've met Matty Gray a few times. He served with Gully and Rose. Jaycee was new to the crew."

Kyra dropped her eyes to her lunch. A heaviness settled in her chest. "Do you know what happened?"

Tarek cleared his throat and turned toward the cove. His own lunch barely touched. He took a sip of his coffee. "Gully, Jaycee, and Matty Gray took the Rose ship to the wreckage site, sometime in the middle of the night. Jaycee and Matty Gray dove under to get images. They were trying to identify whatever is down there. Gully was inside, on the bridge, watching the video feed. According to Terry, everything was fine, and then something happened. Jaycee was the first to signal distress and Matty Gray tried to help her. Gully watched him check Jaycee's equipment, then he tried to share his breathing apparatus. That's when Gully called 911. Gray dropped the camera at some point, and the comms went down. They didn't surface on their own. The Coast Guard pulled them from the water. Jaycee was pronounced dead at the scene."

"Something happened?" she repeated, confused. She'd assumed that Matty Gray and Jaycee were seasoned divers. "Like what?"

Tarek spun his cup on the table. "I don't know yet. Gully isn't a diver. He doesn't know exactly what happened down there. The authorities are going through the footage, but from what very little they told Gully, they believe that the equipment failed." Tarek's voice hardened and a muscle in his jaw ticked.

"Both Jaycee's and Matty Gray's equipment failed? At the same time?" Kyra frowned, tying to make sense of that. It seemed an unlikely coincidence. "But don't they check the equipment first?"

"Yes, they do." Tarek frowned. "They're both master divers. They'd have noticed if something wasn't right. Terry also confirmed all the equipment was checked before they left the ship yesterday afternoon, per standard protocol. The investigating officers wouldn't tell him anything more, and they won't give me access to the equipment or their report. The local department has shut me out."

"Because you're on holiday?"

Tarek paused and turned to face her. Something in his expression made Kyra lean in closer.

"That, and after last spring, my relationship with the local departments is … strained."

Strained? Her stomach dropped, and she sat back. *Oh.* She realized. *Because of me.*

Kyra had had an unpleasant run-in with the Edgartown police last spring. Tarek had protected her. She chewed on the end of her straw. His tone wasn't accusatory or condemning. It made her feel worse that he didn't seem to blame her. Tarek leaned forward and ran his hand through his hair before setting his elbows on the table. He wore it longer, curling at the ends.

"When I arrived at the station this morning, the Menemsha Police Chief not-so-politely told me to fuck off." He sighed and yanked off his sunglasses, tossing them on the table.

"That's my fault," she whispered. "I'm sorry."

"Don't apologize." His gaze snapped to hers. "You did nothing wrong." He loosed a breath and sat back in his chair. "I made a call into my headquarters this morning. I've asked to be assigned to the case."

"Will they give it to you?"

"Unlikely," he huffed, and ran his hand through his hair again. "Technically, I'm on vacation, but there's a bit more to it. In June, I finished my post doc work and received my invitation to Quantico."

Kyra raised her eyebrows. *Quantico?* "The FBI?" she asked.

He nodded, but his eyes shifted like he wasn't comfortable talking about it. "I also received a preliminary offer with a private security contractor."

"You're quitting the police?"

"I'm weighing my options. Nothing's been decided." He attempted a shrug. He sounded more annoyed than enthusiastic.

"Congratulations?"

"Thanks." He completed his shrug. "My captain isn't exactly thrilled that I'm being poached or that I'm considering the offers. I'm not in a position to ask any favors of her."

"And you came to the island for a holiday and to weigh your options?"

"No." He broke eye contact with her and looked down at the table. His long, elegant fingers traced the wood grain. "I came because of Gully and the *Keres*. I had the vacation time, so I took it."

Right then. Kyra bit her lip, against the jab of disappointment. She'd hoped at least some small part of him had come to see her. But it was merely a coincidence that the discovery of the *Keres* happened when she was on the island. She sat straighter. *Understood.*

"So, it *is* the *Keres*, then?"

"Looks like it." He slipped his sunglasses back on. Tarek pulled out his phone and passed it to her. He'd brought up the image of the masthead Kyra had seen on the television news broadcast earlier. It was remarkably close to the drawing she'd seen at Gully's pub. "Unless there was another ship with a similar masthead."

Kyra returned his phone.

He pocketed it, and said, his voice tinged with annoyance, "Unfortunately, thanks to the media, the photos are out now and that'll attract even more salvagers looking for scraps. According to Gully, the hull was laden with Spanish gold and silver, although who knows how reliable that story is. If it did break apart on the shoal, the treasure could be scattered all over the Vineyard Sound."

"But if the treasure was spread up and down the coastline, wouldn't someone have found something by now?"

Tarek shook his head. "Who knows? But even without the treasure, the *Keres* is a big find. The Wraith was one of the most successful pirates in history. He'd amassed a fortune. By Gully's estimates, it'd have been equivalent to two hundred million today." Tarek fell quiet, drinking his coffee.

The amount was staggering. *And that could be sitting at the bottom of the sea?*

Her mind jumped back and forth between the story Gully had told them yesterday and the night dive. Gully said he needed to get eyes on the wreck. She ran her finger along the side of her cup, watching the condensation collect and dribble down. *Was that all they were doing?*

"Do you think they were trying to pull the *Keres* up?"

"Gully said they weren't. Their plan was to identify the wreck and get some video footage." Tarek spoke with a conviction that surprised Kyra, and she realized it was because he believed Gully.

He trusted his childhood friend implicitly. She didn't know Tarek that well. They'd only spent a few days together last April, but when they'd worked together, he'd been skeptical of every clue they found or theory she proposed. He accepted nothing as fact without corroborating evidence. But that distrust didn't seem to extend to Gully's word.

"What's it in?" she asked, after a long moment to fill the silence.

"What?" Tarek turned to her, his forehead creasing.

"Your degree? Post doc? I assumed you finished a … a what? A doctorate?" Kyra waved her hand. "Last spring in Boston, you told Donna and Antonio you only had a master's."

His mouth turned down in surprise, but morphed into an affectionate smile. "I didn't want them to fuss over me, and nothing was official until I completed the fellowship."

The diner owners treated him like a son. They definitely would have made a fuss. She could understand his reluctance to tell them.

Tarek cleared his throat. "Psychology."

"A therapist?" *He's not much of a people person.*

"Not quite." Even under the shade from the pergola, Kyra saw his cheeks flush. "Forensic profiling."

"Profiling what?" She was almost afraid to ask.

Tarek didn't answer. He shrugged and looked away. She realized he was embarrassed by the attention.

"That's brilliant, Tarek. Really." She tried to sound encouraging.

"Thanks." But he said it without enthusiasm. He finished his coffee and shook his cup, rattling the ice. "Have you been to the beach yet?"

It took a second for her to catch up. Apparently, he was done talking about himself. "No. I only just got here. It's already been busy."

Tarek's phone rang, and he pulled it from his pocket. He glanced at the screen. "One second." He walked away a few paces before answering.

Kyra caught a few words, enough to guess he was speaking with Gully. Tarek swore loudly, running his free hand through his hair. He walked further away, closer to the cove. She watched him pace back and forth along the bank. From his troubled expression, she knew it wasn't good news. Needing something to do, she cleaned up their lunch, packing away their barely touched food and wiping the crumbs off the table. When she heard him say goodbye, she looked up, pretending she hadn't been trying to listen.

"That was Gully," he said. "He just spoke to Rose. The investigators confirmed the equipment had failed. It'd been sabotaged. Jaycee and Matty Gray's deaths will be ruled homicides."

A chill broke out on Kyra's entire body. "*Sabotaged?*" she mouthed. "Sabotaged how?"

"They didn't say." Tarek fell into his chair and rubbed his forehead. He looked exhausted. "They'll want to keep that bit of information out of public knowledge."

"You're saying they were *murdered?" And Gully may have had something to do with it?* "But who'd do that? Why?" She frowned and said louder, "Who even knew they were on the island? Or about the *Keres*?"

"I don't know."

"What about Terry Rose? Could he have had anything to do with what happened?" she asked.

Tarek dropped his hand to his side and cocked his head, considering. "According to Gully, Rose didn't know about their plan. When he came to the station at four this morning, he seemed as confused as I was." Tarek fell into the chair across from her. "Terry isn't my favorite person. But Matty Gray and Gully are family to him. Gray saved Terry and Gully's lives in some skirmish. And the girl? Terry probably thought of her as a daughter. Rose has his faults, but he's protective of his people."

Kyra remembered the affection in Terry's voice when he spoke with Jaycee. He'd acted like he cared very much for his crew.

"So, no. I don't think that Rose would tamper with the tanks. He wouldn't hurt them."

Even for a two hundred million dollar buried pirate treasure? Kyra wasn't sure. In her experience, people did terrible things for money.

Tarek looked out toward the cove. "No," he said, his

voice soft, muttering. "Chief Erikson will try to pin it on Gully. He's an easy perpetrator. He had opportunity and motive. They can place him at the scene. Erikson will see it as open and shut." Tarek was mostly talking to himself. "Unless persuasive evidence is introduced, that proves otherwise..." Tarek's voice trailed off.

Kyra rubbed her hands against her bare thighs. She wondered if he'd come to the same conclusion she had—that there was no way he'd be assigned this case. He was too close to Gully, and she doubted he could be objective.

"You saw the news," he said, louder now. It wasn't phrased like a question. She nodded. "The broadcast caught the attention of other salvagers. Rose knows of at least one company, Blue Stream Marine Salvage, that's heading to the island. They'll be here tonight."

"What does that mean for Gully and Terry?"

"I'm not sure. Rose said Blue Stream is one of the biggest in the business, but they don't often do antiquities or cultural excavations. They have military contracts or work with drilling or mining companies."

That made no sense to Kyra. *Why would an industrial salvager come to the island?*

"How can I help?" she asked. Not like this morning, she wasn't being polite. She really wanted to help. She wanted to find the person who'd killed Jaycee and Matty Gray, help Tarek protect his friend.

"I'll let you know." Tarek glanced at his phone screen and pushed his chair back.

Kyra tried to hide her surprise. She'd expected him to shut her down, but he hadn't. A fluttery sensation flickered behind her sternum, something like anticipation but prickli-er and more satisfying.

"I need to get back to Gully." He stood up. "Thank you, again. For this morning."

Kyra followed him around to the front of the house. At his car, he turned back. "I'll give you a call?" he asked, but something in his tone was different, perhaps a little tentative.

"Yes, please. Whatever I can do, let me know."

"I will."

Kyra stood in the yard; thumbs hooked in her pockets. She bit her lip in anticipation as she watched Detective Collins get into an older model Jeep Cherokee and reverse out of her driveway.

Chapter Six

KYRA STEPPED BACK to assess the cheese and charcuterie board she'd assembled.

After Tarek had left, Kyra had gone for a walk. She'd explored her neighborhood, and the trails through the woods. It'd also given her time to clear her mind and ruminate on the tragic dive, Jaycee and Matty Gray, Gully, and the *Keres*. Tarek.

While out, she'd run into Charlie on her way home from her tennis lesson. Impulsively, Kyra had invited the Chamberses over for drinks later, then spent the afternoon scrambling around the island for groceries.

Kyra had little experience hosting. Her depressing flat in London was barely big enough for her. *But*, she thought, adjusting a fig on the board, *this isn't half bad.* A knock sounded from the front. "It's open!" she called, walking into the foyer.

Grace's brilliant smile and coifed blonde bob filled the doorway. "Hello, dear!" She gave Kyra an enthusiastic squeeze. Her still tender ribs twinged and Kyra made a little coughing sound.

"Give her some air, Grace." Charlie patted her wife's shoulder. "Hey, neighbor," she murmured and touched her cheek to Kyra's.

"Come on in." Kyra stood to the side, ushering in her friends.

Charlie stepped past her and held up a heavy-looking basket. "Julia sends her … well, she sends carbs." Charlie shrugged, rolling her eyes. Kyra's lips pressed together in a skeptical frown. "If it makes you feel better, I don't think she poisoned it. She still likes Grace."

Kyra took the basket from Charlie and peeked inside. Julia had packed it with all sorts of delectable goodies. Her gaze lingered on the loaves of fresh bread as she led them to the living room. *Even if she did poison it, it'd probably be worth it.*

"I'm sorry, dear." Grace's lips pulled down, and she patted Kyra's arm. "Our Julia can hold a grudge. Char, remember when she refused to speak to me for a month after I told her I didn't like her moqueca?" Grace's eyes widened. "I swear it wasn't personal. I'm sure it was excellent. I just really dislike cilantro." Grace rubbed her knuckles with her thumb.

"We know." Charlie rolled her eyes again and flung herself down on the couch. She mimicked Grace, "But Char, it tastes like soap."

Julia Silva's son, Wes, and Kyra had not got on when she visited last spring. He'd broken into her home, threatened her, and nearly run her over with his truck. Then she'd ruined his construction business, and his reputation, by exposing his Ponzi scheme. According to Grace, Julia blamed Kyra, *that off islander*, for Wes's financial troubles. But for Kyra, Julia insisted, Wes would have dug himself out of debt with the new housing development on the north side of the island. That Julia had invested heavily in Wes's failed business venture, and was forced to return to work, cooking and catering for the island's summer crowds, probably had not helped improve Julia's opinion of Kyra. However, if this was what being hated by Julia was like, Kyra could live with it.

"This looks delicious," she said.

"I know. That's why I didn't tell her we were coming to see you." Charlie's eyes gleamed and her lips stretched into a conspiratorial smirk. "I said we were visiting an old island friend."

"Char," Grace admonished, but her cheeks were pinched like she was trying not to laugh.

"I'll be right back." Kyra laughed and carried the basket into the kitchen.

She arranged the baguettes in a tray with the pot of Julia's homemade butter. Not for the first time, Kyra wondered who bothered to churn their own butter, but she knew from experience Julia's herb butter was life altering.

She brought the food into the living room. Charlie had already opened the wine, and she handed Kyra a glass.

"This looks scrumptious, dear!" Grace took an olive from the board. "So, tell us everything! How are you? How is work? How is your detective? Your family?" Grace's words fell over each other.

"Let her talk." Charlie rolled her eyes at Kyra over her wineglass. "How is your family? Your aunt and uncle? The baby?"

Charlie's questions, though they came slower, allowing

Kyra to answer, were as copious as Grace's. Kyra filled them in on her job, her loose holiday plans, Ali, Cam, and little Iggy, the ear infection that postponed their trip.

"How disappointing," Grace frowned. "Will they be coming at all this summer? We've heard so much about Alicia."

"They have tentative plans to come this fall, once Cam finishes his contract. Ali goes back to work in January, so they'd like to take a holiday before then."

Kyra stacked a slice of brie on a chunk of Julia's baguette and dribbled it with honey. "Grace, did you learn anything about the wreck at the meeting? Or the accident?"

"Oh right. Do they know what happened?" Charlie wiped her mouth and sat forward.

"Ida didn't want to discuss anything else." Grace heaved a sigh and clasped her hands together. She glanced between Charlie and Kyra. "It's a terrible tragedy, what happened to those young people."

"It is." Charlie's mouth turned down in a sympathetic frown. "You knew them, didn't you?"

"Not really. I'd only just met them." Kyra told them about Gully and the *Keres*.

Grace shifted in her seat and pressed her lips together in distaste. "The council wants to release a public statement that the shoal is dangerous and warn off tourists from the site."

Kyra frowned. "Why?"

"The Devil's Bridge shoal has a nasty reputation for beaching ships. There is a lighthouse there, for goodness' sake." Grace finished her wine. "For centuries, the islanders have warned people away from that shoal. We're worried people will want to see the wreck and charter boats or sail out themselves. Already a few of the island charters are advertising trips to see the sunken pirate ship. The shoal is legally part of the island, and the island towns wouldn't want to be held responsible if something else went wrong."

"It makes sense for the island to mitigate its risk."

"Ugh, lawyers," Charlie teased and Kyra grinned.

"It may sound callous, but it's the council's responsibility to protect the island community." Grace turned to Kyra. "And there is concern this could impact tourism. The environmental activist groups are already raising objections, threatening to file injunctions and stage protests." Grace sucked in a breath and shook her head at Charlie. "And I know you're friends with them, Char, but that Andy has Ida's ear about the salvage ruining their business." Grace threw her hands up. "As usual, everyone is complaining." Charlie patted her wife's knee.

Grace sniffed and shifted in her seat. She lowered her voice as if to avoid being overheard. "Before we left the house, Ida called. I'm not sure if it's public knowledge yet, but the police don't think those young people drowning was an accident. They're calling it *murder*." Grace put her hand to her heart. "After all that awfulness last spring, and now this? The island will get a reputation. Char and I moved here to be safe. So many people did. What's happening to Martha's Vineyard?"

Charlie wrapped her arm around her wife's shoulder. "Grace, it'll be okay." Grace just shook her head, distraught. "Here, eat something, love." She handed her a brie-ladened crostini.

"Thank you," she said her voice breathy.

Charlie pulled away and passed her wine glass to Kyra to fill. "What were you saying about Andy, Grace?"

Kyra's head swiveled between her two friends; her eyebrows raised in a silent request for them to explain. "Oh, sorry. Andy. Andrew Mackey is my classmate from school. He and his brother Joe run a fishing company. You met my friend Lisa, Joe's wife, at my birthday party." Charlie made a face.

"Char, you had a wonderful time."

"I did." Charlie rolled her eyes, then grinned at Kyra, but Kyra was frowning. She'd sworn the man in the kitchen introduced himself as Andrew. *Definitely not Joe.* But she'd been so jet-lagged.

"Dear?"

"Was Andrew, er, Andy at your party?"

"Oh, he was." Charlie tapped her lip with her finger. "I'd forgotten. He wasn't there long. I'm surprised he was able to make it at all. I don't get to see him often."

"You're close with the whole Mackey family, then?" Kyra asked.

"Not really," Charlie said, spreading butter on a piece of baguette. "Andy, Lisa, and I were close as kids. Andy attended college in California and we lost touch. Lisa and I remained friends, but it wasn't until she married Joe that I got to know him. He's older. He'd already graduated by the time we were freshmen. Andy and I reconnected when he moved back with his wife, Sophia, about five years ago, when their dad died and left his sons the business."

"Andy's married to Sophia?" Kyra asked. The night of Charlie's party, she'd walked in on Lisa and Andy. She couldn't say for certain what she'd interrupted, but it hadn't looked like an innocent conversation between Lisa and her brother-in-law. She debated saying something to Charlie and Grace and decided not to. It wasn't any of her business.

"Mmhhmm." Charlie nodded. "Sophia is…" Her voice trailed off like she was searching for the right word.

"A pain in the ass. Is what she is." Grace finished for her.

Charlie choked on her wine. "Grace!"

"What, Char? She is. You can't deny it. Odious woman."

Charlie's cough turned into a cackle. "But you never say those things!"

"Some things are so obvious, my love, they need not be said." Grace peered at them over her wineglass. Her cheeks were tinged pink.

"Grace isn't wrong," Charlie said, still grinning. "But Sophia may get a bad rap."

"What do you mean?" Kyra asked.

Charlie sipped from her glass. "Andy and Sophia want to sell the business and go back to California, but Joe and Lisa can't make it work on their own. Until they can figure it out, Andy and Sophia are stuck here. Andy never wanted the island life. Even when we were kids, he talked about getting away. Both of them want to leave, but Sophia is much more vocal about it." Charlie chewed on her bread thoughtfully.

Grace reached over and took her wife's hand. "She still doesn't have to be so unpleasant," she said, curling her lip with distaste.

"Not everyone can have your sunny disposition, my

love."

"No, I suppose not." Grace sighed and Charlie rolled her eyes. "I hope she behaves herself at the council meeting tomorrow, though."

"What meeting?" Kyra asked.

"Oh, yes, dear. The Martha's Vineyard Community Council is the unofficial, but very official, island-wide voice of the people. Although the island has a few different towns, the council coordinates between them. We have representatives from all the villages. I represent our community, Katama. Ida, who you met, is our chairperson. Tomorrow we're hosting an island-wide meeting to discuss the impact of the wreck and the salvage efforts. The residents will hear from the salvagers, the environmentalists, local businesses, everyone. Then there will be a vote to allow or prohibit continuing the salvage efforts."

"You should come." Charlie picked up a fig and muttered out of the corner of her mouth to Kyra, "If nothing else, it's free entertainment."

"Oh yes, Char, that's a wonderful idea. You are a community member now. You're more than welcome. And you'll certainly learn more about the wreck. We're actually in need of another Katama representative."

Charlie shook her head, crisscrossing her hands in front of her, palms out. *Noooooo*, she mouthed. Kyra pressed her fingers to her lips to keep from laughing. Grace's eyes narrowed as she focused back on her wife. Charlie hid a fake yawn behind her hand.

"Tired, Char?" she asked dryly.

Charlie rolled her eyes. "I am actually."

Grace checked her watch. "Oh, it is later than I thought. We should be getting back." Charlie stretched and agreed. "Thank you, dear. It's been lovely to catch up." Grace reached to help Charlie stand. Kyra stood to walk her guests out. At the door, Grace turned to her. "I'll send you the details for the meeting tomorrow. You'd be welcome. Think about it."

"Thank you. I will. G'night, ladies." She watched Grace take Charlie's arm as they walked toward the path.

Chapter Seven

SOMETHING PULLED KYRA from the fog of sleep, and she groaned.

It buzzed again. Still blind with sleep, she reached for the bedside table. Her hand slapped the top once, twice, before landing on her phone. She brought the screen close to her face. Three a.m.

"Hello?" she croaked. The person on the other end didn't say anything. "Hello?" she said again, although she knew who was calling, and her heart ached for him.

"Kyra?" Chase's voice was rough, barely a whisper, like cotton on sandpaper.

"Hey," she said, and pulled herself into a sitting position.

She heard his breaths. His inhales were short and sharp, like he wasn't getting enough air. She pulled her knees up.

"I'm here, Chase. Deep breaths. In, one, two, three, four, five. Now out, five, four, three, two, one. Again." She breathed with him. In and out, in and out. His breath stuttered as he tried to breathe with her. "It's OK. I'm here." Slowly, his breathing turned normal.

"I'm sorry," he whispered. "I woke you."

"Nonsense." She remained on the call, both of them quiet, taking comfort in knowing the other person was there.

Kyra hadn't received a late-night call from him in a while, and she'd hoped the panic attacks were finally subsiding. But the news of Matty Gray and Jaycee's murders, and with Gully being held and questioned, she wasn't surprised it had provoked an attack. She hoped that he'd called when it started and he hadn't tried to suffer through it alone, but her hope was wishful thinking. He only called when he was breaking and had no other choice.

"Kay?" His voice was soft, not as hoarse.

"I'm here." She paused. Chase was silent on the other end. "Have I told you about the house my parents and I stayed in when we lived in France?"

"No."

Kyra settled back against the headboard, and like many nights before, she told him a story. She told him about the little house they rented in Nimes, the pear orchard, about her mother biking into town every morning for fresh bread and flowers. It mattered little what she said. It was just that she was there.

When she finished, he asked her to tell him another. She heard rustling and creaking as he settled, and she told him about a school trip to the see the Elgin Marbles, drawing it out, filling the air, listening to him until his breathing was deep and steady. It was past four when she finally hung up and dipped back under the covers.

Chapter Eight

KYRA RUBBED HER eyes. The sun shined off the cove. The memory of last night's phone call replayed through her head. Cronk meowed, and she rubbed his ears. Her phone buzzed on her nightstand. She reached for it. The movement disrupted the little abomination, and with a tortured yowl, he jumped to the floor. Kyra immediately missed his rumbly warmth.

"Sorry, Cronkers."

He paused at the door and shot a glare over his shoulder before striding from the room with an indignant tail flip. *I swear he understands me.* Kyra glanced at her phone screen. Chase.

"Be ready by 10."

Kyra frowned, her concern melting into confusion. *Did we make plans?* She checked the time. 9:35. *Shit.*

Twenty-five minutes later, she hurled down the stairs, her arm muscles protesting as she yanked a white tank over her bikini. She had no idea what she was dressing for. Her texts to Chase asking for more information had gone unanswered.

She snapped a coffee pod into the machine with more force than necessary and dribbled kibble into Cronk's bowl.

Kyra took her coffee and sat at the counter. She plugged her nearly dead phone into the charger and scrolled through the news headlines. She was searching for any mention of Terry Rose, the *Keres*, or Gully, *aka* Andre Gould III.

"Where do you think *Gully* comes from?" she asked the cat, who didn't stop chomping. Someone knocked on the front door. "Don't worry, I'll get it." Coffee in hand, she walked to the door to let Chase in.

"Hey, what are we…" Her words died on her lips, and her eyes widened in surprise. Her grip on the mug loosened. "Whoops." Kyra righted the mug before it tipped over.

"Good morning," Tarek said and pulled off his sunglass-es.

"Oh, uh. Good morning." She blinked the sun from her eyes and waited for him to explain what he was doing at her house.

Seconds ticked by before Tarek groaned. "Chase didn't tell you I was coming, did he?" He pressed his lips together and his eyes drifted to the sky like he was praying for pa-tience.

"Um, no. He didn't. But that's okay. Come on in." Kyra stepped aside to let Tarek in and made a mental note to strangle her dear friend later. "I'm having a coffee. Would you like one?" she asked over her shoulder as she led him back to the kitchen.

"Coffee would be great, thank you."

She slid another pod into the machine and pulled a mug down.

Tarek perched on a barstool and Cronk jumped up on the island. "Hello, there." Tarek scratched his chin.

The furry demon's purr could be heard across the room. He never greeted Kyra with such enthusiasm.

Kyra handed Tarek his coffee and waved the cat off the counter. "Black, one sugar, right?"

Tarek's eyebrow quirked up. "You have a good memory."

Kyra shrugged, feigning nonchalance. *For some things, maybe.* She leaned against the counter, sipping from her own cup. "So, what's the plan today?"

"He didn't tell you that, either?" Tarek pinched the bridge of his nose. Kyra shook her head. "Apparently, we're going to the beach." He didn't sound particularly happy about it.

"The beach? But what about Gully? The *Keres?*" It didn't sound responsible or very supportive to go sit in the sun while his friend was defending himself against possible murder charges. "Shouldn't we be doing something to help?"

"Gully is meeting with a lawyer this morning. Just getting him to agree to do that was like pulling teeth." Tarek sighed, the noise frustrated and unhappy.

"And the *Keres*?"

"Rose is filing the paperwork and securing the permitting so he can begin the salvage. He has to put together a presentation requested by the Martha's Vineyard Community Council. They're planning on meeting there later tonight."

"What about the investigation into what happened to Jaycee and Matty Gray?"

Tarek's eyes flashed. "I've been told by HQ that I'm to stay away from the case. That I have a *conflict of interest.*" His jaw clenched. "My captain is threatening to put me on administrative leave if I don't leave it alone."

Administrative leave? Kyra wasn't sure how that differed from a holiday, but by his expression, she sensed it wasn't good.

"You do have a conflict of interest."

"I know that, but I had to try." He rolled his shoulders back, and she got the impression that talking about it was making him feel worse. He spun his coffee mug.

She noticed he was dressed in swim shorts and a threadbare Boston University T-shirt. "And *you* want to go to the beach?" she asked, still trying to wrap her mind around a beach-going Tarek. *I bet he's one of those people that sits under an umbrella all day avoiding the sun like it's radioactive.*

"You say it like it's a weird thing. I lifeguarded on South Beach for years." He reminded her of his connection to the island. He and Gully had worked here during the summers, all through high school and college.

"Oh, that's right. So, do you go to the beach often, then?"

"It's been ten years, at least." He huffed an almost laugh. His gaze met hers and he was suddenly serious. "Kyra, actually…" But he didn't get to finish because at that moment, the front door flew open and Chase bounded in.

"Morning, sunshines!" he sang, his arms spread wide as he entered the kitchen. He pulled off his sunglasses. "Thank god, coffee." Kyra gave him a withering look and added a pod to the machine. He crowded her against the counter, wrapping his arms around her shoulders and dropping a kiss on top of her head. Kyra looked up, and she took in the dark circles and tight lines at his eyes. He looked like he hadn't slept at all, and she wondered if he'd been faking being asleep when she'd hung up.

His eyes searched hers. "Thank you," he whispered. She nodded, knowing he wouldn't want to get into it with an audience.

"How do you take it?" she asked, nodding to the machine.

"Just fake milk." Chase's playboy mask slid into place, and he flashed her a too wide grin. "So, you guys ready?" he asked, rubbing his hands together.

"You never actually told me what to be ready for." Kyra pulled the mug from the machine and set it on the counter.

Chase rummaged around in the fridge. He added an English muffin to the toaster.

"It's a small island. There really isn't that much to do." He gave her a lazy shrug. "Muffin?" he asked Tarek, who shook his head.

"Shouldn't we be helping Gully?" Kyra pressed.

The thought of sitting on a sunny beach while the pub master dealt with defense lawyers made her uneasy. Chase inclined his head toward Kyra, smiling behind his mug. Then he shifted his gaze to Tarek and raised his coffee cup in a mock cheers.

Tarek's mouth slanted down with understanding. "He called you."

Chase grinned. "He may have said something about being smothered by an overbearing mother hen and losing his mind." He stuffed half a muffin into his mouth. "Gully said he'd be free this afternoon and we can stop by then if we want to help him research."

"Research?" Kyra repeated. "Research what?"

"Mmhhmm." Chase shoved in the other half of his muffin, chewed, and swallowed. Kyra made a face. *Gross.* Chase wiped his mouth on his T-shirt sleeve. "He said we can help him go through the historian's papers on the *Keres.*" Now Chase made a face. "Fun times."

Kyra frowned. *Gully should be more concerned with the murder investigation. Not treasure hunting.*

Tarek must have noticed her expression. "When he's upset, he fixates." Tarek sucked in his cheeks. "He's been like that since we were kids. He'll obsess about the *Keres* to avoid thinking about the investigation."

Oh. Kyra's frown deepened. She empathized with Gully. She'd had clients like that–ones who'd become paralyzed with fear or come up with any excuse not to deal with the seeming unsurmountable problem in front of them. It offered them a sense of control. Kyra smoothed her hands over her cutoffs.

"Okay, then. If he wants our help with research, we'll help." She caught Chase's eye, daring him to object, but to her surprise, he didn't. He nodded his agreement and finished his coffee. Chase cleared his throat and wiped his hands on his shorts. "We should get going if we want a good spot." He slid his glasses back on and headed toward the front door. He stopped just as he opened it and called back, "Bring snacks. I'm starving."

Tarek watched him leave, then turned back to Kyra, one eyebrow raised.

"I guess we're going to the beach, then." Kyra sighed. "I think I saw beach chairs in the storage room in the cellar."

Tarek followed her down into the basement. She hadn't had time last spring to clean it out, and it was still full of her father's things. Normal mundane things, the kind of stuff people convince themselves they couldn't part from, then put away to forget about. In the storage room, a few rainbow-striped beach chairs were stacked in front of shelves installed against the back wall.

"Back there." She pointed. She scrambled over boxes and bins to the back of the room. The chairs were wedged between the shelving unit and another stack of boxes sitting on the floor in the corner. The box was labeled, written in her father's unintelligible scrawl, smeared where his left hand slid through the wet ink: *H--t, M--th-'s --e-rd.* Kyra reached for the wrinkled cardboard flap.

"Kyra? What is that?"

She whirled around to face Tarek. "I don't know. Rubbish likely." She wiped her dusty hand on the back of her shorts and reached for the chairs. "Here." She passed them one-by-one, followed by a beach umbrella. "Oh nice," she said, yanking a cooler out from the bottom of the shelves. She held it up.

"Great. Let me help you." He reached for her forearm and steadied her as she climbed back over the clutter.

"Anything else?" he asked, looking around.

"No, don't think so." Kyra shook her head.

"Get whatever else you'll need. I'll take this stuff outside."

Kyra ran upstairs and assembled her beach bag, tossing in a towel, sunscreen, and a paperback she'd plucked off the bookshelf, *And Then There Were None.* Kyra filled the cooler bag with ice and drinks. She surveyed her mostly barren pantry with dismay, pulling out the few bags of chips.

"Ky-ra! Come *on*!" Chase bellowed through the front door.

"Pipe down. I'm ready," she muttered, and slipped on her sunglasses.

Chase had donned one of the chairs like a backpack and had the umbrella strapped across his chest. Kyra snorted. He looked like a colorful warrior. Tarek too seemed cartoonishly burdened with bundles. He took the cooler from her and slipped it over his shoulder.

"Do we really need all this stuff?" she asked, looking between them.

"Yes. That's the fun of the beach. You bring all your shit with you, spend most of the time setting up, sit for twenty minutes, take it down, then lug it home. It's a time-honored tradition." Chase shook his head in mock disappointment, and his long hair fell into his eyes.

"You're an idiot, you know that?" She waved for him to proceed, resigned to follow Chase's lead. "Go on, then."

Tarek took up the rear in their short procession down the path to South Beach. Chase kept up a steady stream-of-consciousness monologue, giving them detailed updates about Barbossa, Mander Lane Farm, the *Elpis*, people he's met at bars. Tarek asked polite questions as if to encourage Chase to continue babbling and received a few glares from Kyra in return, which only seemed to fuel Tarek's inane inquisition. If she hadn't known better, she'd have thought he was *enjoying* himself.

They crossed Atlantic Drive and clambered up the dune

to South Beach. Kyra's chair slapped the back of her bare thighs. At the top, she took a deep breath, inhaling the salty scent of the sea. South Beach was crowded. The sand was spotted with colorful umbrellas and towels. Heads bobbed in the surf.

"This way," Chase said. He slid down the embankment and turned to the right. Sand gave way under their sandals, and Kyra kicked hers off. She yelped when bare feet hit the scalding sand.

Chase found a spot and plopped his things down. He cranked open the umbrella while Kyra and Tarek set up their chairs and towels. Kyra sat. She dug her toes into the soft, white sand and gazed out onto the Atlantic. The waves rolled in with a rumble. Seabirds flittered above the crests.

"It's beautiful, isn't it?" Tarek said softly. She couldn't see his eyes behind his mirrored aviators, but he didn't sound like he was teasing her.

"It really is." She'd been to the seaside a few times in England, and often to the Mediterranean. Italy, Spain, Greece, the regular places, but the western side of the Atlantic was different. Wild and menacing.

"I've missed it. I rarely get to come here in the summer."

"Nice!" Chase crowed, and Kyra turned to see him squatting in front of the cooler she'd packed. She heard the distinct, crisp sound of a can being popped. "You guys want one?" He looked up, his hair flopping over his wayfarers.

"It's barely eleven," Tarek grumbled.

Chase grinned; his eyebrows raised in a challenge.

"Yeah." Tarek sighed and leaned forward. "What do you got in there?"

Chase handed him two cans, wrapped with insulated koozies, and Tarek passed one to Kyra. She slipped it into the little cupholder attached to her chair and settled back against the nylon to people watch.

As the sun climbed, so did the heat and eventually she gave in to the temptation of the cool water. She stood and stripped down to her bathing suit. Chase gave her a whistle from under his hat. She made a face at him and flipped him the finger. She heard Tarek's chuckle as she walked down to the water. Kyra waded in up to her hips. The water was cool without being cold, and the sand was silky under her toes. She dove into a wave. Coming up for air, she pushed her hair out of her eyes and turned back toward their spot on the beach.

Chase was sitting up on his towel, his long legs straight out in front of him, talking over his shoulder to Tarek, who was leaning forward in his chair, his elbows on his knees. She could see Tarek's wry grin and Chase's shoulders shaking in laughter and she couldn't deny the nip of jealousy.

While she'd been in London, Chase and Tarek had become friends. Chase had told her about his frequent trips to the mainland for depositions and other legal proceedings. Tarek had met him each time, coached and supported him as he told and retold the story of Ed Gibson and Brendan Delaney's murders.

"What are you guys whispering about?" Kyra interrupted, pulling her towel from her bag. Even from behind his glasses, Kyra felt the weight of Tarek's gaze linger, perhaps for a second longer than necessary, and she smiled to herself.

"The regatta, then the *Keres*, then ... what else were we

talking about, Tar?" Chase gave Tarek a pointed look and smirked.

Tarek ignored him. He sat back in his chair and raised the can to his lips. Kyra glanced between them, frowning at their odd behavior. *What's going on here?* She caught Chase's eye, and he inclined his head the slightest bit. *He'll tell me later.* She stretched out on her towel, resting her head on her crossed arms, letting the sun dry her back. Her eyes slid closed, and she let Tarek and Chase's conversation about some Boston sports team lull her to sleep.

A stiffness radiating from her hip roused her, and she pushed herself up into a sitting position. Chase was gone, and Tarek had moved to his own towel. He was splayed out on his back, his T-shirt covering his face. He'd taken a swim. Water streamed off his tan muscles. He'd mentioned he'd swam competitively. Apparently, he'd kept up with it. Kyra caught herself staring and looked away. She was flushed, and not just from the afternoon heat.

"Where did Chase go?" she asked, picking the grains of sand from her towel one-by-one.

"Grindr or Tinder or something," Tarek mumbled and waved toward one end of the beach. Kyra lifted her sunglasses and squinted in the direction Tarek had pointed. She huffed a laugh. "He said he'd be back in a few."

"When is Gully expecting us?"

Tarek pulled his T-shirt away and checked his watch. "He'd probably prefer we stayed away, but we can pack up when Casanova gets back. When is that council meeting tonight?"

"I think Grace said five. It's in Chilmark. Why? Were

you planning on attending?" Kyra stood and shook out her towel. She was mostly dry. Her skin felt tight from salt and baking in the sun. *Did I get any color?* She checked for tan lines. When she looked up, she caught Tarek watching her. He didn't look away.

"There's a tiny family-run tavern up island, not far from the meeting house. Popular with the locals." Tarek's tone was casual.

Too casual. Kyra's eyes narrowed behind her glasses.

"Want to grab dinner after the meeting? With me?" She looked away, and folded the towel, lining up the edges perfectly.

"Are you asking me out?" She matched his too casual tone.

"I am." He sounded amused.

"Okay." She bit her lip to keep from grinning and squatted down to repack her bag.

"Okay." He repeated, sounding pleased.

Chase jogged up, water sloughing off his toned body. Tarek tossed him a towel. "How'd it go?" he asked, nodding down the beach.

"Good. I'm meeting them in OB later." He raised his eyebrow at him. "Wanna come?"

"Not even a little." Tarek stood to fold his chair while Kyra pulled the umbrella down.

"Your loss." Chase shrugged. "Are we going to Gully's now?"

Kyra nodded. "Mmhhmm, pack up."

Chapter Nine

"WHAT ARE YOU listening to?" Kyra was sitting in Tarek's old Jeep. Chase had gone on ahead. Tarek had put away the mostly unused beach things while she showered and dressed. Kyra smoothed the skirt of her dress. She'd had major wardrobe indecision, but she couldn't call Ali for help with Tarek waiting downstairs. She'd settled on a blue strapless sundress that was probably too fancy for sitting at Gully's house, or dinner at a tavern, but it showed off her tan and made her eyes pop.

"It's a podcast."

"You listen to true crime podcasts?" she asked, her mouth falling open, and then she grinned. *I cannot wait to tell Chase!*

"Some of their ideas aren't half bad." Tarek glanced at her and back to the road. He shifted in the driver's seat.

Kyra couldn't help teasing him. "Obviously. Tell me, is it exclusively women talking about serial killers, or do you listen to other types of murder?"

His mouth twitched. "I don't discriminate. I listen to all types of crime. Murder, larceny, disappearances." Tarek flipped off the stereo, and Kyra frowned. She'd only been in the car a few minutes, but she'd already become invested in the host's investigation. Tarek glanced at her with a knowing look. "I'll text you my favorites."

"I'd like that, thank you. Where does Gully live?" She peered out the window. They were somewhere inland, but she hadn't been paying close attention to their drive.

"He has a modest compound in the interior of the island."

"A modest compound? A bit of an oxymoron, no?"

Tarek laughed. "The property has five buildings. He fixed them up and rents out the front four houses for the summer or puts up families for school or sports competitions. He stays in a cabin at the back of the property year-round."

Tarek made a left off onto a wooded road. Without the wind and surf to fight, the trees in the island's interior grew taller than the scrub pines near her house. They continued deeper into the thickening woods. He turned onto a dirt road with a PRIVATE PROPERTY sign. The brush had been cut back and a crude walking or bike path had been stamped down alongside the road.

They emerged from the forest into a clearing surrounded by trees. It was indeed a modest compound. Kyra thought it resembled a summer camp from old movies. Four small cape style houses sat on the perimeter of a u-shaped green, dotted with plastic toys. Someone had set up soccer nets in the yard, and Kyra noticed a horseshoe pit tucked to the side. Three cars were parked in a makeshift parking area.

"He normally has renters booked throughout the summer," Tarek said, his voice more serious. "But after the news named him as a person of interest in Matty Gray and Jaycee's deaths, he had cancelations. The family here now has been coming for years. They booked this week, and will take next week that just freed up."

Kyra caught the worry in Tarek's voice. She didn't know Gully's financial situation, but he couldn't make that much money from the pub, especially during the off season. He probably relied on what he earned from his summer rentals, and people would cancel staying with a potential killer. She'd never considered how a murder investigation would impact a suspect's livelihood.

"How about his restaurant?"

"He said there has been some backlash. He's had a few canceled events and when he's in the dining room, he's been hassled by the press. He's been trying to stay out of sight. Luckily, his place is a favorite with the locals, who know him. They won't be scared off easily as the summer people."

Tarek followed the road behind the cluster of houses. Just beyond a natural barrier of trees and brush sat another building. The front of Gully's house was partially hidden by untamed rhododendron bushes. Unlike the other houses on the property, his didn't have a front porch, and two chimneys, one on either side, framed the little two-story cabin.

"This is it." Tarek parked on the grass next to a beat-up Tacoma and Chase's Bronco. Tarek rapped on the Dutch door before pushing it open.

"Gully! We're here," he called out, stepping into the room. Kyra slipped in behind him and stepped to the side to allow Tarek to close and latch the door.

Kyra took in the space. It was bright and open, with exposed pine beams and brick accents. On one side was the living room area, with an enormous sectional sofa and matching armchairs arranged around a brick fireplace, and a gargantuan flatscreen TV. On the opposite side was a modern kitchen with an island instead of a table. Sliding glass doors opened up to a patio with a picnic table and barbeque. Stairs in the back led up to a second story, where Kyra assumed the bedrooms were. Everything about the pub master's house was too big for the space but it didn't feel crowded. It was warm and cozy, a *hyggelig* house. *It looks like him.*

"Be right up!" A gruff voice came from below and Kyra noticed a door open to a descending stairwell. Tarek helped himself to a few bottles of water from the fridge. He handed her one and nodded toward the couch.

"You made it." Chase bounded up the stairs two at a time, balancing two boxes stacked one on top of the other. He dropped them unceremoniously on the floor next to the coffee table, releasing a cloud of dust. Kyra coughed and glared at him.

"Watch it," Gully growled from behind him. A scowl creased his brow. He stooped to set down his own set of boxes. "How was the beach?"

"Nice," Kyra said at the same time Chase said, "Sandy."

"South wasn't too windy or crowded. Not yet anyway. We probably left at a good time." Tarek answered. "How did the meeting with the lawyers go?"

Gully's brown eyes flashed and his eyebrows slanted. "As well as one could expect." He turned an accusing glare on the detective. "You didn't tell me you hired the biggest firm in Boston."

"It's not the biggest firm. And Connors owed me one. They're giving us reduced fees." Tarek shrugged, but something flickered behind his eyes, and he looked down at his feet.

Gully grimaced. "The reduced fees are a joke."

"Gully."

Gully raised his hand, cutting him off. "I know, Tar. They're sending over the engagement paperwork today. Connors has a call into the investigators. He told me to lie low, keep out of trouble, and refuse to answer any more questions without my attorney present. All the things you told me yesterday for free." Gully opened the boxes, folding back the flaps. "Satisfied?"

Kyra watched Tarek from underneath her lashes. His head bobbed in a curt nod, but he looked like he wanted to say something more. Gully's forehead was creased in a scowl. He yanked open the box.

"Gully?" Her voice came out soft. Gully looked up. "I just wanted to say how sorry I am. With what happened to Matty Gray and Jaycee. And this whole … thing. I didn't know them, but they seemed like lovely people." Kyra wrung her hands, knowing that nothing she said would be adequate, but still feeling like she needed to say something.

Gully swallowed, and his expression softened revealing his grief. "I appreciate that, London."

They were all quiet for a moment, until Kyra clapped her hands together and said with forced enthusiasm, "Right. Well then, what are we looking for?"

She sat on the couch and peered into the box closest to her. The cardboard was old, crumbling at the corners and covered in dust. *Please, no spiders.*

"Good question," Gully said with a grateful dip of his chin. He gestured to the boxes. "These are Aaron Hart's files."

"Who's that?" The name sounded familiar, but she couldn't place it.

"He was a local historian," Gully explained. "He researched the Wraith and the *Keres*."

Chase slumped onto the couch and yanked a box closer to him. He pulled it open, his nose wrinkled, lip curled.

"After he died, some of his files were donated to the library in Vineyard Haven. When the library moved to the new location, they didn't have the room, or the interest, in keeping or cataloging it all, so I offered to take them. Technically, it's all *on loan*." Gully made air quotes. "I've been meaning to go through it, but I haven't gotten around to it. Now, since the wreck was uncovered, the head librarian wants it all back for an exhibit. And since I have fuck all to do, I'm going through it today." Gully stood and strode into the kitchen. He returned with a folder.

"Jaycee and Matty Gray got a few good images of the wreck. Terry brought them over earlier. He had more than what the press leaked." Gully swallowed.

Kyra thought his hand trembled as he pulled the eight by ten photographs from the folder. He dropped them on the coffee table and took a seat in one of the big chairs.

Tarek leaned forward and arranged them for a better view, his shoulder brushing against hers. She peered around him. The photos were close-ups of the grainy image she'd seen on TV. Although it was partially buried under the sand, it was definitely a woman's face carved from wood. Her visible eye was open wide, with pinpoint pupils. A mouth, baring sharp pointed teeth, was open in a scream. Her tongue, which might have stretched over her bottom jaw, had broken off. Kyra rolled her shoulders, unsettled by the image. Seeing this coming at you, emerging from the mists, it would have been petrifying.

"Anything more we can find that would help us prove the wreck is the *Keres* or what's on board and where to look once she's hauled up would be helpful. Terry's exclusivity to the wreck doesn't last forever. We need to prove it's the *Keres* for him to salvage it."

"Is there any question?" Kyra asked, tapping the image of the masthead.

"Unofficially, I'm the expert, but it would be helpful if I can point to some evidence supported by someone qualified and credentialed, but I'm pretty sure it's the *Keres*."

"How sure?" Chase asked, waggling his eyebrows.

Gully frowned. He stared down at the images on the coffee table. "I'd bet my life on it."

Chase quirked an eyebrow at Gully and pushed his hair out of his eyes to stare into the depths of his box. He made a face at Kyra, something between a plea for help and disgust.

"This'll be fun," he said, his voice flat.

Kyra observed the pub master. She was still circumspect that he was pursuing researching the salvage when his friends had just died, when he could have been trying to build a defense, but she remembered what Tarek said about how Gully processed emotions. Even with the distraction of the wreck, Gully seemed despondent. *Maybe he needs this.* Kyra resolved to help anyway she could.

She scooted down to the floor, folding her legs underneath her skirt. Tarek gave her shoulder a gentle squeeze and excused himself to take a shower, earning a glare from Chase.

"Lucky bastard," he muttered.

They worked in silence.

Kyra soon found herself immersed in the documents. It brought back memories of long nights digging through records during due diligence reviews when she was a junior lawyer in New York. She'd secretly enjoyed the research part of the job, going through documents, talking to people, hunting down the facts. As she'd progressed up the ranks at her law firm, she'd become more client-facing, relying on her own junior lawyers to handle doc-review and researching legal precedence.

Aaron Hart had assembled an impressive collection. There were copies of ship logs, manifests, and sail charts tracking the movements of the *Keres* across the western hemisphere. Hart had put together William Robert's entire maritime history, mostly from original source accounts. He'd filled notebooks with data, all neatly printed with what she thought looked like ink from an old-fashioned fountain pen.

Despite his notoriety, William the "Wraith" Roberts was reportedly quite the gentleman rogue. He attended posh society events in Port Royal, Jamaica, and the Bahamas. His crew was infallibly loyal to him, many even taking his place on the gallows on less pirate-friendly islands where he was a wanted man. His story echoed the legends of Robin Hood. Personal accounts told tales of the pirate distributing his stolen wealth amongst the needy in Port Royal, and Douglas on the Isle of Man. He'd been a sort of folk hero to the people, and his name was mentioned with reverence by the residents.

"Find anything?" Tarek asked, coming downstairs.

He'd changed into slim trousers and a crisp white button-down shirt, the sleeves rolled up his forearms. She still wasn't used to seeing him in anything but his rumply television detective uniform and she'd forgotten how well he cleaned up. *He really should dress like that more often.* Her appraisal was appreciative and his eyes lit up.

"Kay, look at this," Chase said, his brow furrowed. "These are photocopies of an old journal, I think." He passed yellowing pages to Kyra. Tarek sat beside her on the couch and read over her shoulder. She skimmed its contents, written in swirly old-fashioned script.

> *14 September 1709*
>
> *The journey has been difficult, but we have been blessed with fine weather. The captain says we will reach Boston in a week's time, if the weather holds. It cannot come soon enough. My dearest Helena has taken to her bed since we left Douglas and has remained there for the entirety of this long journey to the Colonies. The ship's doctor believes she is burdened with an illness of the mind, a melancholia. Kitty says our youngest suffers from an ailment of a more feminine nature, a broken heart. I pray the fresh air and new opportunities in Gloucester revive her.*

Tarek took the pages from her and read them through before returning them to Chase. She frowned and glanced at

Gully. "Was Roberts married? I think the writer is talking about his wife and daughter."

Gully motioned for the pages. "To my knowledge, he wasn't married. He died trying to unite with his love. I don't know about children."

Chase passed her another page. "It looks like Hart only made copies of certain entries. Read this one."

Kyra read it aloud. "'9 March 1710. Our family is ruined. Helena has birthed a bastard. She claims she was married in Douglas. In secret. That the child's father will come for her. My dear Kitty has taken to her bed in shock. Our relations in England have abandoned us.' Are there more?" Kyra asked, and Chase handed her the rest of the pile.

She skimmed them. The rest of the entries were about the writer's merchant business, but here and there, he mentioned his daughter and a child named William. Kyra set the pages down, and Tarek picked them up. "Who are these people?"

"Is Helena's baby the pirate?" Chase asked.

"No." Gully rubbed his beard. "The dates don't match up. Roberts would have been an adult in 1710." He frowned. "Does it say whose journal this is?"

"It doesn't say." Tarek flipped through the pages.

Gully pulled a binder down from a bookshelf. "This is my research," he explained, flipping through. "What year were those entries?"

Tarek checked. "September 1709 and March 1710."

"That family is from the Isle of Man?"

Kyra nodded. "I think so, unless there's another Port

Douglas in the UK?"

Gully scratched at his beard.

"When was the *Keres* lost, Gully?" Tarek asked.

"Late summer 1712, based on local accounts. There was a bad hurricane that year. I think it was on or around the eighteenth of August." Gully's jaw worked as he thought.

Kyra chewed her bottom lip.

"What are you thinking?" Tarek asked.

"I'm not sure yet," she said honestly. "I'm trying to piece it together." She didn't yet have enough information.

Gully snapped the binder shut and dropped it on the table. Chase picked it up.

"He was born on Man, by all accounts. Took up as a sailor. Eventually got into pirating." Gully walked to the kitchen, returning with four beers and passed them out.

"What's this?" Chase asked, holding out the binder and pointing to a page.

Gully took it from him. "Oh, the lighthouse at Gay Head. It was built in 1799, way later than the *Keres*."

"No, not that, about the smugglers?"

"Hmm. Oh, right. I was looking for accounts of the *Keres* running aground, but all I found were these stories."

"What stories?" Tarek asked.

"The legends about the site of the lighthouse? It's special to the native people, the Wampanoag."

"Like a cursed burial ground?" Chase sat up straighter.

"No, you idiot." Gully snorted. "All of Aquinnah is a heritage center and significant to the Wampanoag culture even today. I'm sure it's been exaggerated, turned into a myth or folktale, but the Wampanoag did use the cliffs and

Lost Beach. They used the sea caves. Eventually smugglers learned of the caves and used them, too. The legends say the sea caves go deep into the cliffs, all the way to the top. But like I said, it's probably blown out of proportion. Those caves fill with water during high tide. I doubt there's much truth to the stories."

Tarek opened their beers. She placed hers on the table and rested her head against the couch cushions. Despite the air conditioning, Kyra's skin felt prickly and hot, her body drained and lethargic. Kyra pushed her hair away from her face and tried to focus on the article she'd been reading about Port Douglas.

"Hey," Tarek's voice was soft at her ear and his hand came to her shoulder. "Are you OK?"

"Yes, fine." She pulled herself upright and gave herself a mental shake. "How often did William Roberts go back to Man?" she asked. "Does anyone have a box with accounts from there?"

"Yeah, mine has stuff." Chase pulled a notebook from his box. He wiped it off with his shirt and opened it. The taped spine cracked. "This one contains information on his early life. Says here, Roberts was listed as a sailor on a merchant vessel sailing for Virginia, the *Patience*." He squinted at the notes. "I think this says he left Douglas in June 1709. The journal family and Roberts were on Man together, then. Could they have known each other?"

Kyra considered that. Was it possible and if so, what did that mean?

Tarek cocked his head to the side, considering. "Do you have any more boxes, Gully?"

"We haven't gone through this one yet." Chase pulled over the last box and opened it. "More notebooks. What's this?" He pulled out a thin packet of pages bound with an alligator clip and handed it to Kyra.

She flipped through the document. "It's an outline."

"For what?" Tarek peered over her shoulder.

"Looks like a book," she mumbled. "Did Aaron Hart write a book?"

"Not that I know of." Gully shook his head. "But he was a history professor. He probably wrote lots of things."

History professor? Kyra frowned at something niggling in the back of her mind. Chase caught her eye and cocked his head. She shook her head. *It's nothing.*

"Can I?" Tarek reached for the outline. His eyes flicked back and forth while he read.

Kyra scooted closer to Chase's box and peeked inside. "What else is in this one?"

Chase grunted and kicked the whole thing over.

"Hey!" Kyra snapped, and she scowled at him.

He raised a shoulder in a lazy shrug. The contents of the box lay scattered over the rug. Her eye caught on the corner of what looked like an old Polaroid photograph, peeking out from the mess.

She grabbed it, expecting to find something related to the shipwreck. She held the photo up. Chase leaned in behind her, his body warm against her bare shoulders. It was an image of an older man and two girls. They were standing in front of a cedar shingled house. The man, in round glasses, wore shorts and a T-shirt with a dog printed on the front. He was grinning widely for the camera, his arms around the two children on his either side. The taller girl, perhaps in her teens, had long, dark hair and a secretive smile. The other, much younger girl, was laughing. She was hugging a goat nearly as big as she.

Kyra's breath hitched, and she froze. She knew that smile. She knew that laugh. She'd recognize them anywhere.

"What'd you find?" Tarek asked.

Kyra looked up to see them all watching her. She pulled her phone from her purse and snapped a picture of the photograph before passing it to him.

"It's my mom."

"Your mom?" Chase craned his neck like he could see the image Tarek held.

"It is." She angled the phone so Chase could see. "And that's my aunt." She pointed to the younger girl on her screen.

"But Ali's blonde," Chase said.

"She's been dying it since she was a teenager," Kyra mumbled, only half paying attention. She stared at the image of Isabel, her mother, smiling the same smile Kyra saw some days in the mirror. "Their maiden name is Hart. I didn't put it together."

"Aaron Hart was … your grandfather?" She looked up into Chase's eyes. She recognized concern there. He put his hand on her shoulder.

"The name sounded familiar, but I didn't place it. I don't remember him or my grandmother. They died when I was young. They were older when they adopted my mom and Ali." Tarek passed the photograph back to her. "Do you think the library would care if I kept this?" Kyra asked Gully.

"I won't tell if you don't."

"Thank you." Kyra slipped it into her purse.

"Actually…" Tarek stretched his arms above his head. "We probably need to get going if we're going to get seats at that meeting."

Gully glanced at an old-fashioned clock on a side table. "You're right." His chest expanded with a sigh. "This was kind of a bust, huh?"

"I don't know," Kyra mused, her hand moving to her purse.

Gully made a gruff noise that could have been in agreement, then asked Chase, "You coming?"

"Fuck no." Chase drained his beer and grabbed Kyra's that sat still untouched on the coffee table. "I'm meeting some friends in OB in a few hours. I'll pack all this shit up and take a rideshare over later."

Kyra picked up the empty bottles. "Friends?" She threw him an incredulous look over her shoulder as she headed to the kitchen.

"Call me an optimist." His smile turned wicked as he stood to follow her.

She dumped the bottles in the recycling bin. "Be careful." She narrowed her eyes at him.

"Always." He pressed a kiss to her temple. "I'll give you all the sordid details tomorrow. Promise." His eyes sparkled when Kyra wrinkled her nose. *Please no.*

Chapter Ten

THE MEETING HOUSE parking lot was full, and they were directed to park at the church across the street. Cars sped by, honking at the chaos created by well-meaning but inept volunteer traffic directors. A man leaned out of his window to yell at an elderly woman in an orange visibility vest. Tarek grabbed Kyra's hand and pulled her across the street, narrowly avoiding oncoming cars in a real-life game of Frogger.

The meeting house was a large building set back from the street, behind a graveled yard, bordered with trees for shade. It had a wide covered front porch scattered with wooden rocking chairs. People loitered outside. From the way the attendees greeted each other, clasped hands, and others polite nods, Kyra could tell many of these people were acquainted.

She recognized a few faces from when she'd visited in the spring. Nina from Café Joy, Mrs. Lisbon from the general store. Even one of the police officers who'd come to her house after her altercation with Wes Silva. *These are the islanders.* She stepped a little closer to Tarek, and his hand around hers tightened for a second before he let her go and ushered her up the stairs.

A man approached; hand outstretched. "Collins, I thought I'd find you here."

Tarek shook his hand. "Taking a bit of a vacation."

Kyra stepped away to give them a moment and studied the bulletin boards posted on either side of the double doors. Flyers announced various events – a weekly farmer's market, artisan and agricultural fairs later in August, summer concerts. There were even postings offering summer work, including a few help-wanted ads for the farm stand at Mander Lane.

"Sorry about that. Ready?" Tarek's hand rested on her lower back.

"Yes. Who was that?"

"He runs one of the island's newspapers. He thought I was here investigating the murders. Wanted to ask me some questions."

She heard the irritation in his tone. The doors were propped open, and Kyra stepped through into a wide antechamber. Just beyond the entryway, inside the main room, plastic folding chairs had been set up in rows. Tables pushed against the walls were laden with pitchers of lemonade, iced tea, and baked goods covered by little netted tents.

She stepped into the meeting room and reared back. The heat hit her like a punch. It had to be at least fifteen degrees hotter in here, and it wasn't even full. Ceiling fans spun slowly, and floor fans spaced around the room whirred, moving the air like a spoon through hot soup. It did nothing to temper the heat.

"I forgot," Tarek muttered and let out an exasperated sigh. "No AC." His eyebrows furrowed as he straightened to scan the room. "Go find seats. I'll get us some drinks." Tarek cocked his head toward the refreshment table, where a queue was already forming.

Kyra moved through the crowd looking for the Chamberses. She felt eyes on her, heard questions asked in hushed tones.

"Who's that?"

"Is she new?"

"Did someone sell?"

She squared her shoulders—against the heat and the stares. Sweat gathered where her dress clung to her body. Her hair stuck to her neck and back. She spotted Grace waving from a row close to the front of the room, strategically positioned right in front of an industrial fan. Kyra raised her hand in acknowledgment and made her way through the crowd.

"Hi, dear, you made it!" Grace waved her forward. "Come sit. We saved seats." She gestured to the chairs next to hers. She'd slung jackets across the chair backs and placed bags on the seats. "Your handsome detective is with you." It wasn't a question. Kyra opened her mouth to object, but Grace cut her off. "We'll need more seats. Put your bag on that one. We don't want someone stealing it." Grace hoarded the row like the chairs were priceless.

"How many people are you expecting?"

Grace blinked at her and cocked her head to the side. "What do you mean?"

Kyra pushed her now limp hair off her shoulder and set her purse on the chair. Grace had reserved nearly half the row. Grace plopped in a chair three over from Kyra and leaned in. She rolled her lips and narrowed her blue eyes. Kyra stared at her helplessly, unsure what her friend was doing.

"Grace?"

"Where is he?"

"Who?" she asked, before realizing and she sighed. "Tarek's getting us drinks. Where's Charlie?"

"Kay!" Charlie appeared at the far end of their row, carrying two large plastic cups. She muscled through the people, stepping over legs, bags, even a small, miserable-looking dog. "No, stay sitting." She pushed past them, handing Grace a cup, and took the seat at the end in front of the fan. "Christ, it's hotter than a billy goat with a blowtorch in here."

Kyra gaped at her. *What?* Charlie wiped her forehead with the back of her hand, then wiped her hand on her powder blue shorts. She pressed the side of the cup, already glistening with condensation, against her neck and forehead.

"Char, are you sure we should sit here?" Grace spread her hands, gesturing to their reserved space. "With the fan, we won't be able to hear anything. It's going to be a very important presentation. We really will need to pay attention."

"We won't be able to get seats together." Charlie rolled her eyes. "And I'll die before I give up the fan," she said behind her hand to Kyra and turned her face into the blowing air.

"Oh, I suppose you're right. This is why I wanted to get here early, Char. We don't have many options." Grace made a grumbling noise. She straightened in her seat and looked up at the front of the room, then tested the seat next to that one. "This will have to do." Kyra watched her neighbors, half wondering if the heat was giving her a fever dream.

Charlie turned to Kyra and said, her voice low, "Are you prepared to witness the full insanity of island politics?" She glanced around and lowered her voice even further. "At least fifty percent of these people are certifiable and should be committed."

Kyra grinned.

"Char," Grace hissed from a closer seat, neck craning toward the front of the room. No one had taken the seats in front of them. They had an unobstructed view of a podium with a microphone and the six chairs arranged to the side, facing the audience. Charlie rolled her eyes again and turned her face into the fan.

Where's Tarek? Kyra lifted her hair off her neck. She wished she'd had the forethought to bring a hair tie. Her skin prickled uncomfortably. She swiveled in her seat, looking around the hall just in time to see Gully enter the room.

He was hard to miss. His bulky frame almost took up the entire doorway. He'd changed into a starched short-sleeved button-down shirt and his beard seemed less wild and bushy. His head moved slowly as he scanned the crowd. Spotting someone, he raised his hand in greeting. Kyra followed his line of sight across the room and recognized Terry Rose standing in the corner, close to the front.

"Water?" Tarek appeared at the end of the row. He handed her a plastic cup full of mostly ice. It was cool in her hot hand. Kyra took her purse from the chair next to hers and motioned for him to sit. "Sorry, I got stuck talking to one of Gully's neighbors."

The woman occupying the seat directly behind them glared at Kyra and muttered loudly about rude tourists.

Tarek gave the woman a toothy smile. "Ma'am," he said with a nod, and turned around.

He leaned back in his chair. Kyra pressed the cold cup to her clavicle. She sighed when the icy drops of water hit her feverish skin. Tarek's cheeks were flushed too, his shirt not as crisp.

He cleared his throat. "Grace, Charlie. Nice to see you again. How have you been?"

"Lovely!" Grace crowed. "It's so nice to see you too, Detective! How has your summer been?" She talked in a singsong voice over Charlie's greeting. Charlie rolled her eyes and turned her face back into the fan.

"It's been busy, but I'm glad to have some time off."

"It's wonderful that you get to spend time on the island, and with our girl."

Kyra stiffened. If it was possible, she'd have blushed, but if her skin got any hotter, she'd ignite.

"It is."

There was some shuffling as a group of official-looking people walked up the center aisle. Tarek pointed to the man in an almond-colored suit at the center.

He leaned forward and said, his voice low so only Kyra could hear, "That's Frank Kapowski, with Blue Stream Marine Salvage. Terry's competition. Looks like he came prepared."

Kyra noticed an aide carrying a projector screen. Frank and his entourage moved to the side of the makeshift stage next to where Gully and Terry were standing off to the side. Frank greeted Terry, gripping the smaller man by the shoulder while he leaned in to say something. Terry nodded; his expression solemn.

A man in a Hawaiian shirt strode toward the podium. He tapped on the mic and cleared his throat. “Can everyone find their seats, please? We’d like to get started.”

A woman asked Charlie if they could all shift down a few seats.

“No, Barb, but you can take those.” Charlie pointed to the center of the row. The woman grumbled and turned away. “Like I’m giving up the fan,” Charlie muttered.

Kyra’s eyes met Tarek’s. Like her, he was trying not to laugh. A noise came from the front of the room.

“Thank you!” The man’s voice boomed over the PA system and the chatter quieted. “Welcome to the third unscheduled Martha’s Vineyard Community Council meeting this year. As you know, we’re here to discuss the wreck that was discovered off the coast of the island and potential salvage efforts.” A few voices came from the back of the room and the speaker made a *settle-down* motion. He mopped his forehead with paper napkins and stuffed them in his pocket. “Yes, you’ll all get a chance to ask your questions, *at the end.*” There was the sound of a chair scraping on the floor.

“Okay, let’s get started. First, Terry Rose with Rose Marine Salvage and Frank Kapowski with Blue Stream have put together a presentation.” Frank raised his hand at the mention of his name. Terry turned to say something to Gully. “Frank, you go first.” Hawaiian-shirt man stepped back and motioned to the podium.

As Frank stepped forward, Kyra watched Hawaiian shirt man back step across the front of the room and duck out through a side door. It banged shut with a loud thud. She cast a glance at Tarek, who returned it, his eyebrows raised.

"Er … right." Frank's eyes lingered on the door, then turned back to the crowd.

"And the insanity begins!" Charlie whispered, rubbing her hands together like a cartoon villain.

At least three people shushed her.

Grace threw a glare at her wife that any exasperated mother would be proud of. Charlie winced. Kyra bit her bottom lip. Tarek's shoulder bumped against hers. His nostrils flared, and his eyes were wide, holding in a laugh. *This is straight lunacy.*

"Thank you all for your time." Frank turned back to the room. Despite the suffocating heat, he looked cool and calm. He pushed the podium and mic off to the side and gave the crowd a gracious smile, sliding his hands into his pockets. "These things are so formal." He chuckled and some of the tension in the room eased.

Frank reintroduced himself and his company, then launched into his proposal. He motioned to his assistants, who projected a presentation on a temporary screen at the front of the room. He showed the audience a short animation depicting the salvage, and explained, using graphs and other visual aids, how Blue Stream planned to raise the *Keres* to preserve the ship. His tone was polite but conversational. He emphasized the historical significance of the find, and conveniently, Kyra thought, left out the potential financial value of the treasure rumored to be in this ship's hold. Frank paused and his eyes swept over the crowd. A clamor from the back of the auditorium had everyone turning around. A man in an aqua and blue polo shirt was standing. He'd crossed his arms over his chest.

"I'm sure you have many questions." Frank raised his hands, palms out. "I'm happy to answer every one, but I request you hold them until after my colleague speaks." The man sat back down. "May I present Terry Rose with Rose Marine Salvage." Frank waved Terry over, but remained next to him.

Terry thanked Frank, then summarized his own company's proposal in excruciating detail. He explained the mechanics of the salvage efforts, his cadence slow and monotone.

The heat was unbearable. Kyra set her cup of now warm water on the floor. She tried to unstick her hair from the back of her neck, but the damp strands just tangled in her fingers. The chair's knobby plastic irritated her heat-sensitive skin, and she shifted in her seat.

Terry was losing their attention, and the audience became restless. People were on their phones, fanning themselves with paper plates, chatting in hushed, hurried tones. The atmosphere had changed. It felt charged, staticky.

Charlie moved her chair, so it was facing away from the front of the room and positioned directly in front of the fan. Her body swayed with the oscillations and her hair stirred in the artificial breeze.

On the drive up island, Tarek had explained that marine salvage efforts like this one were often about who got there first. There was no doubt Terry had a superior claim, having arrived on the scene days prior, but he needed the support of the community to raise the wreckage. Unlike Frank, who had a much larger operation, Terry couldn't afford to give up other jobs to remain on the island and slog through administrative red tape and file lawsuits for access. If Terry was stalled too long, he would have to abandon the *Keres*.

"Blue Stream and Rose Marine are wholly committed to working with the community. This find should benefit us all," Frank's booming voice interrupted Terry, and he stepped in front of him. It was clear to Kyra that Frank was implying he and Terry were aligned, but that he and Blue Stream were the strategic leaders of the effort. Without saying it, he conveyed to the audience that he was the decision-maker.

Terry's shoulders drooped and gave a slight shake of his head. His forehead glistened with sweat and his clothes stuck to his body. Kyra chanced a glance at Gully, but his expression was blank and unreadable.

"Thank you, Frank. If you're ready, we can open the floor for questions?"

"By all means."

"What do you intend to do about the fishing?" a voice demanded from the back of the room.

"That's my livelihood!" called another male voice.

There was a *screech*, metal chair legs on wood. Kyra, along with the rest of the audience, turned around. The same aqua-shirt man from before was standing. His arms were crossed over his chest. He held his chin high as if challenging the front of the room. The audience quieted, all eyes on the man.

"Terry, Mr. Kapowski," the man said, his voice steady and clear. "We … *I* make my living fishing through the summer and fall. The fluke are biting now and the stripers start soon. You pull up a wreck, you'll disturb their runs. You'll ruin my business. How am I to feed my family while you get rich pulling that trash up?"

"We should be able to pull her up in just a few days, so the impact on the fishing in the sound should be minimal." Frank shrugged, and turned his attention to another audience member, but the man wasn't finished.

"Not so fast. My family has had an oyster farm on that shoal for the past thirty years. You pull a settled wreck out; you'll pollute the water with sediment. That will ruin my harvest. So now I've got no fish and no oysters. How are you going to compensate me? Do I … we islanders get a part of whatever you haul up? What if it's garbage? What then? No one here believes that whatever's down there is worth shit."

Voices murmured their agreement.

"Joe, please." A woman sitting next to him reached for his arm.

Kyra recognized Charlie's friend Lisa Mackey.

"No, Lees." He brushed her hand away and glared at the salvagers. "I'd like to hear what the *mainlanders* have to say. How they're going to justify ruining our livelihood for a treasure hunt."

Lisa's hands dropped to her lap, and she turned to a dark-haired woman sitting next to her, but the woman ignored her, and tucking her hair behind her ear, turned to the man at her side. Kyra recognized him from Charlie's party, too. It was the man in the kitchen. *Andy. That must be his wife.*

"I assure you we'll do whatever we can to contain the debris." Frank held his hands up. He'd made a cursory mention of the potential impact on the water quality and nearby seabed, brushing over it to focus on the expected tourism income. Given how he was dismissing Joe Mackey, Kyra bet the omission had been intentional.

Terry was in front of Frank's laptop. He pressed a few keys and a marine chart depicting the Devil's Bridge shoal appeared on the projector screen.

"Joe," he said without raising his voice. The room quieted. He moved the cursor. "Let's talk, after." He pressed his lips together and tapped the screen with his finger. "I think we can come up with something if we re-scope our approach."

"What about the rest of us?" A voice called from behind Joe. "I got forty traps sitting on that shoal. You gonna buy my lobsters, too?"

Joe jerked his chin toward the back of the room. "You'll be meeting with all of us?"

"If that's what it takes." Terry said, his expression grim. He shared a look with Frank, who nodded. More people stood up.

"What is the environmental impact?" Another man's voice rose above the hum of the crowd. Frank's head snapped in the direction of the voice. "The Vineyard Sound is home to a unique ecosystem, and there are rich habitats along the ravine and on the shoal. Pulling up a wreckage this large will have a significant impact on seabed life."

Kyra peered around Grace to get a better view of the person speaking. Her vision darkened at the edges. She shook her head, blinking it away, and ran her hand across her dry forehead. *It's so fucking hot in here.*

"Do you have a plan to protect the sea life, Mr. Kapowski? Mr. Rose?" The man stepped forward from where he'd been standing against the wall.

He wore too large clothes in unmatched shades of khaki. His shaggy, sun-bleached hair gave him a crunchy granola appearance. Kyra squinted at him, focusing. The man was familiar-looking, but she couldn't place him.

"Dr. Seth Hammond." He pointed to his chest. "I'm with the Oceanic Conservation. We're prepared to file a lawsuit and will pursue an injunction."

Tarek shifted in his seat. Kyra turned toward the front of the room, where Frank and Terry were conversing. Frank glared at Dr. Seth Hammond with unconcealed contempt, his mouth set in a thin line.

"Preliminary video of the wreckage suggests it's buried in the sand. There is no evidence that it's acting as a manmade reef or that there is significant sea life," Terry said and raised an arm to wipe his forehead on his sleeve.

"And how do you know that, Mr. Rose?" Hammond pulled out a notebook and flipped through the pages. "I don't see that any permits were issued for an exploratory dive. It's still island property, is it not?"

"Oh, get off it, Hammond!" Frank snapped. He said the man's name with enough venom Kyra realized they knew each other. "Everyone on the island and likely the whole of the East Coast knows about the unsanctioned dive and the video." Frank threw his hands up in frustration. "Go ahead and try for your TRO. You know we have claim." Frank's eyes swept the crowd. His voice was steel, challenging the community. "Are there any more questions?" His friendly demeanor had vanished, likely melted in the god-awful heat.

"I have some questions." Ida Ames stood up.

Kyra hadn't noticed her sitting at the other end of their row.

"No need, Ida." Frank cut her off. "We've already talked about this. We understand your concerns."

"Ida," Terry said, his tone more diplomatic. "I'll come see you. I'm sure we can work together on this." He looked like he was going to say more, but Frank stepped in front of him, blocking him from the crowd.

"Thank you for your time this evening. We're eager to get this project moving. We're happy to take any additional questions by email. Please help yourselves to the refreshments." Frank pointed to the back of the room.

While they'd been listening to the presentation, someone, presumably Frank's team, had replaced the lemonade and homemade baked goods with catered canapes and hors d'oeuvres. Poster-size artistic renderings of the *Keres* sat on easels strategically placed around the room.

She felt the barest breeze across her hot skin and noticed Charlie had left her seat. Kyra scanned the room for Charlie's dark curls but couldn't find her. Grace, too, was already up and speaking with Ida and Terry. A cool hand grazed her scalding skin.

"Did you want to stay any longer?" Tarek asked, his voice low in her ear.

"No," she said. Her mouth and throat felt dry. "I'll just say goodbye to Grace and Charlie."

She stood up. Her legs were unsteady beneath her as she made her way down the aisle. A wave of dizziness hit her, and her toe hit a chair leg. She stumbled. Tarek grabbed her elbow, holding her up.

"Hey, are you okay?" he asked, peering into her face.

Kyra attempted a smile. "Oh yes, sorry." She tried to swallow. She put a hand to her forehead and blinked a few times. "I'm fine. Head rush."

"Mmhhmm," Tarek hummed and ran an assessing eye over her.

Self-conscious, she smoothed the bodice and skirt of her dress. She felt strange, prickly. Her mouth was cottony.

"Do you need to say goodbye to Gully?" she asked and scanned the room for the pub master. He was beside the podium, talking with Frank Kapowski. A scowl creased Gully's brow, and his arms were crossed over his massive chest. Frank's hands were flying through the air as he spoke.

"I'll catch up with him back home," Tarek said. Kyra took in Gully's stormy expression and agreed that might be for the best.

"Excuse me, Grace." Kyra touched her friend's elbow. "Tarek and I are going to go."

Grace's eyes glittered, and she grinned. "Go on, dear. You two have fun. We'll see you tomorrow."

"Rick?" a silky voice cut in.

Tarek started. Together, almost synchronized, they all turned around.

Standing before them, seeming impervious to the heat,

was a gorgeous woman. She was tall, wearing one of those slim, tailored business suits that was more fashion statement than office wear. Her blazer was buttoned over the matching form-fitting dress, and her long box braids fell to her waist.

"Rachel?" his voice came out hoarse, strained. His eyes had gone wide. "What are you doing here?"

"I'm here with the Oceanic Conservation. I got in a few nights ago. I thought you might be here once I heard Andre was involved." Rachel approached Tarek, stepping a little closer, but moving slowly like she feared he might bolt. A smile played at the edge of her mouth and her dark eyes drank him in. "It's good to see you," she murmured.

Kyra's stomach clenched and a pain, knife sharp, pierced the space behind her eye. She put her fingers to her temple. Her gaze shifted between them. *What the hell is going on?* Tarek rocked back on his heels and slid his hands into his pockets. His jaw clenched. Rachel's eyes flicked to Kyra, and she inclined her head. The light caught the tops of her cheeks, highlighting her delicate bone structure.

"Hello," Rachel said. She held out her hand, her glossy nails glinting in the light. "I'm Rachel Collins."

Kyra might have responded with her name, or she might have just stared at the woman. *Rachel Collins?* She blinked. Her brain was so fuzzy. The pain behind her eyes intensified. Her vision swam, darkening at the edges. Kyra stepped back, away from Tarek and Rachel. She pushed a limp, damp tendril of hair off her hot shoulder. She threw a confused glance at Tarek, but he wasn't looking at her. He was watching Rachel Collins.

"It's a pleasure to meet you, Ms. Collins." Grace shook

Rachel's offered hand. She glanced at Kyra, worry creasing the corners of her eyes.

"Please, call me Rachel." Rachel glanced at Kyra then returned her gaze to Grace.

"Ah, very well, Rachel," Grace stumbled over her name. "I'm Grace. Grace Chambers, this is my wife, Charlie, and this is Ida Ames. She and I are with the council."

"Ah," Rachel said, focusing on Ida. "Ms. Ames, I'd love to get on your schedule. The OC has concerns about the salvage efforts and we'd love to work with the community."

"Yes, of course. Let me check my calendar." Ida pulled out her phone.

"Rachel, a word?" Tarek interrupted.

"Oh, yes, of course." Her brown eyes flicked to his, and she gave him a brilliant smile, all white teeth and full lips. "Ms. Ames, I'll call your office in the morning to confirm." She pulled a leather cardcase from her bag and selected a business card. "My contact information." She handed it to Ida, then motioned to Tarek. She followed him to a corner, a little away from the mass of people.

Kyra pressed the pads of her fingers to her eyes. She coughed against a wave of nausea. *What's happening to me?*

"What was that about? Who is that?" Charlie leaned in, her eyes searching Kyra's.

She glanced at Grace. Ida and Grace were already chatting with another man. Kyra sucked in a breath, but the air held no oxygen in this unbearable heat. She felt like she was breathing underwater. Kyra's blurry gaze drifted to Tarek and Rachel. His expression was dark. Rachel's mouth was pressed into a lovely pout. They could be arguing. Or not.

She shook her head. Her headache intensified.

Charlie's eyebrows drew down in concern. "Kyra, do you feel okay?"

Kyra nodded feebly and put her hand on the podium to steady herself. She was disoriented. Her heart pounded at the base of her throat. *Something is wrong.*

"And what are you going to do about it, Andre!" a voice bellowed from the other side of the room. "This is fucking ridiculous! You're going to ruin me! For fucking what? A fantasy!" The other Mackey brother, the one from Charlie's party, Andy, was in Gully's face. He poked the larger man in his broad chest and Gully stepped back.

"You push this, I'm warning you! I'll take it all. I'll come after you, that campground, the bar. By the time I'm done, you'll have nothing but the shitty pieces of driftwood you pulled up from the sound." Andy's voice rang out among the now quiet crowd.

Then Tarek and Rachel were there. Next to Gully. Rachel's hand on Tarek's arm. Tarek between Andy and Gully. Tarek said something, and Joe Mackey pulled his brother back.

"Char, we should go," Grace said, watching Kyra.

Kyra's grip on the podium tightened. She shut her eyes tight, then peeled them open.

"Now?" Charlie's mouth dropped open. "It's just getting good."

Kyra almost missed the pointed look Grace flicked in Kyra's direction. She was just so dizzy. She needed fresh air.

"Oh, yeah. Let's go." Charlie's voice sounded so far away.

I'm going to pass out. Kyra gasped. Her heart beat in her ears. Her knees gave out, just as hands gripped her elbow, an arm wrapped around her back, supporting her, guiding her. She leaned on Grace and Charlie.

"Is she alright?" a worried voice. Ida? "Here take these."

"Thank you. We've got her." Charlie.

Kyra glanced back once more at the scene Tarek was trying to contain. Gully's arms were crossed over his chest and now Joe Mackey stood next to his brother. The brothers wore identical scowls. Behind them, the dark-haired woman was speaking and Lisa stood off to the side. Tarek turned, and his gaze met Kyra's. His expression changed, but Kyra was too muddled to interpret it. And then she was pulled outside.

Kyra stumbled. Grace and Charlie held her up and pressed her back against the wall. The first thing she noticed was that it was blessedly cooler.

"Breathe."

"Here, dear. Drink this."

An icy bottle of water was pushed into her hand. Grace helped her take a few tentative sips. The cool liquid helped. Breathing became easier. The sound of blood pumping in her ears subsided. Kyra raised her hand to her head. Her vision was clearer. The dizziness seemed to be abating.

"Stay with her, Char. I'll get the car."

"What's wrong with me?" Kyra asked. Her voice came out weak and raspy.

"Probably heat exhaustion. It had to be over a hundred degrees in there, and you're not used to it." Charlie pressed another cold bottle of water against Kyra's neck. "If it makes you feel better, at least one person passes out at each of these summer meetings."

It did not make her feel better. At all.

Grace's Subaru pulled up, and Charlie helped Kyra into the back seat. She turned all the vents so cold air blasted her. At first it was refreshing, but then it stung her over sensitive skin. Grace pulled out of the parking lot.

Charlie turned around in her seat. "How are you feeling?"

"A little better." Her mind was clearing, but her skin still felt raw. She was more embarrassed than anything. She finished the bottle of water. Charlie opened the second one and handed it to her.

"Who was that woman? The one who called Tarek, Rick?"

Kyra shrugged. "I don't know. She said her name was Rachel Collins." She touched her skirt where droplets had fallen from her water bottle. Kyra tried to remember her conversations with the detective last spring.

"Sister?"

Kyra moved to shake her head and winced. She leaned back against the car seat. "I don't think so." At some level, she knew Rachel wasn't a sister or a cousin, but to her knowledge, he'd never mentioned he was married. He hadn't said much about himself at all, really, now that she thought about it.

"Wait, his *wife*?"

"Char, not now."

The sweat on Kyra's arms and shoulders had dried, leaving a film that pinched her skin. She felt awful, and it was made worse by the thrumming behind her eyes, and the knowledge that she almost passed out in a room full of people, and had been shocked stupid by Rachel Collins. Kyra was acutely aware that she wasn't handling any of it well. She was embarrassed and hurt and pissed off, at herself mostly, for trusting Tarek *again*, for having to rely on Grace and Charlie, for needing their help. Kyra hated being vulnerable.

She sneaked a glance at the Chamberses. Grace's attention was on the curvy road. Charlie was playing with the temperature controls. She knew they wouldn't consider taking care of her an inconvenience and they were glad she was feeling better and that made the whole thing worse. Her stomach sank further into the dark bottomless pit that had formed inside. She wanted to crawl under a rock or preferably an iceberg.

The car pulled to a stop and Kyra realized Grace had driven her right to her front door. She sat up, her limbs heavy and cumbersome.

"Oh, you didn't need to bring me all the way."

"Don't be silly, Kay," Charlie said, turning around. "Are you feeling any better?"

"Yes, much," she lied. "Thank you for keeping me from fainting away in there."

"Don't mention it, dear. We were all melting." Grace's light tone was forced, her lips pressed together with concern.

"Sweet baby Jesus, was it hot in there." Charlie fanned herself. "I wouldn't be surprised if more fights break out. Did you see Andy Mackey charge up to that bearded fellow? Andy has balls. That man was twice his size."

"That's Gully. He owns the Wraith & Bone pub in Edgartown."

Charlie's eyes widened and her voice dropped to a whisper. "The man who's involved with those divers' deaths?"

"I'm not sure he was involved," Kyra said softly, bunching the skirt of her dress in her hands.

"I'd have put money on the big guy." Charlie's eyes twinkled and she grinned.

Kyra huffed. *Gully is probably a pacifist.*

"Char." Grace's tone held a warning.

"Fine." She sighed, rolling her eyes. "I'm glad the Mackeys didn't punch the mainlander, but it'd have been fun to watch."

"Char, help Kyra inside."

"Oh, no, please. I'll be okay."

Charlie frowned, studying Kyra. "Drink lots of water. Take a cold bath or shower and go straight to sleep. Take some ibuprofen as well." Charlie reached back and squeezed her hand. "You sure you don't want me to come in?"

"No, thank you. I'll be fine, really." Kyra reached for the door handle.

"We'll call you tomorrow," Grace promised.

Kyra entered the house before the Chamberses left the drive. She suspected Grace had waited until she opened the door before leaving. She walked straight to her bathroom, peeled her dress from her salty skin, and stepped into a cold shower. The icy stream hit her like a thousand papercuts. With her hands on the tiled wall for balance, she slumped to the floor and sat. Her body slowly returned to normal, but the headache persisted, now a drill barreling through her skull from one temple to the other.

As her body temperature cooled, her cheeks and chest burned with embarrassment and anger. She'd been blindsided by the existence of Rachel Collins. She'd been wholly unprepared and had acted like a dumbstruck fool, notwithstanding her fainting episode. Tarek had lied to her, even if it was by omission. She should have been warned or informed. Kyra leaned against the shower wall, let her fingers and toes whiten and wrinkle. Not until she was shivering, did she reach up and turn off the water.

Kyra pulled her wet hair up into a topknot and climbed into bed. She heard a soft padding and, with a chirp, Cronkite jumped up. He made a few turns before settling down next to her. She scratched his ears. His purr rumbled, and he dropped his chin on her hip. It was like he knew she needed comfort and came to sit with her. She swallowed the tightness in her throat, thankful for the tiny terror.

Her phone buzzed, and she pulled it from her purse on the nightstand. There were two missed calls from Tarek and a text that had come in while she was in the shower.

"Are you OK? Where did you go? Call me."

Ali had also texted her earlier. It was still early on the east coast, half seven, but it was past midnight in London. She sent a text that she'd call her in the morning and set the phone down. It started ringing.

"Hello?"

"Kay!"

"Why are you whispering?" Kyra asked her aunt.

"Iggy just fell asleep." Kyra heard the weary relief in her aunt's voice. "How's the island? Wait, why did you answer? Where are you? What's wrong?"

"Home."

"The date was that bad?"

Kyra winced. "Um, no, it was canceled."

"Canceled? Why?"

Kyra sat back against the headboard, careful not to disturb Cronk.

"Kay?"

Kyra told her aunt about the meeting, the heat, almost passing out.

Ali sucked in a breath through her teeth. "Fucking hell. Are you alright? How are you feeling now? Did Tarek take you to hospital?"

"I'm fine, just tired and headachy. Grace and Charlie helped me. They brought me home. Charlie said it was heat exhaustion." Kyra's eyes slid closed.

Ali made a humming sound. "Your neighbors? But where was Tarek?" Ali's voice pitched with concern and Kyra could picture the crease between her eyes, the one she accused Kyra of creating when she was a teenager.

"There was a woman there," Kyra said reluctantly. She really didn't have the energy to get into it with her aunt, but she knew Ali wouldn't let it go, not now. "She introduced herself as Rachel Collins."

"Rachel Collins?" A long pause. "He's *married*? The fuck?" Then Ali laughed a humorless chuckle. "Only you."

"I know." Kyra groaned.

"What did he say when you asked him about it?"

"I didn't have a chance. I was so dizzy, I thought I would vomit right there, and then Grace and Charlie were pushing me outside." It was still fuzzy in her mind. "He called, but I haven't called him back."

"Are you going to?"

"Hmm?"

"Will you call him? Give him a chance to explain?" Kyra was quiet for a long time. "Kay?"

"I don't know." She heard Ali's disappointed sigh, but before her aunt could launch into a lecture about the value of good communication, Kyra said, "Ali, I was going to call you tomorrow, but since I have you, before the meeting, we learned some more about the *Keres*. Did you know your dad … er, Grandfather, was researching it?"

"What's that?"

"Gully has Aaron Hart's papers. I found a photo." Kyra sent Ali the picture of the polaroid she'd taken. "That's your old house, isn't it? You, your dad, and Mom?"

"Yes," Ali said, her voice far from the phone. Kyra heard her suck in a breath. "Oh my god, that's Bubbles!"

"Bubbles?"

"My pet goat. I found him when he was just a baby. None of the farms claimed him, so Dad let me keep him. Mother was furious. She hated that goat. He'd eat all her flowers. Where did you find this?" Ali's voice was breathy.

"It was shuffled in with Aaron's research about the pirate who crashed off the coast of the island, William Roberts."

"I remember Dad being obsessed with some shipwreck in the area, but honestly, Izzy and I paid little attention to his work. I don't think I knew it was a pirate ship. If I had, maybe I would have listened." She breathed a sad laugh. "Though, really, probably not." Kyra could picture her aunt shrugging. "I was pretty wild as a child, and Dad always had some research project he was working on. He was a history professor."

"Do you have any of his research there?"

"No, not really. I have a few of his published books. Maybe this will inspire me to finally read one."

Kyra doubted it. Ali was a voracious reader. Of fantasy romance. Exclusively.

"I'll look through what I have and let you know."

Kyra yawned and sank deeper into her pillows.

"And Kay? For what it's worth, I think you should call him. Give him a chance to explain. And if you don't like what he has to say, I'll help you key his car, or set his clothes on fire when I get there."

Kyra huffed a tired laugh. Ali would make good on such promises.

"Sweetheart, you need to learn to give people the benefit of the doubt," Ali said in her adult Ali voice. "Sleep on it tonight. I love you."

"I love you, too."

Kyra swiped through her messages. Tarek hadn't left any voicemails just the text. She tossed the phone on the nightstand.

Maybe tomorrow.

Chapter Eleven

KYRA LEANED AGAINST the kitchen counter, sipping her coffee. Cronkite stared up at her. His tail swished back and forth. He didn't break eye contact as his pink tongue swept over his white cheeks.

"No. You already had breakfast. Twice," she said, and she swore the cat narrowed his eyes at her. Her phone buzzed. Again. It'd been going off every few minutes. She frowned. She'd been ignoring it, thinking it was Tarek, but he wouldn't keep texting her. Ali would, though. She was relentless. Kyra reached for it and unlocked the screen. *Chase.*

8:02: "I feel like a workout or brunch … Is it too early for burnch?"

8:06: "Brunch after."

8:08: "Yogat @ 9."

8:08: "Tofa @ 9."

8:09: "I want to tell you all about my night! Yoga @ 9."

8:10: "His name is Gryphon. He definitely gave himself that name. Yoga @ 9."

8:12: "Wake up!"

8:14: "I think his real name is Gerald. Shit."

8:16: "Yoga @ 9."

8:37: "Reserved us space. Meet you there."

The last one at least had the address of the studio in Vineyard Haven.

"What do you think?" she asked Cronk, who had splayed himself out on the granite island like it was his own personal dais. He yawned and dropped his head onto his paws. "You're right. It does sound horrible." She didn't really have the energy for a heavy workout, but an easy Vinyasa flow? Stretching out her weary muscles might be just the thing to make her feel better. And it had the added benefit of giving her an excuse to put off thinking about last night and whether she'd speak to Tarek again.

Kyra found the yoga studio across from the ferry and entered the reception area. The woman behind the desk seemed vaguely familiar, but Kyra couldn't quite place her.

"Good morning. Have you been here before?" she asked, not looking up from her computer.

"No."

The receptionist pulled a pen from a cup on the counter and slid it into the clip of a clipboard holding a stack of forms. "Here, you'll need to fill this out." She slid it across the counter, and then the woman looked up. The clipboard stopped moving, her hand splayed atop.

"It's you. You're that police consultant. From last spring."

It clicked. *Daphne.* The bartender at the Crow's Nest. The woman who had driven Chase home the night Kyra's father died. She'd given him an alibi and probably saved him from a prison sentence.

"Oh, no… Well, yes. That's me, but I'm not with the police. I was just helping a friend." Kyra stopped talking, not sure how to explain her involvement in the murder investigation. "Actually, he's coming too. He set up our reservation. Chase Hawthorn."

Daphne looked down at her computer monitor. "You're Kyra Gibson?" When Kyra nodded, Daphne gave her an odd look, like she wasn't convinced. "Hmm." She sniffed. "You'll still need to fill this out. You can leave it here. When you're done, you can go on through." Daphne pointed to a hallway. "The changing room is through there. Extra mats and equipment are stowed on the shelves. We start in five minutes." She gave Kyra another long look before standing and disappearing down the hall.

With only seconds to spare, Kyra entered the warm yoga studio. Chase was already on his mat, stretching and chatting up two blushing elderly women.

"You made it!" He beamed at her as she laid her mat next to his.

"Greta, Dot, this is Kyra. She has a house over near Katama. Kay, this is Greta and Dot. They're here for the summer, too."

"A pleasure to meet you both."

Greta's expression darkened. Kyra noticed her nose and cheeks were red from a nasty sunburn, not Chase's flirting.

"We're in Dodger's Hole." Dot grinned. "Been here every summer for the last thirty years, right, Greta?"

Greta nodded, her eyes still on Kyra. "Longer." She said it like a challenge.

Kyra glanced at Chase. *What is going on?* His eyebrow hitched up, and he patted her mat.

"You look pale. What's wrong?"

Kyra waved off his concern and sat down. "Just tired. You didn't say Daphne worked here."

"She doesn't. Well, I guess she does. She owns it."

"I'm not sure she likes me." Kyra reached for her toes coming up very short, the tips of her fingers dancing over her shins. Chase's chest nearly touched his thighs. She sighed. *This is going to suck.*

"Oh, don't mind her. She hates everyone," Dot scoffed, eliciting a snicker from Chase. Dot's cheeks flushed redder than Greta's sunburn.

"She does," Greta piped in, her voice raspy, like her vocal cords had been damaged. "She's the least Zen instructor I've had, but this is the best class on the island. Dot and I have tried them all over the years."

"We have tried them all, and we keep coming back to this one." Dot's voice dropped, and she whispered, "It's popular with the celebrities. Once we saw that nice girl from that comedy show, remember Greta?"

"I do, the blonde one."

"That's her. She was supposed to be funny. You know her."

Kyra didn't know her. Thankfully, Daphne walked in at that moment, saving Kyra from acknowledging her ignorance of supposedly funny blonde celebrities.

Daphne clapped her hands together. "Let's get started. Please lie back on your mats." Soft meditative music filled the space and Kyra closed her eyes.

Ninety horrible minutes later, Kyra stumbled out onto the sidewalk and into the bright morning sun. Even the July heat was refreshing after the steamy hell that was the yoga session.

"You didn't say it was a power class." Her voice came out in a gasp. She was going to die of dehydration. Just shrivel up like a raisin and die. She attempted a glare at Chase, but her eyelids stuck to her parched eyeballs.

"I didn't know." He at least had the decency to look equally miserable and disheveled. He pushed his damp hair from his eyes, making it stand at gravity-defying angles. "I think Daphne changed it on purpose." He picked at the T-shirt clinging to his sweat-drenched abdomen. "I need coffee. And water." Kyra was still breathing hard. "Iced coffee. Definitely iced."

She looked up at him. She hadn't even realized she'd eased herself down and was sitting on the curb.

"You're going to have to carry me." Iced caffeine did sound good, but so did giving up, and melting away.

"And you call me dramatic. Come on." He reached out a hand to help her up, then pulled it back, wiping it on his shorts with a grimace. "Better not."

"See you next week, Chase!" Dot waved at them. She and Greta skipped out of the studio, looking no worse for wear. Kyra took in their fresh faces and bright smiles and silently cursed them.

"I hate you," she said to Chase and stood.

"I'm not a fan myself at the moment." Chase led them up the street to the coffee shop. The few short blocks felt like miles. They dropped their things on a tiny bistro table on the covered patio and Chase went inside to order. Kyra fell into the chair and pulled out her phone. She had a text from Ali encouraging her to talk to Tarek, and another from the detective himself.

"Kyra, are you OK? Call me. I'm worried."

Guilt twisted in her stomach, and she made a face.

"Uh-oh, what happened?" Chase set their iced coffees and two paper wrapped bagel sandwiches on the rickety little table.

"Nothing, really."

Chase unwrapped his straw, tied the paper in a knot, and waited expectantly. Kyra sighed and told him about the community council meeting, about how she'd nearly passed out, and Charlie and Grace having to take her home.

"Shit, Kyra." His voice came out gruff. He pushed his wayfarers into his hair and studied her. "You should have told me. We would have skipped yoga. Sat on the couch. Recovered."

"I'm fine. I actually feel better." After a little caffeine, she could admit the class had made her feel better. Her mind was clearer, less foggy, and she'd worked out the stress knots in her shoulders and back. She rolled her shoulders, enjoying that satisfying, energized, yet depleted feeling of a rigorous workout.

Chase narrowed his eyes at her.

"Really. Promise." She shook the plastic coffee cup. "Tell me about Gryphon."

Chase sucked in his cheeks, as if he was about to object, but let it drop.

"I met him and his friends at the Oyster House for

drinks. Have you been?" Kyra shook her head. "It's dark, and there's always a lot of people. Anyway, I found them immediately, because they'd coordinated their outfits."

"Coordinated?"

"Yes." His eyes were wide with mock horror, his lips set in a grim line. "Gryphon was wearing a shirt embroidered with lobsters. Maximus." Chase shuddered like saying the man's name pained him. "Maximus wore a sweater vest with the same lobsters but in reverse, so the lobsters were white. The girls, June-Bug and Prim, were wearing lobsters too, red and white respectively."

"June-Bug and Prim?" Kyra repeated and rolled her lips to keep from laughing.

Chase's eyes slid closed, and he gave her an exaggerated nod.

"Did they explain why they were dressed like that? Was it performance art?"

"Gryphon said something about a family party, and it was tradition to always wear lobsters. Who does that?"

Kyra couldn't hold it back. Her cheeks hurt too much and she collapsed into a fit of giggles. Chase hated theme events. "And? What happened?"

"Stop laughing." Chase took a savage bite of his breakfast sandwich. "After an hour when Maximus wasn't able to convince anyone but Prim to hook up with him, he wanted to go. Their cousin, or Prim's cousin's brother-in-law or something, keeps a boat moored in OB, so Max convinced us to check it out."

Kyra's laughter stopped, and she straightened in her chair. "Chase, what did you do?"

He shook his head. "No, nothing like that. I only looked at the boat. From the dock. The cousin-brother-in-law-relative runs a charter company. Prim was telling us how he was one of the first people to see the wreck. He's been taking people to see it. Has runs out there every day." Chase picked up his phone and tapped the screen.

Kyra heard her phone buzz and looked down at it. It was a photo of the boat, with the company name, website, and phone number.

"Every day Prim said?" Her heart beat a little faster. She looked up, her grin mirrored Chase's.

"Every. Single. Day."

"The captain may have seen something. Maybe he saw Matty Gray and Jaycee." She had a sudden urge to text Tarek and, just like that, her excitement dissipated. "Thank you for this." She slipped her phone into her bag. "Then what happened? After you saw the boat?"

"I decided to head home, or at least somewhere else. Gryphon offered to come with me. Great, right? And that's when June-Bug yelled, 'Where are you going Gerry?' and Gryphon answered, "With Chase, Sissy!"

"Sissy?" Kyra repeated, and her eyes came back to his. She took a deep drink of her coffee to keep from laughing and said a quick prayer she didn't spit it up.

"Yeah. Gryphon and June-Bug are siblings, and somehow Prim is married to or related to someone who is married to a cousin. I don't know how Maximus fits in, but I'm sure it's Hapsburgian."

Kyra gaped at him, but he didn't notice her surprise.

"They're staying at their family's place in OB. When I

confronted Gerald/Gryphon, he confessed. His sister's real name is Jeralyn."

"Gerry and Jerry?" Kyra started laughing, harder than before. *Amazing. Ah-MAY-zing!* Chase dropped his head in his hands and groaned. When she could catch her breath, she asked, "Did you leave?"

"No, it was still early, so I made out with Gerry/Gryphon in the alley, then went home. He texted me this morning. He wants to see me again." Chase's lips turned down in an exaggerated frown.

"And?"

"I don't know. Maybe?" Chase made a frustrated noise in his throat. "He was so much hotter when his name was Gryphon."

Kyra gave him her best make-good-choices look, and he mimicked it back at her, making her grin.

He checked his phone. "Shit. I need to get back. What are you doing today?" He stuffed the rest of his sandwich in his mouth.

Kyra wrinkled her nose. "You're disgusting." Chase lifted a shoulder in an apathetic shrug. "Charlie and Grace invited me to dinner at an inn in West Tisbury. I may go to that. I haven't decided." She'd received the text inviting her during yoga.

"What time?" Kyra checked her phone and showed him Grace's text. "I know the place. Get there an hour earlier. I'll meet you for a drink." He stood and pulled his keys from his pocket. He leveled a look at her, causing Kyra to pause.

"Kay," he said, his voice unusually serious. "Promise me you won't go see that charter company without me or

Tarek." And before she could protest, he said, "I mean it. Promise."

"Fine," she huffed. "I won't." Chase cocked an eyebrow. "Jeez, I promise."

"See, that wasn't so hard. I'll see you later."

Kyra sat at the table and finished her coffee. She didn't have anything she had to do before dinner. The idea of sitting home alone, procrastinating working or cleaning out the basement, and obsessing over her episode at the meeting, Tarek, Rachel… She didn't want to face any of it. Not yet.

She bought another iced coffee and walked up Main Street, peeking into the shops. She hadn't spent much time in Vineyard Haven yet. The little town center had its own atmosphere, a unique vibrancy that catered to tourists and islanders alike. Kyra knew from her conversations with Grace and Charlie that many of the businesses were open year-round. She stopped outside of a bookstore. A black and white cat snoozed in the window, the display behind him featuring books by local authors. Her phone buzzed, and she fished it out of her bag.

"Hello?"

"Hi! I remembered something." Ali didn't wait for Kyra to respond. Her words stumbled over each other as she gushed. "Dad moved back to Abingdon after Mom died, but we kept the island house. When he died a few years later, Izzy and Ed went to the island to clean it out and sell it. My sister wouldn't have thrown away Dad's research. Who knows what Isabel found, if anything, but Ed may have held onto it." Kyra's heart raced. *Ed may have held onto it. But where would he have put it?* "Kay?"

“I’m here.” Her voice came out breathy. “You think he could have kept it?”

“He may have done. Call me immediately if you find something. Ugh, I wish I was there.”

“I wish you were here, too. I’ve got to get back to the house, but I’ll call you.”

She slipped her phone into her bag. Kyra spun on her heel, nearly taking out a small child with her yoga mat. She hollered an apology over her shoulder as she ran to her car.

Chapter Twelve

KYRA PULLED HER car into the garage and did a cursory search. The shelves were neat and organized. She found mostly unused garden supplies—extra hoses, a birdfeeder, a snow shovel. Her heart skipped when she pulled a thick paperback book from underneath a tarp, but it turned out to be the owner's manual for the massive snow blower she had no interest in ever using.

"The office."

Kyra dropped her yoga mat by the door and disabled the alarm. She pushed open the French door to her father's old office. Cronk followed her inside and leaped onto the desk.

"Cronk, where would Dad have kept boxes of Mom's stuff?" She found herself looking expectantly at the cat. Cronk just plopped over on the desk.

Kyra spun around the room. She'd gone through most of Ed's junk last spring. She'd thrown out reams of Ed's papers. Story research, drafts, junk mail, magazines, and newspapers. It wasn't impossible that she'd found Aaron Hart's files and thrown them out, thinking they were Ed's. Kyra bit her lip. *I hope not.*

The desktop was mostly clear but for a neat pile of recent mail. *Grace must have dropped it off.* She made a note to go through it later and checked the desk drawers, but they were all empty from when she'd cleared them last spring. She checked the small closet. Nothing. Her eyes wandered to the bookshelves.

She ran her finger along the spines as she searched shelf after shelf. Mostly trade publications, and a few industry tomes, shelved in no particular order. Knickknacks had been randomly stuffed here and there. She crouched down. The shelves closest to the bottom held photo albums and yearbooks. She reached for one. Her father's college yearbook. Kyra cracked it open, and a white head bumped it to the ground, with a growly *rawr*. She rubbed Cronk's ears.

"You're right. Ali would want to go through these with me." She slipped the book back onto the shelf. Cronk bumped her leg again, and she stood up. "I don't think there's anything in here."

Kyra remembered the attic hatch she'd seen in one of the guestroom closets. She tried there next. She stuck her head above the opening. Plywood lay across the joists, creating a makeshift floor. It was hot and empty. She glanced down to see the cat staring up at her from the base of the ladder.

"It's empty," she told him and hopped down. The hatch slid shut with a soft *plonk*. Kyra put her hands on her hips. "Where else?" She wandered back to the kitchen.

She poured a glass of water and leaned against the counter. Should she call the Chamberses? Kyra frowned and put her water glass down. Her eyes fell on the basement door. *The storage room?*

Kyra hurried downstairs. She stepped into the musty room. Tarek had neatly stacked the beach chairs and umbrella near the door for easier access, but the rest of the room was still disorganized. She scanned the contents of the shelves.

Ed had labeled plastic containers for things that people stored until needed, Christmas lights, ornaments, board games, extra glassware. Her breath caught. She stumbled over a vacuum in her haste to get to the corner, to the stack of cardboard boxes sitting on the floor beside the shelving unit. They were crumbling from age and damp. She pressed her fingers to her father's handwriting. If she squinted, she could make out some of the smudged letters—*H*, *t*, *M*, *t*, *h*, *s*, *e*, and *rd*.

Hart, Martha's Vineyard? Could this be it?

Kyra lugged the boxes upstairs to the kitchen and set them on the floor. The cardboard disintegrated around her fingers, leaving them sticky with dust. She yanked one open. It was full of books. Kyra's pulse quickened and she pulled one out.

Family photo albums. She thumbed through the images lovingly displayed behind milky sheets of plastic. The pictures were of the Hart family on their island holidays over the years. Photos of her mom and Ali playing on the beach, riding bikes, jumping off the dock at their house. Of Aaron and Laura hosting dinner parties or drinking iced tea on the deck. She wiped the dust from the books and set them aside to shelve in the office. *I'll show them to Ali when she visits.*

Kyra opened the second box. It contained lumps of fabric. She reached inside.

"Gaahhhh!" She fell back. Something had nested in there. Recently. "Ew. Ew. Ew." Her entire body shuddered. Cronkite blinked at her and yawned, nonplussed. Kyra scowled at him and inched forward. The fabric could have been a quilt. Once. Maybe. But now it was moth eaten and littered with droppings. Kyra swallowed back a gag. Careful not to let the infested box touch her skin or clothes, she wrapped the entire thing in a trash bag and dumped it in the bin. At the sink, she scrubbed her hands and arms raw.

"Please be mice," she mumbled. "Please be moved out, mice." She shuddered again, wiping her hands on a towel. "It's your job to keep them out!" She glared at the cat.

Cronkite jumped up on the third box and pawed at it. His pink nose twitched before he let out a sneeze that should have been too big for his body.

"That's what you get for letting me touch the mouse box." She nudged him down. The cat made a harrumphing noise and sat a few feet away to clean his whiskers. Kyra stared at him before shaking her head and turning her attention back to the box. She pushed back the flaps and looked inside. "Please, no mice. And no spiders," she prayed to all the gods.

This box was neatly packed and contained just four books, and a few brown accordion-style expanding folders. She pulled out one of the folders. Inside were yellowing sheets of thin printer paper. She thumbed through the folder and yanked out the first page. A title page.

The Voyages of the *Morgana* and the *Keres*
by Dr. Aaron Hart

Her mouth went dry.

"It's the manuscript." Her voice came out in a whisper.

She pulled the rest of the book out of the sleeve and

flipped through the pages. It looked like a final or at least submission draft, with pages and pages of endnotes. She slid the manuscript back inside the folder and set it aside. She pulled out one of the books.

The cover was leather, not faux or vegan leather, or leather-looking plastic, but actual leather. She ran a hand over it. Its texture was dry, almost papery. She opened it, taking care not to tear the delicate sheets or damage the binding. The paper felt thick, but brittle, its edges raw and uneven. *These are old.* She turned the page. It was covered in straight lines of neat cursive writing. Kyra looked closer at the unevenness of the letters and dabbed drops of ink. She ran her finger across the first line, squinting at the cramped text. It looked like …

"Business records?" She turned the pages. There were repeated references to Douglas, and other ports, lists of inventories—wine, molasses, grain, tea. Fees and taxes paid. The second half of the book was filled with names. *Passenger manifests? Sailor records?*

She pulled the next book from the box. This one was smaller than the first, about the size of a modern-day paperback. It wasn't as high quality as the ship's log. The spine cracked when she opened the book and Kyra winced. The paper was thin, dry, like it could turn to dust between her fingers. Kyra carefully turned the page to the first entry. Her heart skipped when she saw the date.

9 March 1710

My son is strong and healthy. I am truly blessed. No matter what Mother and Father say, he's perfect. He's mine and William's. Mrs. Bell gave me this journal, while Father shuts Liam and I away. She said writing will be a comfort.

She scanned down the page for the next entry.

11 May 1710

Mother is pressuring me to lie. To say that I am widowed, to take a new husband, but I refuse. I will not deny my dear William. He is alive. The husband of my heart. He will come for us. Mr. Lewin will hold my letters for him. I pray the hotel proprietor in Port Royal will do the same. He must come, if not for me, for Liam.

Kyra sucked in a quick breath and clasped the journal to her chest, her mind wrapping around what she'd just found. She was almost certain. The woman from Gully's boxes was William Robert's sweetheart. *I have Helena Robert's journal.*

Chapter Thirteen

KYRA PULLED INTO the parking lot of the Lady Slipper Inn and checked the clock. She was late. Kyra took off her sunglasses and rubbed the space between her eyes.

After finding her grandfather's boxes, she'd spent the rest of her day reading his book between calls from work. During one particularly boring call with Assaf and a potential social media influencer client, she'd looked up her grandfather. She wondered why it had never occurred to her to do it before today.

Aaron Hart had been a marine historian at Amherst College. He researched trade routes during the late seventeenth and early eighteenth centuries. He'd written eight books. *The Voyages of the* Morgana *and the* Keres, presumably his latest, was a history of the ship's travels through the various ports in the Caribbean Sea and the cargo it carried first as a trade vessel then as a pirate ship. Aaron's research was … *thorough.*

It had taken all her self-control not to read Helena's diary. But she'd told herself; it wouldn't be fair to Gully. Instead, she'd set it aside and ignored the itch to call the detective, to tell him and Gully what she'd found.

Tarek hadn't reached out again since the morning. She knew she couldn't avoid him forever, and her silent treatment was beginning to feel childish and obstinate. He'd only asked her to call him, to confirm she was okay. She could hear Ali's voice in her head scolding her.

Give him a chance, Kay. Don't push people away, Kay. Don't do the you-thing, Kay.

Ugh. Ali's the actual worst. "Because she's always right, and she knows it," Kyra grumbled, and yanked her phone out of her bag.

She texted Tarek.

"Sorry. I'm fine. I fell ill at the meeting. Grace and Charlie took me home. Found some of my grandfather's research that may interest Gully. Please let him know."

She stared at the text, hesitating. It was cowardly to put Gully between them. The knot in her chest that she'd thought had finally gone slack, tightened, and lodged itself at the base of her throat. She swallowed, but it didn't move.

Kyra slid her finger over the send icon. She regretted sending it almost immediately. She dropped her head to the steering wheel.

"Why am I like this? What the hell is wrong with me?" Kyra slipped her phone back into her purse and stepped out of the car.

Inn was a quaint misnomer. The Lady Slipper was a large Victorian-style mansion, complete with turrets. The hotel's website said it offered five-star accommodation in each of its forty guestrooms and ten guest cottages surrounding a private lake. There was also an on-site spa, an eighteen-hole golf course, and the award-winning restaurant.

The hostess, dressed in an orchid pink blouse and a light gray pencil skirt, pointed her to the bar. Chase was already there, chatting with the bartender. Kyra inhaled, trying to push past the guilt that she knew would eat at her until she spoke to Tarek. She squared her shoulders and slid onto the stool beside Chase.

"Hi."

"Don't you look good enough to eat," he murmured, his eyes never leaving the bartender.

"You're an asshole." Kyra elbowed him in the ribs and the woman behind the counter snorted, like she was used to Chase's antics.

He raised one shoulder in a halfhearted shrug.

"A scotch on the rocks, please." The bartender stepped away to pour Kyra's drink, and Chase swiveled in his chair to face her. "How was the rest of your day?"

"Exhausting," Chase groaned and rubbed the back of his neck. "Muscles I didn't know I have hurt." Kyra sympathized. Her back, bum, legs, arms … all of it ached. "You?"

Kyra told him about talking to Ali and finding her grandfather's research in the basement. "Hopefully, Gully will find it helpful." Chase's expression shuttered, and he shifted his gaze away. "What is it?"

He pushed his hair off his forehead and turned his attention to his drink. He played with the straw, swirling it around the glass, once, twice. Kyra put her hand on his arm, worried. "Chase?"

"It's the investigation. It's not looking good for Gully," Chase said, his voice quiet.

"You talked to Tarek?"

"I did. A few hours ago. I take it you still haven't."

Kyra shook her head. "I know." She heaved a frustrated sigh. "I'm being a shite. But what's happened?"

"The prosecutor is considering first degree murder charges. She's saying they have sufficient evidence to prove the equipment was sabotaged. That the crime was premeditated. She's pressuring Gully to implicate Terry. She said she'd offer him a deal, reduce the charges, but Gully insists they took the boat out without Terry's knowledge and that Terry wasn't involved."

Kyra stilled. *First degree murder?* England didn't have the death penalty, but it was still used in America.

"The death penalty?" she asked, her voice barely a whisper.

"No, thank god. Massachusetts doesn't have the death penalty. If they'd been a few miles out, it'd have been federal jurisdiction. Gully's lucky. Sort of."

To Kyra, nothing about Gully's situation sounded lucky.

"I don't understand. Why do they think Gully would kill Jaycee and Matty Gray? What motive does he have to hurt them? He needed them to help him identify the *Keres*."

"Yeah." Chase let out a long breath and fixed his gaze somewhere beyond the wall of liquor bottles. "The police are saying that Gully and Rose didn't want to share the treasure. If Gully is right, the wreck could be worth millions. They wanted it all for themselves."

Kyra took a sip of her drink. The liquid burned down her throat. It did little to ease the tight knot in her chest. The prosecution's story didn't add up. Even if the motive was monetary. Gully still needed the wreck raised. *Why would he kill them before they pulled it up?* She wished she could talk to Tarek.

Chase rubbed his temple and, as if reading her mind,

said, "Tarek wants Gully to file a complaint against the Menemsha department."

"What? Why?"

"Apparently the chief of police at the department is an uncle to some guy who's been after Gully for ages." Before she could ask, Chase shook his head. "I only know it has something to do with the pub. Tarek didn't get into specifics." Chase turned his body so he faced her. "He didn't get into specifics about Gully," he said, meaning dripping from each syllable.

Kyra sat up straighter.

"Kay, it's not what you think."

"And what do you think I think?" she asked, her tone sharp. She finished her drink and placed it back on the gray coaster. The hotel's logo, the outline of an orchid, was printed in a metallic pink.

"You?" he scoffed, shaking his head. "I'd bet Barbossa you're thinking the worst." He wasn't wrong. "He's worried about you, but I'm not going to tell you that you should talk to him."

"You're not?" Kyra watched him from the corner of her eye. Her defenses were up.

"You wouldn't do it, just to spite me. Nose, face, all that."

Kyra's eyes widened. *That sounds like me.* She felt raw and exposed, uncomfortable with being seen so clearly. How did he know her so well?

"Miss Gibson?" Kyra turned around to see the hostess. "The rest of your party has arrived. They're in the dining room."

"Oh, thank you." Kyra opened her purse.

"No, I've got it." Chase waved her off. He gripped her elbow, stopping her when she stood. "I'm going to Menemsha tomorrow. I'd like to show you the new sailboat."

"Chase," she said, her voice shaking. "I don't know."

"Please? We don't need to take it out. Not unless you want to."

Kyra swallowed and took in his hopeful expression. Chase wanted to share this with her, out of everyone he knew. She felt herself nodding. "Okay, I'll see it," she said at last.

Chase beamed. It wasn't the calculated smarmy smile he used with the press or to charm people, but the rare one reserved for when he was truly delighted. He gave her a crushing hug. "Brilliant," he said, mocking her accent. "You'll love it. Promise."

Charlie and Grace were already seated at a table near the window. Grace spotted her once Kyra entered the dining room and waved.

"Hi, dear!" Grace sang. "How are you feeling?"

"Hello. Much, much better. Thank you for taking care of me yesterday." Kyra sat next to Charlie and leaned over to give her shoulders a quick squeeze.

"Don't mention it. How's Chase?" Charlie asked, handing her the wine list.

"We saw you two at the bar," Grace said. "He's looking so much better these days. Healthier."

"Oh, you should have said hi." Kyra pushed the wine list back to Charlie. "You pick."

"Dear, if we sat at the bar with you, that boy and Char

never would have left. We'd be sitting there until the Lady Slipper closes for the season. Possibly forever." Grace pressed her lips together in mock austerity.

Charlie rolled her eyes.

"He's good," Kyra said. "I'm going to see his new sailboat tomorrow."

Charlie's smile fell away. "Not in a million years," she hissed, then tried to laugh it off like she was joking, but Kyra could tell it was forced.

"Char, love, we live on an island. You'll need to face your fear of boats, eventually." The corners of Grace's eyes wrinkled with concern. She reached over and took Charlie's hand in her own.

Charlie rolled her eyes again, an exaggerated movement, an entire half circle. "I'm not afraid. I've just developed a healthy respect for the ocean that keeps my feet firmly on dry land." Charlie was smiling, but her tone held a warning.

Grace shifted in her seat and glanced at Kyra. Charlie pulled her hand away. Kyra opened her menu and studied it. Clearly, this wasn't the first time the Chamberses had discussed Charlie's new phobia. Kyra didn't think Charlie's fear of boats or the ocean was unwarranted. Being stranded on a drifting boat during a storm did that to a person.

"Have you ladies decided on drinks?" the server asked, and Kyra sent him a silent thank-you for interrupting an imminent-sounding argument between the couple.

"Oh, I think so, yes," Grace said her voice wavering. She gave herself a little shake. "Char, did you choose something?" Charlie opened the wine list and asked the server questions about vintages and regions. Kyra listened with half an ear as they finally settled on a bottle, and he left to fetch it.

"Excuse me, you're Grace Chambers, right?"

Kyra looked up from her menu. The khaki man from the council meeting was standing beside Grace. His pleated pants were a light shade of khaki tonight, the color of dry sand. He wore an army green utility shirt, buttoned to the collar. He looked strangely formal and yet still out of place in the elegant dining room.

Grace glanced between the man and Charlie; her brows drawn in confusion.

"You're with the Martha's Vineyard Community Council, correct? You met my colleague, Rachel Collins?" The man pointed to a table a few over from theirs.

Rachel Collins was watching them. She raised her hand in acknowledgment. Grace swiveled her head back to the man and tucked her hair behind an ear.

"Yes? I'm Grace. Can I help you?"

"Actually, yes!" the man said with enthusiasm, and took the empty seat at their table before any of the women could object. "I'm Dr. Seth Hammond, with the Oceanic Conservation." He shot his hand out and grabbed Grace's. He pumped her arm up and down a few times before Grace could extricate herself. She pulled back and dropped her hands in her lap.

Kyra chanced a glance at Charlie, who looked equally bewildered.

"Of course, Dr. Hammond. I remember," Grace said, her courteous smile melting.

"I'm here to ensure the protection of the delicate oceanic ecosystem."

Charlie shifted in her seat. The movement caught Seth's attention, and he refocused on her. Confusion flashed across his face, like he just realized there were other people at the table.

"Oh, hi, uhhh..." He left the question unsaid hanging in the air.

"My wife Charlene and our friend Kyra Gibson," Grace said.

"Mmhhmm. Nice to meet you." He nodded his head once, then turned back to Grace, dismissing them.

Charlie's eyebrows flew up. She caught Kyra's eye and mouthed, "What the hell?"

Kyra shook her head. *No idea.*

"Did you need something, Seth?" Grace's voice was polite.

His mouth flattened in annoyance. "Yeah. I need to get a meeting with Ida Ames and the other members of the council. I want your support when I file the injunction. We need to stop those excavators before they cause more damage. Rachel said you're the person to talk to."

Grace glanced back to the table where Rachel was sitting, but Kyra couldn't see their table now with Hammond in the way.

"If you call the office, someone will assist you during business hours."

"But we're here now and every moment that the salvagers are on the water, they're causing irreparable damage."

"The efforts are paused until the town issues the permits, subject to the council's vote," Grace said, frowning. "The ships are just parked there. They may take photographs, but that's all."

"That's too much." Hammond waved his hands around. "Just *being* on the water is impacting the sea and avian life."

Avian? Birds? Kyra started. *He's that birdwatcher from my flight.* Kyra narrowed her eyes, focusing on Seth Hammond. *It is him. I think.* She was 90, no 80, percent sure.

"I'm not sure what you'd have me do," Grace said. "As you can see, I'm at dinner. With my family and friends."

"Seth, stop harassing these nice people." A hand dropped on his shoulder. Her lime green manicure was bright against the dark olive of Hammond's sleeve.

"Ms. Chambers," Rachel said in her silky voice. "Apologies for the intrusion. I'll call your office first thing to set up a meeting with the council." She flashed a toothpaste model smile, but it melted away under Charlie's glare. She looked at Kyra, and her lips formed an *o*.

"You were also at the meeting last night. With Rick."

"Pardon?" Kyra's skin flashed hot and cold.

Out of the corner of her eye, she caught Charlie waving to someone.

"Are you involved in the council as well?" Rachel asked.

"No, I'm … I'm friends with Gully." It wasn't quite a lie.

"Ah." For a second, Kyra thought she looked … *disappointed*? Rachel seemed to shake it off. "Another treasure hunter. Tell him hello for me."

"You're one of the salvagers?" Hammond glared at Kyra.

"Um, actually…"

"Excuse me, Mr. Hammond, Ms. Collins. We kindly request you return to your table."

Charlie must have been waving to the hostess. Behind her, their server held a wine bottle and four glasses.

"Yes, we're so sorry to have disturbed you," Rachel said. "Thank you, Grace. I'll be in touch. Come on." She patted Seth's shoulder, and he got to his feet.

He mumbled something that could have been an apology, all the while glowering at Kyra. Then he followed Rachel back to their table.

"Our sincerest apologies for the disturbance, Grace," the hostess said. "I'd like to offer you a complementary bottle of champagne as an apology for the inconvenience. We can also move you to a new table if you'd be more comfortable." She nodded in the direction of Rachel and Seth's table. They were sitting, heads close together, having a conversation. "I can assure you; you won't be bothered again."

"Oh." Grace put a hand to her heart. "That's not necessary," she said at the same time, Charlie exclaimed, "We'd love champagne!"

"Very well. Thank you, Kristen, champagne would be lovely, but we can stay here. We don't need another table. Do we?"

"No, we're fine here," Charlie agreed when Kyra gave her a nod.

The server stepped forward with their wine. Kyra noticed he'd lost the fourth glass he'd been holding since Seth had left the table.

"Apologies for the delay ladies, I had some trouble finding your bottle." He brandished it and presented it to Charlie.

"That was strange," Charlie whispered once the server

left. "What did Rachel mean when she said treasure hunter?"

"I suppose Gully is a sort of treasure hunter. He's been searching for a lost treasure ship for years," Kyra said and snuck a peek at Rachel's table.

She was leaning over her plate, talking to Seth. Her long hair obscured much of her face. His jaw was set, and from her hand movements, Kyra thought Rachel might be reprimanding him. She jerked her chin toward their table, and Kyra shifted her gaze before she was caught staring. She peeked again from under her lashes to see Rachel watching her. Rachel inclined her head in polite acknowledgment, then turned back to Dr. Hammond. Kyra wasn't sure what to make of Rachel Collins.

Charlie and Grace kept up a steady stream of conversation. When their food came, Kyra pushed it around her plate and picked at it, her appetite gone.

"Char, how was the open house today?" Grace asked.

Charlie rolled her eyes. "The Wheelers are a pain in the ass." Charlie ignored Grace's admonishing lip purse and launched into an exaggerated story about the open house she'd held earlier that day, and her clients' exotic reptile collection's strict feeding schedule. Kyra tried to listen, but even the tales of Charlie's crazy clients couldn't hold her attention. She snuck another peek at Rachel and Hammond's table, but a new party sat there. She hadn't seen them leave.

Dinner was endless. Kyra excused herself before dessert, laughing at Grace's mortified expression, when Charlie accepted the champagne and slid the bottle into her purse. She gave quick hugs to Grace and Charlie and made promises to check in with them tomorrow.

When she was safely locked in her car, Kyra released a long breath. She couldn't stop rehashing the strange conversation with Hammond or forget how he'd looked at her when he'd thought she was a salvager. Kyra rubbed her forehead, and with an uneasy pit in her stomach, she turned the car toward home.

Chapter Fourteen

THE SUNSHINE DID nothing for Kyra's stormy mood as she parked her SUV in the Menemsha parking lot. She yanked her sunglasses off and flipped down the visor. She looked at herself in the mirror. With the pads of her fingers, she tried to pat out the dark smudges under her eyes. She'd woken up in a cold sweat, the recurring nightmare of being trapped on the *Neamhnaid* leaving her exhausted and raw. She'd almost caved and called Chase, just to hear his voice. He'd have answered, sat with her like she'd done for him at least a dozen times, but she'd never made a late-night call to him before and she couldn't bring herself to pick up the phone.

Kyra wrapped her arms around herself and let her forehead drop to the steering wheel. *I can do this. Chase won't let anything happen to me. There is no storm. This is not the* Neamhnaid. She'd been repeating this mantra over and over in her mind all morning. It wasn't helping. She replaced her oversized sunglasses, forced her lips into a weak smile. *Fake it 'till you make it, right?* Gathering the vestiges of her courage, she stepped out onto the sunbaked pavement.

Kyra's senses were overwhelmed by Menemsha in the summer. The tiny harbor bustled with boats of all sizes. The breeze carried scents of diesel fuel and fish. People were already camped out on the beach. Children flew kites dangerously close to a sculpture of a spearfisherman.

She made her way down the docks to the enclave of private boathouses. The Hawthorn shed had been refreshed since she'd been assaulted there last spring. It'd been painted a bright blue, and the faded decorations removed. The island's would-be national flag replaced the dingy American one that used to fly on the pole. She bit into her lip and grateful tears welled in her eyes. Chase had done it for her. Not for the first time, she wondered how much of the party-boy persona was an act for the public, and the real Chase was the empathetic person she had come to cherish these last few months.

"Morning," she called through the open door.

"Oomph!"

Something hit the floor, and Chase swore. There was another muffled bang, and he emerged from the boathouse holding a few sorry looking life jackets. He flashed her his playboy smile, half teasing, half devious, and pushed his hair out of his eyes.

"You need a bell."

Kyra laughed, but it came out high-pitched and nervous.

Chase's eyes narrowed and his smile faded. "Couldn't talk Grace and Charlie into coming?"

"No." Kyra made a face. "I think Charlie has been turned off sailing for life."

"Hmmm, makes living on an island more challenging…"

Kyra huffed another strained laugh. "Her fear is understandable." But since the easiest way on and off the island was by ferry, she hoped for Grace's sake, Charlie's phobia was limited to sailboats, especially since Charlie had regular visits with specialists on the mainland for her diabetes.

"I know," he mumbled, more to himself than to Kyra. "Let me take those." He eased her bag off her shoulder and dumped it on the floor of the small dinghy tied alongside the dock. Kyra eyed it skeptically, her stomach tightening. She looked out at the boats in the harbor and shifted her weight from foot to foot. Chase's hands came to her shoulders.

He turned her around to face him.

"You'll be fine, Kay." He wrapped his arms around her and rested his chin on the crown of her head.

She let him comfort her. *I can do this. He won't let anything happen to me.* He gave her a squeeze before pulling back and stooping a bit to peer into her face. She swallowed. The lines at the corners of Chase's eyes became more pronounced when he pressed his lips together.

"I'll be with you the whole time. I promise."

She nodded. The rational part of her brain believed him, but her heart was still beating out of control, banging against her ribs.

"Whenever you want, say the word, and I'll bring you back. If we get out there, and you don't want to get on the *Elpis*, I'll bring you back. If you don't want to go out at all, we won't. We can do something else."

"I know." She stepped out of his arms and squared her shoulders, feigning courage. "I want to see the *Elpis*."

"We have one more person coming." Chase grinned, but he still eyed her with concern.

"Who? Gryphon? Sissy? Please let it be Sissy." Even her

teasing sounded strained.

Chase shook his head, then nodded over her shoulder. "Don't be mad."

Kyra jerked back.

"I said I wouldn't tell you what to do. I didn't say I'd leave it alone."

What did you do?

But before she could say anything, Chase raised a hand and called, "Hey! Over here!" He winked and stepped around her.

Kyra whirled around. Tarek Collins was walking toward them, a bag slung over his shoulder. She gritted her teeth. *Just. Fucking. Brilliant.* She scowled at Chase, but he just gave her a smug grin.

"Chase," she hissed.

"Good morning." Tarek pushed his sunglasses onto his forehead. His tone sounded off, like he was forcing himself to be chipper. He clasped Chase's hand, then glanced at Kyra. His expression faltered. "I brought coffee and pastries?" He held up a tray of three coffees and a paper bag. "And lobster rolls from the good place." He held up the cooler he was carrying in his other hand.

Apparently, he knew she'd be there. Kyra turned to glare at Chase, but he was no longer next to her. He'd already hopped down into the boat.

"Come on. Time to go." Chase coaxed her down, holding his hand out to her.

She hesitated. She felt Tarek watching her and her resolve clicked into place. She didn't want him to see her afraid. Kyra placed her hand in Chase's and let him help her down into the dinghy. He settled her near the bow.

Tarek handed Chase their breakfast, and he passed it to her.

"Don't let it get wet," he said with a smirk.

She glared at him, knowing it didn't have the same effect with her oversized sunglasses. She held the coffee tray in her lap with one hand and gripped her seat with the other. Chase moved to the stern to start the outboard motor.

Tarek unlaced the lines from the boat clips and hopped down, the impact causing the boat to rock. Kyra's grip tightened. She wouldn't be surprised if her fingers were embedded in the underside of the wooden bench. The motor roared to life and Kyra's heart skipped, then pounded. She could feel its staccato rhythm against her sternum, hear it in her ears. Her vision blackened around the edges. With a soft tug, the dinghy pulled away from the dock.

Chase steered the boat beyond the inner harbor to the deeper water, beyond the breakwater. Kyra swallowed and squeezed her eyes closed. She sucked in a deep breath. *I can do this. There is no storm. This is not the* Neamhnaid. She let it out in a long whoosh, and then did it again. A warm hand wrapped around her leg, just below her knee. Her eyes shot open. Tarek was leaning forward, watching her from behind his mirrored sunglasses.

"You're doing great." His voice was so soft. It barely carried over the outboard's rumbling. Kyra stiffened. Now she was not only on the verge of a panic attack but also mortified. "We're almost there."

"There it is!" Chase was pointing over the starboard side. The new sailboat was older and much smaller than the

Neamhnaid. "It was built in '63 and was fully restored three years ago. It has a small cabin, and the manual says it can sleep four. Realistically, it can sleep two tiny people." Chase grinned. "It'll just be a day sailor. The trip up from Baltimore was a nightmare." He made a pained face and despite her panic, Kyra huffed a strangled laugh. She caught Tarek smirking, too. Anything less than five-star accommodations would be torture for Chase.

"You rename it?" Tarek asked.

"Yeah, the guy I bought it from had named it after his wife, the *Lovely Lily* or something. Lovely Lily, divorced him and left him with nothing but the boat, so I figured it should be rechristened."

Elpis. Kyra bit back a smile. *Hope.*

"Isn't it an administrative hassle to rename a boat?" Tarek asked.

"Not really. It's more superstition than anything, but I offered the name back to Poseidon."

"You did what?" Kyra asked.

"You write the old name on something that will sink, slip it into the ocean offering the name back to the sea god, then make a sacrifice." Chase reached up to rub the back of his neck.

"A sacrifice?" Kyra didn't know if he was kidding or not. Tarek was also confused.

"I poured out some whisky." Chase raised one shoulder; his cheeks went a little pink. "Single malt, too." Chase made an exaggerated frown and put his hand over his heart.

He pulled the dinghy alongside the *Elpis* and clipped it to the mooring. He turned to Kyra. "Did you want a tour?

On board?" he asked, his tone hopeful.

Tarek was watching her. They'd turn around and take her back to the harbor without question if she asked. Knowing she had some control helped. She was still scared, terrified, but she also felt ... supported. She worried her bottom lip, thinking. It wasn't something she was used to, feeling like she could rely on anyone other than her aunt. Tarek turned his face into the sun. They didn't rush her. Finally, after what was probably too long, she dipped her chin in a tentative nod.

Chase clapped his hands together and grinned. He sprang up onto the deck of the sailboat and reached down for her. "Step here and use this to pull yourself up."

I can do this. She passed him their breakfast, and following his instructions, pulled herself onto the *Elpis*. Chase guided her to a seat. A moment later, he handed her a cup of coffee. She sipped it while he and Tarek made short work of unloading the dinghy and stowing their things. When they were finished, Chase sat at the helm, and Tarek took the seat next to her.

"Captain, a tour?" Tarek asked, handing Chase a cup from the tray.

Chase was like a kid with his favorite toy. He gave them a tour of the boat, pointing out all its classic idiosyncrasies with pride. His enthusiasm had a calming effect. He was so surefooted, and his excitement was almost innocent. The biting edge of her terror dulled, moved to the periphery and Kyra relaxed the slightest bit. She leaned back against the sun warmed cushions.

"Down there are the bunk rooms, the galley, and the

head. I haven't really set any of that up yet. So, there isn't much to see." He pointed to the cabin door. He was providing an excuse, so she wouldn't feel pressure to go below. "That's pretty much it. Do you want to go out?"

Kyra stilled as her pulse quickened.

"We can also just hang in the harbor," he added quickly, and pulled a donut from the paper bag. "Or," he said between bites. "I can take us up the coast. There's a hidden beach and a swimming area. It's only accessible by boat, so it's not crowded even in the high season."

"Or we could just sit here..." Tarek said.

"No, let's go." Kyra surprised herself. The two men watched her closely. "If you want to. I'm okay." Her gaze flicked between them, and she swallowed. "I'll *be* okay."

"Just say the word, and I'll Jack Sparrow us right back." Chase stuffed the rest of the donut in his mouth and wiped his hands on his swim shorts. He stood up. "You'll love it. I promise."

He moved about the rigging with the confidence of someone who spent their life on the sea, humming the pirate song loudly enough for them to hear.

"Tar, gimme a hand?"

Tarek made an affirmative sound and began unclipping and tying down ropes.

"You know how to sail?"

"I learned the basics one summer," Tarek said as he knotted and looped ropes.

Kyra pulled herself onto a spot that felt as much out of their way as possible. *Looks like more than basics*, she thought as he tied off a complicated knot.

"Unclip us." Chase pointed and started the engine. The boat rumbled to life. Tarek unhooked the *Elpis* from the mooring and Chase guided the boat out of the harbor.

Kyra watched the tiny village shrink as the *Elpis* moved out into the Vineyard Sound.

"You, okay?" Tarek asked, and his hand gripped her shoulder.

She wasn't. Her body tingled and her heart beat in her ears. She was on the verge of a panic attack. She took in a deep breath. *Ten, nine, eight, …* Down to one. She shut her eyes and gripped the seat, her nails digging into the cushion, and she counted down again.

"Kyra?" Her eyes popped open, and she was peering right into Tarek's face. He'd kneeled down in front of her, his sunglasses in his hair. His hand slid down to her biceps, and she shivered. "We're right here."

"I know, thank you. I'm just nervous." Chase yelled something and Tarek responded he was coming. "Go on. I'll be okay." She knew she wasn't convincing.

He released her, stood, and stepped away to untie the sails. He shouted something to Chase, who was fiddling with lines on the mast. Chase returned to the steering column and cut the engine. Tarek yanked on a line. The sails unfurled with a *whoosh*, catching the wind. A gentle tug, and the *Elpis* moved forward, cutting through the crests.

Kyra sat on the bench behind Chase, watching as the boat moved through the waves. Glistening sea spray flew over the sides, misting her.

"Come see the view from over here." Tarek guided her to the bow. She settled on the teak decking, holding the railing to keep steady. From up front, her view was unobstructed, and she could see the coastline as they sailed by.

"Don't listen to a word he says," Tarek said, rolling his eyes in Chase's direction. He sat down beside her. His long legs hung over the side, and he rested his elbows on the rails.

"What is he saying?"

"There's no such thing as the Nightingale Reef, or Dead Man's Bluff. He's just making shit up," Tarek said loud enough for Chase to hear.

"Is that true?"

"What? Absolutely not," Chase scoffed. "And over there is where Moby Dick first met the whale."

Tarek raised his hand as if to say, *see?* But it didn't deter Chase. He continued to point out fictional landmarks, each more ludicrous than the last.

"How's Gully?" Kyra asked during a lull in Chase's fantasy tour.

"As well as can be expected." Tarek rested his chin on his crossed forearms. "He's back at the pub today. We met with his legal team again yesterday." Tarek moved his sunglasses to rub his eyes. "Connors spoke to the prosecutor. He expects Gully to be charged. The prosecutor has been looking for a high-profile case, one that will give her career a boost, and the chief of the Menemsha police force is pressuring her to move quickly."

"But why?"

"Closing the case quickly looks good for him. And for her." Something about his tone made Kyra look over at him.

"Tarek?"

He ran his hand through his hair and sighed. "I don't

know. I think it's more than just ambition. This investigation feels malicious. It feels personal." Tarek glanced back at Chase and lowered his voice. "I haven't worked with Chief Erikson much, but in the few instances I have, he's always been pretty hands off, more administrative. In this case, though, every order is coming directly from him. And he's pursuing Gully relentlessly. He's not interested in considering alternative theories, not that anyone has come up with anything credible." Tarek looked like he wanted to say more when a whistle interrupted him.

Kyra looked back over her shoulder.

"This is it!" Chase called from the helm. "We can stop here." He steered the *Elpis* into a small inlet. "Tar, help with the sails." Tarek helped Chase bring the sails down. Kyra watched them, feeling useless but not knowing how she could help. Chase tossed in the anchor and nodded to the shoreline.

Rocky outcroppings protected the small natural harbor. Boulders were scattered along a sandy beach that seemed to go right to the base of the wall of the clay cliffs towering above. Birds swooped down from cliffs to skim the water.

"This is perfect." Kyra's voice came out breathy as she took in the scene.

Chase joined Kyra at the bow. He pointed to the cliff side. "See the colors?" Bands of sediment cut through the cliffs horizontally in shades of charcoal, rust, and ochre. Chase told her about the ribbons. Each color represented a different prehistoric era. "The black ones are thought to be from the Mesozoic." Kyra frowned at him, unsure if he was teasing her. He put a hand over his heart. "I swear, that's true."

"It is," Tarek said from behind them, and Kyra turned around. In his hands, he held a bottle of champagne and plastic flutes. He sat on her other side and handed her the glasses so he could open the bottle. "The only true thing you've said all day," Tarek said, filling their glasses.

Chase *tsked* and reached for one.

"Cheers." He tapped his against Kyra's.

Tarek tipped the bottle and poured a splash of champagne into the water. He grinned, his white teeth flashing. "For the sea god."

KYRA'S FEET FOUND the silty sea floor, and she stood up. She sucked air into her lungs. Chase grabbed her hand and held her steady against the waves. He snickered as she double checked her swimsuit. Thankfully, it'd remained mostly in place during the swim from the *Elpis*.

The beach was pristine. Theirs were the only footprints marring the otherwise unblemished sand. Kyra wandered to the back of the beach, to the clay wall. This close, Kyra could see it wasn't as steep as it appeared from the water. The incline was more gradual, with lots of outcroppings on the way up. Seaweed clung to the crags far above her head.

"That's why it's called Lost Beach," a melodic voice spoke over her shoulder. Tarek pointed to the seaweed clinging to the rocks above. "At high tide, the entire beach gets swallowed. Over there, you can see remnants of the old trail." Tarek's hand rose a few yards above the waterline. An overgrown path switchbacked up the cliff. "It starts at the top and goes all the way down to the sea caves over there." Kyra could just make out dark spots where the clay met the sand that must have been the caves' mouths.

"Not that long ago, you could walk down from the top and wander the caves. Legend says the caves will take you all the way to the lighthouse."

Kyra's eyes traveled back up the cliffs. She couldn't see a lighthouse from the beach.

"The lighthouse?" she asked.

"They had to move it back some years ago, to save it. Erosion undermined its stability."

She remembered reading that the lighthouse sat on the bluff warning sailors away from the Devil's Bridge shoal, the same that had beached the *Keres*.

"It's all a protected nature preserve now. I think nesting grounds for birds. You can't climb the cliffs anymore."

"And the caves?" she asked, looking toward the entrances.

"When the tide comes in, the caves fill up. About thirty years ago, a few teenagers got lost exploring and were drowned. They've been closed ever since."

Despite the sunshine, goose bumps broke out along her arms. She walked closer, right up to the signs staked into the sand. Weather worn, red lettering on a once white background notified visitors of the danger and to KEEP OUT.

Kyra waded through the surf and climbed up one of the larger boulders. The wet rock was slippery and covered in black seaweed and mussels at the base. The waves and sea spray didn't reach the top, though and she sat down to dry off in the sun. From her vantage point, she could see Chase and Tarek. Tarek was walking along the shoreline, toeing the sand, while Chase was sitting, knees bent, tossing stones into the waves. Their voices carried, but couldn't make out what they were saying over the sounds of the surf.

She observed them, a little envious of their easy friendship. She'd been stuck in London, nursing broken ribs and a bruised psyche, while they had grown close. Kyra didn't have many close friends, preferring to keep people at a distance, but watching them, Chase's easy laughter, Tarek's indulgent smiles, she wondered if she'd been missing out. If her transient, isolated existence wasn't quite the safety net she'd thought it was.

She laid back and stared up at the cumulus clouds. When she'd moved out of her London flat before leaving for the island, she hadn't made plans for when she returned. She'd stored her few possessions with Ali, and they decided she'd figure it out later. At the time, Kyra had been surprised her aunt accepted Kyra's non-plan. Now she wondered if Ali had known that Kyra would want to make a home of Martha's Vineyard long before Kyra knew herself.

"Wake up, sleeping beauty."

Someone poked her in the ribs and her eyes fluttered open. She hadn't meant to doze off. Chase. "Getting hungry? We're heading back to the boat."

"Oh, yes, I'm ready." She checked her arms for sunburn.

"You've only been up here a few minutes." Chase held out his hand to help her down. "Look at this." He opened his other hand to show her a large half shell. White and purple swirled together on the shell's underside. "It's a quahog, a type of clam. The Indigenous people made beads for currency and jewelry from the shells."

Kyra ran her finger along the glass-smooth surface.

He dropped it on the beach. "Let's go back to the boat."

They made the swim back to the *Elpis*. Chase staying close to her. She wasn't a strong swimmer, and when she reached the boat, she was panting. Tarek reached down to help her up and handed her a towel.

"I'll grab lunch and bring it up." Tarek disappeared beneath the deck.

"Should we help?" Kyra asked Chase, stepping into her shorts.

"Probably." Chase shrugged and climbed up to the bow. "Let's eat up here."

"You're a right wanker, you know that?"

"Love you, too."

She grinned. Kyra paused at the entrance to the cabin. But before she could talk herself into climbing down, Tarek appeared.

"Do you need help?" she asked.

"Yes, thanks. Can you take this?" He passed her an ice bucket containing their drinks. "I'll be right up with the sandwiches."

She nodded; grateful she didn't have to venture below. *Baby steps.* Kyra waited on the deck while Tarek grabbed what else he needed from the galley, and they climbed up to the bow. Chase had spread some cushions around a blanket under the shade of the sails, creating a sheltered seating area. The sea breeze kept the heat at bay. Tarek arranged their food on plates, and Chase poured their drinks.

"How far away is the *Keres*?" she asked.

Chase pursed his lips and looked out toward the ocean. "Forty minutes that way-ish."

"Would we be able to see it?"

"We can sail by it, probably even over it, but I doubt we could see anything from the surface." Chase peered over the edge of the boat. "The water isn't clear enough to see that far down. We can't even see the ground here, and it's not that deep. Eight, ten feet?"

Kyra stretched her neck to see over the side and sure enough, she couldn't see the seafloor through the cloudy water. "Oh."

"We can still sail by it, if you want." Chase glanced at Tarek and took a bite of his lobster roll.

"I'd be up to see it," Tarek said. "Would we still be able to see the island?"

"Mmhhmm," Chase hummed as he chewed, nodding his head. He swallowed. "We'd get a great view of Gay Head and the lighthouse." Chase checked his watch. "We can go once we're done eating, then head back to Menemsha."

Tarek raised an eyebrow over the frame of his sunglasses. "What do you think?" he asked her.

He wasn't asking if she wanted to go, but if it was too much, to be out on the open water, far away from land.

Kyra glanced out at the ocean, searching inside for anxiety or discomfort, but she wasn't afraid. Protected under the sails of the *Elpis*, sitting with Chase and Tarek, she felt safe. *I am safe.*

She looked back at them and said confidently, "Let's go. I'd like to see it."

Chapter Fifteen

THE *ELPIS* CUT through the white-capped crests as they sailed toward the wreckage site. Chase had turned on music and classic rock played over the boat's crackly sound system. Kyra sat on the bow, her legs hanging over the edge, the tips of her toes kissing the water. Salt clung to her eyelashes, and the wind pushed her hair off her shoulders. It had become her favorite place on the boat.

Tarek climbed up next to her. "Over there. Boats," he said, pointing.

Kyra scrambled to her feet to see what he was looking at. A wave hit the port side, throwing her off balance.

"Whoa." Tarek grabbed her arm, keeping her upright.

"Thanks," she muttered, trying to regain her footing.

"Here, put one hand on the mast for balance." Tarek placed her hand on the beam next to his. He pointed with his free hand. "Over there, see them?"

"Are those the salvage boats?"

"Need the glasses?" Chase called from behind, holding up a pair of binoculars.

"Nah, they're not that far," Tarek called back.

Kyra could already make out the writing on the two large vessels, *Blue Stream* and *Rose Marine*.

"Both Kapowski and Rose are out there. I can't make out the other two. They could be fishing boats." Tarek pointed to the bimini on the smaller one. "See the rods?" he asked her.

"That one, with the stripes? That's one of Mackey's." Chase pointed to a large vessel trimmed in aqua and royal blue colors. "What are they doing out here?"

"What was the name of Gerry and Sissy's cousin's boat from last night?" Kyra asked.

Chase made a face at her. "Marlin Tours or something? And can we please agree to call him Gryphon?"

"That's Gerry and Sissy's boat. That one." Kyra pointed to a smaller, weathered-looking fishing boat circling the larger vessels.

"It's not … never mind. Really?" Chase tried to peer around the sail.

"Chase, can we get closer?" Tarek yelled back. Chase gave an affirmative nod and gestured to the sails.

Tarek pulled on a rope, and the mainsail slackened, slowing their momentum. Chase guided the *Elpis* and pulled alongside Mackey's fishing boat.

Chase used two fingers to blow a sharp whistle. "Mackey!"

Kyra recognized the man from the council meeting. He'd been the one who'd stood up, demanded answers. His windbreaker, in colors matching the boat's trim, snapped in the wind. He raised his hand.

"Hawthorn!" he shouted; his tone friendly. Joe Mackey turned and yelled something to his crew and the engine cut down to idling. "She looks good." He gestured to the sailboat.

Chase ran his hand proudly over the ship's wheel. "Thanks." He waved and pointed to the salvage boats. "What's going on?"

"They're scanning the wreck." Joe pointed to the two salvage rigs. "We're here to monitor. Make sure they aren't bringing anything up without a permit."

"And them?" Chase pointed to the Marlin Tours boat that was already retreating, returning to the island.

"Tourists and reporters, I gather. A few of the charters are doing it now."

"Did you see anything?" Tarek asked, pointing to the water.

"No. Too cloudy. They need to get divers down there." A man came up behind Joe and said something to him. Joe nodded, then turned back to them. "They're done for the day, so we're heading back. See you around." Joe waved and disappeared back into the wheelhouse.

"Guess that's it," Chase said with a shrug.

Kyra peered into the water. This far from shore, it was dark and ominous. Her grip on the mast tightened.

"Let's get the sails back up," Chase said. "Kay, you may want to sit back here for the trip home. We'll be sailing with the wind. It'll be a little rougher, but a lot faster."

"Have you heard anything more about the investigation?" Chase asked when Tarek joined them at the back of the boat.

Tarek stretched out on the bench behind Chase and tucked his hands behind his head. He reminded Kyra of Cronk splayed out on her floor in a sunspot.

"No, not really. Since I'm technically here on vacation, and my request to be assigned the case was denied, I have no access to the files. I know only what Gully and his lawyer know, but I guess that's even too much."

"What do you mean?" Kyra asked.

Tarek's hand waved in the air, and his tone was bitter and clipped when he said, "Chief Erikson went to my captain. Told her I was being a nuisance and disrupting the investigation. He requested my removal from the island. Like he has the authority to make me leave." Tarek huffed, and then he said, his voice softer, barely loud enough for Kyra to hear, "Not that it matters. Even if I was given leave to work the case, after last spring, I don't have a lot of friends in the departments here."

Kyra's stomach dropped, and she wondered not for the first time if he regretted what he'd done for her.

"When do you have to go back?" Chase asked.

"I have a lot of vacation time. I can see this thing through."

"And your other options?" Chase asked over his shoulder.

Sunlight glinted off Tarek's sunglasses. "I've the invitation to train at Quantico," he said with little enthusiasm. "And yesterday, the official offer came in for a position with a private security company as a profiling consultant. I'd work with law enforcement agencies on cases all over the country."

"What kind of cases?" Chase asked.

Tarek sat up, looked out toward the horizon and said, his voice soft and heavy, "Violent ones."

Kyra didn't know how to respond. Tarek sounded defeated by the proposition. She had an unfamiliar urge to comfort him, but she didn't know how, or if he'd even appreciate it.

"We're coming into the harbor. We need to get the sails down," Chase said, interrupting Kyra's thoughts.

She looked up. They had made it back much faster than she'd realized.

Tarek stood. He held a hand out to Kyra. "Come on, I'll show you." She put her hand in his, and let him pull her up. He guided her to the mast. "When I say to, pull that one—the downhaul." Tarek pointed to a rope and moved to the other side of the boat. "Now!" he yelled.

Kyra yanked on the rope, and with a *whirr*, the sail collapsed. She grinned, delighted. Chase whooped. Tarek showed her how to wrap and stow it.

"Good job."

Chase turned on the boat's engines and guided it through the harbor to his mooring and the tiny dinghy that would take them back to the docks.

Once everything had been stowed away, the covers snapped into place. Chase helped her into the dinghy and started the motor. She gave the *Elpis* a last look and smiled to herself. *I had fun.*

"Are you going to talk to the Marlin Tour people?" Chase asked over the rumble of the outboard.

"I think so. I was planning on calling on my way home. Did you want to come?"

"I wish I could, but I promised to cover Sara's rounds at the farm tonight. I can meet you tomorrow, though."

"I'll come."

Kyra turned around to face the front of the boat. Her reflection in Tarek's sunglasses stared back at her.

"Only if you want to."

"I do."

Kyra frowned. She really didn't need either of them. She could ask questions on her own.

"You promised," Chase said as if reading her mind.

She shifted in her seat and nodded. *Fine.* "I'll let you know when or if they're willing to talk to me."

That seemed to mollify Chase. The dinghy slid against the dock and he cut the motor. Tarek hopped onto the dock to tie it off. Kyra handed him the bags, and he lined them up on the deck before helping her.

"Thank you. For today. For pushing me to come."

Chase's grin was so wide it almost split his face.

"You're going to love the regatta."

"We'll see." Kyra chuckled and, with a wave, headed back to her car.

The SUV was stifling from baking in the sun all day. She rolled the windows down and blasted the air conditioning. She pulled her phone from her bag and searched for the contact information for Marlin Tours in Oak Bluffs.

"Marlin Tours," a gruff voice answered.

"Hi. I was calling about hiring you to see the wreck site."

"Yeah?" The voice cleared his throat. "When did you want to go out?"

"Can you do it tonight?"

"Tonight? One sec." Kyra heard some muffled voices, like the man had covered the phone's microphone. "Yeah, we can do it. What time?"

"Would six work?"

"Six is fine," the voice paused. "That'll be six hundred for the charter. Cash, or mobile payment. There are no refunds if you can't see anything."

"No, of course. Thank you." *Six hundred dollars? Jeez.* The man gave her the slip number and hung up. She texted Tarek that their appointment was at six p.m., slip seventy-seven in Oak Bluffs.

Chapter Sixteen

THREE HOURS LATER, after a shower and a nap on the couch with a snoring cat, Kyra drove to OB. She ran through the questions she wanted to ask the Marlin Tours captain as she circled Ocean Park, looking for a parking spot. On her second round, she squeezed into a semi-legal spot in front of a green and red Victorian mansion.

The village was bustling with a chaotic energy. Teenagers jaywalked across Circuit Avenue, holding up traffic. Tourists balancing shopping bags and ice cream cones navigated the crowded sidewalks. Children ran in and out of the large double doors of an old-fashioned arcade clinging to hard won prizes.

She dodged the masses and made a left past a line of people waiting their turn at an ancient-looking carousel. She walked along the marina, studying the numbers painted on the pavement in front of each slip. Seventy-five … seventy-six…

"What are *you* doing here?" A voice snarled.

Kyra jerked to a stop. Her entire body broke out in a cold sweat. Wes Silva sat on a folding beach chair on the deck of a shabby fishing boat. She stepped back. Her gaze slid to the ground. *Seventy-Seven.*

Shit. Shit. Shit. Her heart stuttered.

Kyra raised her chin. "I have an appointment." Her voice came out thin and reedy. "What are *you* doing here?" Despite her brain telling her to calm the fuck down, she had no control over her body's flight response to coming face-to-face with the man who broke into her house last spring. Her mind scrambled. *Why is he here? Chase would have told me if Wes ran these tours. Wouldn't he?*

"Excuse us!" a cheery voice sang from behind her. Kyra stepped out of the way of a bicycle tour. The sight of them, of the tiny orange visibility flags attached to the rear of each bike, the children's traffic cone orange helmets, waylaid her increasing fear. They were surrounded by hundreds of people. Wes couldn't hurt her, not in front of all these potential witnesses. Kyra swallowed and looked back at him, doing her best to appear calm.

"This is my cousin's boat." Wes focused on something behind her, and his rugged features twisted. He scoffed a mirthless laugh, like he was almost as unsettled as she was. Kyra blinked.

"Silva," a familiar melodic voice edged with warning, spoke from right behind her. Tarek's hand came to rest at the base of her spine and it took all she could, not to sag with relief. "Nice to see you again," Tarek's polite words juxtaposed his threatening tone.

Wes Silva's glower intensified. His upper lip curled.

"Yo, Wes." A man emerged from the wheelhouse. He was looking at his phone. "I've got some people coming to check out the wreck now." He looked up and came to a halt.

His head swiveled between Tarek and Silva, and he

frowned. Tarek shifted away from Kyra, and he slid his hands into his pockets. She snuck a glance at him, but he was staring at Silva, his jaw clenched.

"They're here." Silva huffed his annoyance and pointed his beer bottle at them. He took a long swig.

Silva's cousin turned to Kyra. Something in his expression changed, the lines in his face sharpened. She steeled herself. This would not go well.

"Rene Ramos?" Tarek asked, stepping forward.

The captain's eyebrows shot up, but he nodded.

"What do you want, Collins?" Silva made a noise that sounded like a sneer. "You and your..." He paused and ran his eyes up and down Kyra's body, making her skin crawl.

"Careful." Tarek's voice was low.

Silva shrugged.

"Yeah, I'm Rene." The captain shot a warning look at his cousin. He glanced between them, his eyes landing on Kyra. "What's this about?" he asked her, seeming to determine she was the safest one to talk to.

"My name is Kyra Gibson. We spoke a few hours ago about the charter?"

"I'm not sure it's a good idea." Rene's gaze shifted between Tarek and Wes. "I don't want any trouble."

"Please. We're working with Gully's team, investigating the circumstances surrounding the deaths of the two divers a few nights ago."

Tarek raised an eyebrow at her, but she ignored him. With Wes here, she assumed honesty, or something close to it, would get her further than subterfuge. The islanders had seemed to embrace Gully as one of their own. Maybe Wes and his cousin would be inclined to help, if they knew it was for him, and not *some summer person.*

"I heard that you've been taking people out to see the wreckage of the *Keres*, and I was hoping you could answer a few questions. We don't want any trouble either. I just want to help Gully."

"He doesn't have to tell you anything," Wes snapped.

"No, he doesn't," Tarek said. "It would be appreciated, though."

"I don't know what's going on between you two." Rene shifted a pointed finger between his cousin and Tarek. Wes threw him an annoyed sneer. Rene sighed and turned back to Kyra. "I've known Gully for years, ever since he bought that old bar. We play softball together two nights a week. He brings homemade lemonade to each game. He didn't hurt those people." Rene glared at his cousin. "Erikson is full of shit. You know Gully wouldn't hurt anyone."

Wes frowned, but didn't disagree.

Rene heaved another sigh and waved them forward. "Come on board. I'll tell you what I can."

Tarek and Wes Silva stared at each other for a half second before Tarek jerked a nod and climbed aboard, turning to help Kyra jump down. They followed Rene into the wheelhouse. Silva came in last and closed the door behind them, but left it unlatched. Tarek leaned against the wall next to her, his shoulder bumping hers. He caught her eye, and he tilted his head toward Rene, a sign for her to take the lead.

"Can you tell us about the trips you've been taking out there? To the wreck?" she asked.

"I've gone out a few times, mostly with reporters and some environmentalists, to view the site." Rene pulled a tablet computer from the steering console. "I'll share the charter manifests with you." He jabbed a thick finger at the screen. Kyra's phone buzzed in her pocket.

"Anything that seemed strange about the trips or the requests?"

"No, not really." Rene shook his head. "The clients were all disappointed. You can't see the wreck from the surface. The water is too cloudy, and it's only been made worse by the salvagers doing scans, disturbing the seafloor. One reporter demanded a refund. He was really rude about it, actually, but other than that, nothing odd." He rubbed at the scruff on his jaw and frowned. "Well, the environmentalists were strange, but I figured that was because they're do-gooders, morally invested, you know?"

"What do you mean?"

Rene opened a cooler in the corner and pulled out three beer bottles. "We're not going out to the wreck, are we?"

Kyra shook her head, and he raised the bottles in an offer. "No, thank you." Tarek declined with a wave and Rene dropped two back into the cooler. He popped one open, leaned against the control console, and took a long drink.

"Well, the guy wanted photos. I explained he wouldn't get anything from the surface, and it was too dark down there without extra lighting equipment. But he wasn't interested in the wreck. He wanted photos of the salvage rigs. Had one of those big telephoto lenses and everything. He made me circle the Rose boat a few times the first time, and then we went back to photograph the Blue Stream boat."

Rene took another drink. "He didn't even want to go see the wreckage site. Had no interest in it. He was happy getting his pictures of the rigs docked in the Menemsha Harbor." Rene shrugged. "I thought it was strange, I guess." He looked at his cousin, who was frowning.

Kyra glanced at Tarek, but his expression wasn't readable. "Anything else?" she asked.

"Not really. The reporters wanted photos of the big rigs doing something. Looks like they're just doing imaging right now, so there's not much to see, but I get paid whether they get a shot or not. That's the deal."

"Did you see the Rose ship at the wreckage site on the night of the accident?" Tarek asked.

Rene pursed his lips, then shook his head. "I don't think so." He checked his tablet again. "No, the night that those divers died, I wasn't out." Rene glanced at Silva, then back at Tarek. "I had one charter that afternoon, though. The environmentalist wanted photos of the Rose boat, then a tour of the island. We followed the coast up to Aquinnah. He took some photos."

"What time was that?" Kyra asked.

Rene tapped on his tablet. "I was booked for the 2-6 slot." *When we were at Gully's pub.* "Oh, yeah." Rene squinted at his screen.

"What?" Wes asked, leaning forward.

"I forgot. Tide was high when we got up island, so I couldn't show him Lost Beach, but we did a little tour of the cliffs, the lighthouse, the Coast Guard station. You know, the normal tourist stuff." Rene shrugged. "But then he asked if I could drop him off in Menemsha." Rene looked over at

Wes. "You know how they are up there with the docking fees, so I had to unload him quick before the harbormaster noticed. He said he was staying at one of the inns up island … the Lady Slipper, I think. I don't know why he came out here to get a charter. He could have caught one right out of Menemsha." Rene huffed and shook his head. "But I guess he liked the service. He's a repeat."

"You've taken him out again?" Tarek asked.

"You'll see in the charter log." Rene pointed at his screen. "Twice more, now. He had another person with him once, another environmentalist. I took them out to the wreckage site. The lady wanted to see it. Then we went back to the marina to get more photos of the Blue Stream rig."

Kyra frowned. It wasn't entirely unexpected the environmentalists would want to see the salvage boats. It was disappointing Rene hadn't seen anything helpful, though.

"I think that's enough." Silva stood up. "Pay my cousin and get out." He grabbed another beer from the cooler.

"Thanks for your time, Mr. Ramos." Kyra pulled a wad of bills from her back pocket and peeled off six.

"Ramos, what did you mean about Erikson?" Tarek asked.

Wes bristled.

"I know you're buddies with him, but come on." Rene rolled his eyes at his cousin. "Gully outbid him for that old bar, fair and square."

Wes made a noise in the back of his throat and threw his hand out in a *whatever* gesture. Kyra's mind raced as she tried to place who Tarek was talking about.

"Erikson's been running his mouth about Gully for

years. He's full of shit. No one pays him any attention. Except for my cousin." Rene gave Wes a pointed look. "His kid plays on the hockey team Gully sponsors. Albie just likes to hear himself talk."

His explanation seemed to satisfy Tarek because he reached a hand out to Rene. "Thanks." Kyra placed the money on the console. "If you think of anything else, you have her number."

Rene raised his bottle to them in salute, and Kyra slipped out the door, Tarek close behind her.

She stepped onto the pavement. "What was that about?" she asked. Tarek quirked an eyebrow. "Albie? Chief Erikson?"

"Oh." Tarek wet his lips. "Albie is Chief Erikson's nephew. The whole Erikson family is involved in island services. Firefighters, police, sanitation. Chief Erikson runs the Menemsha department. Albie is a police officer in Edgartown. You've met him, actually."

"When?"

Tarek shifted his weight. He was acting strange, like he didn't want to have this conversation, which only made Kyra more curious. She waited impatiently for him to continue.

"He was one of the officers who arrived at your house last spring after the altercation with Silva. Erikson's the bald one." Tarek's expression darkened.

"The one who accused me of stealing from Wes?" *The one who protected him.*

Tarek nodded.

"But why would they care about Gully and his pub?"

"Albie, the nephew, he's had it out for Gully since he

bought the Wraith & Bone years ago."

Kyra was even more confused.

"When the pub was put up for sale, Albie Erikson put in a lowball offer. It was rumored he warned other potential buyers off, but Gully made a bid for the place. He made a fair offer, and it was accepted. It should have just been business. Albie should have let it go, but Gully is a mainlander."

More of this mainlander nonsense.

"Gully's been here for years. He lives here year-round. Like Rene said, he sponsors a children's hockey team."

"Maybe now, but not then. Then he was an outsider. An outsider who undermined an islander." Tarek shrugged.

It didn't make sense to her, but Tarek seemed to think it explained everything. "And this man's uncle is persecuting Gully because he made a business deal years ago?"

"Memories here are long."

And, as she'd learned last spring, the islanders protect their own.

"Did you know Rene was Wes's cousin?"

"No." Tarek shook his head and ran his hand through his hair. "If I'd known, I wouldn't have let you come."

Kyra jerked back. "Wouldn't have let me? And you have that authority, do you?"

"I … Kyra." His tone was frustrated.

She scoffed and leveled an icy glare at Tarek. "You have my thanks for being my chaperone, Detective."

Without waiting for a response, Kyra turned on her heel and crossed Lake Avenue.

Chapter Seventeen

WHEN KYRA PULLED into her driveway forty minutes later, she was surprised to see a banged-up Jeep parked in front of her garage. The porch light was on, and Tarek was sitting on her front steps, looking at his phone, his legs stretched out in front of him, crossed at the ankle. He knew the lock code, and he could have let himself in. He was waiting for her. *The hell?* She parked and grabbed the takeaway bag that had given him the opportunity to beat her home.

Kyra strode past, ignoring him, and climbed the stairs. She jabbed in the code and stepped inside to disarm the alarm system. Tarek remained sitting, his elbows now resting on his bent knees, waiting for an invitation.

"I suppose you want to come in?" She turned away so he couldn't see her face.

She dropped her keys and purse on the console table and, leaving the front door open, she strode toward the kitchen. The door click closed, and then silence.

At the kitchen entrance, Kyra looked over her shoulder. Tarek was squatting down, giving Cronkite—her cat—belly rubs. She swore the cat grinned up at her, his jaws stretched in an exaggerated yawn. *Treasonous little bastard.* She narrowed her eyes at the white demon and stomped into the kitchen.

Kyra left her food on the island. She eyed the teakettle and the coffeemaker before settling on booze. Whatever it was he wanted to say, she'd need a drink. A strong one. She reached for the bottle of scotch and poured a glass. *Where the hell is he?* She refused to call or look for him. She sat to wait, sipping her whisky, taking comfort in the smokey burn as the alcohol moved down her throat. Eventually, he walked into the kitchen, sliding onto one of the island stools like it was no big deal, like he wasn't ambushing her. She tore into the takeaway bag containing her salad with grilled lobster and an extra serving of fries. She'd been looking forward to a quiet night on the couch with Cronk. Perhaps a reality television binge.

He invited himself over. He can sit there. Kyra picked up a French fry and studied it before taking a bite, her teeth crushing the crispy salty exterior.

Tarek reached for the scotch bottle and poured himself a measure. He spun the glass on the granite. The whisky sloshed up the sides of the glass. Kyra waited.

Finally, he looked up. "What was that? In OB? Why did you run off? Again." He sounded … annoyed.

Her spine snapped straight, and she sucked in a breath, prepared to go on the defensive.

The glass stopped moving, and Tarek continued, "I can't figure you out, Kyra. You're going out of your way to help my friend. Not just with his case, but also with his absurd obsession with that pirate. But you're avoiding me. Shutting me out." Tarek placed his hands on either side of his glass.

"What has you so upset with me?"

"I'm not *upset*. What could I possibly be upset about?" *That you lied. That you think you can tell me what to do? That you pop in and out of my life on a whim?* The back of her neck felt hot, and her stomach flip-flopped, her body's reaction to the onslaught of changing emotions. Hurt, anger, embarrassment, exasperation. It was a lot.

"Obviously." Tarek snorted.

Kyra took in his eyes, dull in the soft kitchen lighting, his hands splayed out in front of him. Now, he looked ... wounded, and her anger extinguished, like it'd been doused with cold water.

She took a gulp of courage-building whisky. "It's nothing. You didn't do anything." But it came off passive aggressive, and Tarek cocked his head to the side and frowned.

"Are you really upset that I don't want you to be alone in the same room as the man who assaulted you?" Kyra flinched. "I'm not going to apologize for wanting to keep you safe."

Kyra glared at him. "You're off duty, Detective. You don't need to do your job now."

His eyes flashed. "It has nothing to do with my job. And you know that."

"I didn't ask for your help," she snapped.

Tarek studied her before turning his attention to his glass. He was quiet for a long time, but he finally said, in a soft voice. "You don't have to. I'll always help you. But you have to meet me halfway. You have to talk to me."

"Like you talk to me?"

Tarek's eyes narrowed, like he was unsure what she was getting at.

"Who was that woman at the council meeting, Tarek? And why did you stop returning my calls when I was in London?" Kyra stood up to pour a glass of water to avoid having to look at him.

"You mean Rachel."

Kyra turned around.

Tarek let out a breath and stared into his glass. He shook his head. "She's, my ex-wife." His voice was soft, but Kyra heard the undertone of irritation and something else that made her stand up straighter. *Disappointment?* He rubbed his palms along his thighs.

"Ex-wife?" Kyra repeated.

"Mmhmm. Nearly five years now." Tarek slung back his whisky. "I haven't seen her since she moved to Michigan six years ago. I was just as surprised to see her as you. I knew she worked with the OC, and probably should have anticipated it, but it never occurred to me." Tarek spun his empty glass. "Who did you think she was?" His mouth twisted into a rueful smile. "You thought I was married."

Kyra shook her head. "I didn't know what to think."

"You could have just asked me. Or answered the phone. I was worried. You left and wouldn't return my calls. Charlie had to tell me you'd gotten sick, nearly passed out, and they'd taken you home."

"You called Charlie to check up on me?"

"Of course." He gave her a look like she'd lost her mind.

"But you didn't talk to me when I returned to London. You just stopped responding with no explanation." Kyra winced at the hurt and resentment in her voice.

"I had to." Tarek frowned.

Kyra looked up. *What?*

"I was finishing the work on your dad and Brendan's investigation. Interactions between us that weren't strictly professional could have endangered the case against Adele Hawthorn. I thought you knew I had to cut off communications until Adele's plea was accepted." Tarek rubbed his eyes before looking at her. "I'm sorry. I didn't intend for you to think I'd deserted you."

And now she felt stupid.

She should have known. She wasn't a litigator, but any first-year law student knew cases were built on optics. Her friendship with the lead investigator on her father's murder case could be seen as a compromising factor or a conflict of interest. While she'd thought he'd abandoned her, he'd been working to ensure her father's murderer went to prison. He'd been helping her. *Chase was right. I do always assume the worst.*

Kyra pushed the container of fries closer to him. "Are you hungry?"

Tarek's eyes met hers and he dipped his chin in a tentative nod. "I could eat."

"Chip?" She pointed to her dinner. It looked worse for wear after sitting on the counter, the lettuce wilted and the fries cold.

"I'd love one." His mouth stretched into that half smile and he reached for a fry. He chewed it thoughtfully, before asking, "Do you want to go through that list Rene gave you?"

Kyra swallowed and nodded. "I'll forward it to you. Let me grab my laptop."

When she came back downstairs, Tarek had moved them into the living room. He was sprawled on the sectional with Cronk, scrolling on his phone and munching on her fries. He looked content, like the awkward conversation in the kitchen hadn't just happened. She still felt jittery and exposed, embarrassed, but despite the residual discomfort, she was glad she knew the truth, and she was glad he was here.

"Did you recognize any of the names?" she asked, taking a seat a safe distance from him, but still within easy reach of her pathetic dinner.

"Just two," he said, his voice was flat with annoyance surprising her. He angled his phone so she could see the screen. There were six customers listed. Four names she didn't recognize and two she did. Dr. Seth Hammond and Rachel Collins.

Chapter Eighteen

THE BEDROOM GLOWED with the bright, hazy sunshine of late morning on the island. Kyra was still in bed, holding her phone above her face. She'd slept in, after a late night, and had been scrolling through her social media and work emails for the last two hours, procrastinating getting up. Pins and needles spread through her hand. She dropped her phone and shook it out.

After the cringey conversation with Tarek, they'd researched the names on Rene's list and shared the rest of her dinner. Three of them were journalists with various national news outlets, another a freelance photographer. They had found the articles the journalists had written about the *Keres*. One of the articles even quoted Rachel criticizing the salvagers' activities and commending the conservation efforts in Aquinnah.

The other two people who'd engaged Rene were Seth and Rachel. Seth had chartered the boat three times—first on the afternoon before Jaycee and Matty Gray's dive, then the morning of the council meeting, and again on the following day. According to the log, Rachel had accompanied him only on the second trip.

"But it makes sense, doesn't it?" She'd argued with Tarek. "They represent the Oceanic Conservation. They're opposing the efforts to raise the wreck. It's only logical that they'd want to see what Kapowski and Rose were doing."

Tarek had been suspicious. "It doesn't take three trips." He wanted to know why Hammond had chartered so many. "What is he looking for?"

Without his police credentials, the only way they could get the answers they needed was if Hammond or Rachel were willing to talk to them, Tarek had admitted. He'd pulled out his phone and offered to call his ex-wife, but Kyra had declined, perhaps with more ferocity than she'd intended, because Tarek had conceded, agreeing they'd talk to Hammond and Rachel together, his smile uncharacteristically smug.

Kyra groaned. She threw her arm over her eyes.

"I'm such a bloody idiot."

Ali was going to flip. Kyra could almost hear her aunt's high-pitched squeals. She rubbed her eyes. A yowl from the doorway reminded her that there were stomachs in the house requiring immediate attention.

"Fine. Fine. We'll get you your breakfast, you beast." Last night the little goblin had crawled onto Tarek's lap and fallen asleep. She scowled at Cronk, not ready to forgive him for sharing his affections with the detective.

Coffee in hand, Kyra watched Cronk gobble down his kibble, his feather duster tail swishing along the floor. Her phone buzzed. A group message. Chase, Tarek, and a number she didn't recognize.

Chase: *"Gully wants your grandpa's research. Can you bring it to the house?"*

Tarek: *"Please, just throw it all away."*

Unknown Number: *"London, Do NOT throw anything away. I'll pick it up myself."*

Kyra grinned.

Kyra: *"I can bring the boxes by this morning if you're home."*

Gully: *"I'm under house arrest now, so I'm always home."*

Kyra frowned. Tarek hadn't mentioned that last night.

Tarek: *"In Edgartown. Pick you up in an hour."*

Kyra responded with a thumbs up emoji and hurried to get dressed.

She'd just finished getting dressed, when her phone buzzed with a video call. Ali. She answered the phone and her aunt's wide grin filled her screen. "Hi."

"Kay! How are you? How's Cronkite? How's the house? The detective? Tell me everything!" Ali was breathless, and outside.

"Where are you?"

"I'm on a run." Ali was walking.

"A run?"

"Yes, I'm *exercising*. You should try it." Kyra gaped at her aunt. Ali's idea of exercise was the six-minute walk to the local wine bar.

"I do. Often."

"Fine." Ali sighed. "The baby is asleep, and Cam is working from home, and I just *needed* thirty minutes to myself. Then I got out here and didn't know what I was supposed to do. What did I do with my time before children?"

"Drank mostly." Kyra grinned at her aunt's feigned scowl.

"A drink does sound brilliant. A crisp G&T, some baked brie, crusty bread." Ali's eyes went distant. Kyra would have to remember to bribe the Chamberses for Julia's bread and butter when Ali and Cam came to visit.

Ali asked, "What are you doing today?"

"I'm taking Aaron's research to Gully's house. We're going to go through it."

Ali frowned.

"Your dad's? Grandfather?" Kyra wasn't sure how to describe him.

"Ah. We?" Ali's dark blue eyes sparkled, and her smile grew, eliciting a disapproving frown from Kyra. "And who is *we*?"

"Gully, obviously. Chase, I think, and probably Tarek, since he's staying there. At Gully's house." Kyra's eyes went to the ceiling, and she let out a breath. Why did this conversation make her feel sixteen years old again? "Tarek's picking me up in a few minutes." Ali's grin grew so large it ate her face.

Kyra huffed a resigned sigh through her nose. "Stop it."

"You talked!"

Kyra nodded and filled her in on the night before. The boat trip. Silva. The charters to the wreck site. Tarek's ambush.

"I knew it. You do this to yourself. You know that, don't you?"

"What?"

"You assume the worst about everyone and everything," she said in her serious Ali voice. "I get it. It's an effective defense mechanism that a therapist would kill to unpack, and it's served you well. You're independent, smart, successful, and *lonely*. If you let yourself be vulnerable and let people in instead of pushing them away before they have the chance to hurt you, you may be surprised."

"It's not like that," Kyra protested. It was exactly like that. She just wasn't sure what to do with this revelation.

"Come off it, Kyra. I'm thousands of miles away and even I can see that man cares about you and you're besotted with him. And that scares the shit out of you."

Kyra winced. "I wouldn't say besotted," she grumbled.

Ali was more perceptive than she had any right to be. Kyra hated it when Ali saw through her, and even more when she said it out loud. Speaking it made it too real.

Ali's face went slack. "Fuck, Cam is texting. I have to get back. I'll call you later. Think about my sage wisdom. Love you!" Ali ended the call before Kyra could respond. She stared at the darkened screen, dumbstruck.

CRONKITE FOLLOWED KYRA to the office and leaped onto the desk. He watched her with one half-open eye while she took an inventory of the crumbling boxes, she'd hauled up from the basement the other day. She pulled out her grandfather's folders and journals and slid them into tote bags, careful not to damage the old bindings.

"Hello? Kyra?" a voice called from inside the house.

Cronkite jumped down and scampered out to investigate.

"In the office," she called back and smiled when she

heard Tarek's soft murmurs. Maybe she could come to terms with her cat's preference for Tarek over her.

"Hey." His lean frame appeared in the doorway. At his feet sat the feral cotton ball.

"Hi." Kyra finished filling the bags and stood, wiping her sticky hands on the back of her shorts. "I think this is everything. Well, everything I found. These were in the cellar." She toed one of the old boxes. "There could be more down there. Ed wasn't the most organized person."

"Kyra," Tarek said her name, his voice soft, rough.

She started. He was right next to her. When had he moved so close? Her breath caught and the right side of his mouth hitched up, amused. She stared into his eyes, watched them dilate until she could only make out a sliver of green. Each thump of her heart pulsed through her entire body.

She didn't know if she reached for him, or he for her, but suddenly the inches between them had vanished. His mouth was on hers. Her hand fisted in his shirt. He threaded his fingers through her hair, deepening the kiss as he pulled her flush against him. Her hands slid up the smooth planes of his chest, to his shoulders.

Something vibrated against her hipbone.

Kyra huffed a laugh against his mouth, and Tarek paused for half a beat. Then his lips moved to her jaw, skating along the bone to that place right below her ear. Her breathing quickened, and she ran her fingers through the silky strands of his hair at the back of his neck. *More.* He guided her backward a step, two, until the backs of her thighs hit the desk. Kyra's phone buzzed behind her.

"Ignore it," he whispered, his voice sandpaper and his

lips found hers again.

His fingers skimmed the sensitive skin along her waistband, and she shivered. His phone went off. Again. The repeated staccato buzz insistent.

Kyra pulled away, laughing against him. "It must be important."

Tarek made a strangled noise and ran his hand through his hair. "Fuck." He pulled his phone from his pocket. His other hand clutched her hip, like he was afraid she'd disappear. "What?" he barked. "No. I'm here."

Kyra couldn't make out what the caller was saying, but she couldn't help but grin at Tarek's increasingly resigned expression.

"Yeah, no. Fifteen, or twenty." He hung up and turned to her, his expression bordering on sheepish. "That was Chase. He's needed back at the farm."

"Okay…" She pulled away and rested her weight against the desk, her hands gripping the edges. She waited for him to explain.

Tarek ran his hand through his hair again. "Connors, Gully's lawyer, called early this morning and recommended Gully agree to immediate voluntary house arrest. He thinks they're preparing the arrest warrant, and it will look better if we cooperate. I had some business at the Edgartown station. Chase came by a few hours ago to stay with him." Tarek swallowed. "I don't want him to be alone. If they arrest him, I'll need to bail him out."

The gravity of Gully's situation struck her. She shook her head, ashamed that she'd let herself get swept up in her own drama when a man's life was on the line. From his expression, Kyra suspected Tarek felt the same.

She stepped away. "We should go."

Tarek caught her hand. He raised it to his lips and placed a soft kiss in the center of her palm, his eyes boring into hers. He let her go, sucked in a deep, steadying breath, and nodded to the bags on the floor.

"Get whatever else you'll need. I'll take these to the car."

TAREK PULLED HIS Jeep onto the lawn in front of Gully's house. The homeowner was outside with a hose, watering the flower beds. He cut the engine and turned to Kyra. "Don't bring up the case unless Gully does. He pretends it's not getting to him, but it is. This thing with the *Keres*? He's using it as a distraction, and until I find something to transfer suspicion from him, I'm going to let him."

"Okay," Kyra said and looked out the window. Gully's hand was raised in greeting. "Whatever you and Gully need, Tar."

Tarek gave her hand a squeeze before opening the door.

Gully walked over as Kyra jumped out of the SUV. "Hey, London. What did you bring me?" he asked in an overly cheerful tone.

Kyra noticed the strain around his red-rimmed eyes. "I didn't go through all of it, but there are some old journals and ship logs. The final or near final draft of Aaron's manuscript is in there, too. Tarek put it in the boot."

"The boot," he repeated, waggling his eyebrows and opened the trunk. He slung the tote bags over his shoulder.

"Come on inside. Tar, you'd better have picked up food. I'm starving." Gully leveled a stern look at his friend.

Tarek grumbled under his breath but handed Kyra a grocery bag from the back seat.

"Oh good! You're here." Chase came barreling out of the house. "How was your meeting?" Tarek grimaced. "Yeah, that good? Tell me about it later. I gotta run. One of the ewes had an accident. Sara is meeting with the vet."

"I told you, I don't need a babysitter," Gully grumbled.

"You owe me a breakfast." Chase pointed at Tarek, both of them ignoring Gully's protests. He gave Kyra a quick hug and dropped a kiss on the top of her head. "I'll call you later." Before she could respond, he was jogging to his car.

"Finally. That kid is like a puppy with ADHD." Gully opened the door to the house. "Come inside. I can feel myself getting skinny." Gully's body shook with an exaggerated shudder.

Kyra swallowed a laugh. Even a skinny Gully would be a giant.

Inside, Gully nodded Kyra toward the kitchen, where she unpacked the groceries. Tarek brought in another bag, leaving it on the counter. He turned on the coffeemaker and wandered into the living room.

Gully came back and eyed the items on the counter. He closed his eyes and rubbed his forehead. Kyra could have sworn he was counting down from ten as if to rein in his temper.

"Now it makes sense." Gully held up a package of English-style rashers. "You bribed the kid with brunch? A full English, Tar? Really." There were also cans of beans, fresh sausages, mushrooms and tomatoes, and a loaf of fresh sourdough bread from Café Joy, her favorite, second only to Julia's. Kyra's mouth watered. She wondered how much of this had actually been for Chase. She hadn't had a proper fry-up in years.

"Wouldn't want you to get skinny, Gul. I want poached eggs."

Gully swore. Tarek pointed to the coffee table and the tote bags sitting there. His eyebrow quirked.

"Fine. How do you take your eggs, London?" Gully pulled down coffee mugs, placing them on the island.

"Whatever is easiest."

"She'll take poached, too." Tarek was grinning.

Gully scowled. "Who in their right fucking mind eats poached eggs with a full English?" Gully muttered and yanked down pots and pans from the pot rack above the stove.

Kyra had to agree. It was probably some sort of blasphemy. The English took their breakfast very seriously.

"You know how to make all this?" She gestured to the counter.

"Mmhhmm, learned to cook when I was stationed in the UK. Go on and help him, London. I'll bring our plates over."

Kyra handed him the carton of eggs and prepared two coffees. She handed Tarek a cup and sat on the floor next to him.

"Thanks. What are we looking for?" Tarek emptied a bag onto the coffee table.

"I'm not sure."

"Gully, what are we looking for?"

"Everything," Gully called, over the sound of sizzling.

The delicious scent of bacon wafted through the living room, and Kyra's stomach growled.

"Alright," Tarek sighed, kicking off his shoes. He slid down next to her, his leg pressing against hers. Before he could see her blush, she reached for the other bag.

Kyra pulled out the books and flipped through the larger journal. It contained manifests and ship logs from the *Keres* on an island-hopping voyage in the spring of 1712. She studied the lists of goods they bought, stole, pillaged, traded, and sold. For a pirate, the Wraith kept excellent records. Among the supplies William Roberts purchased that spring were several dresses, children's clothes, art supplies, books, and toys.

Gully walked over and handed them each a plate. He returned with his own and a steaming cup of coffee and sat in one of the large armchairs.

"Find anything?" he asked, balancing his plate on his knee.

Kyra set her plate to the side. "It's the ship's manifest for 1712. He purchased clothes and supplies for women and children in the spring before the wreck."

"Crew members?"

Kyra ran her finger down the list of toys William Roberts bought in Saint-Domingue. It troubled her seeing this list of items the captain had purchased. She slid it across the coffee table to Gully.

"What is it, London?"

"I'm not sure." She pressed her lips together, thinking.

"It's just that, if all of this stuff—the stuff the Wraith was carrying—is supposed to be at the bottom of the Vineyard Sound, how did Aaron Hart get the manifest?"

Gully's expression turned contemplative. She dipped her rasher in the gooey center of her egg and bit into it. *Ohmagod.* She nearly moaned out loud. *What kind of wizard is he? It's delicious.*

Tarek bumped her leg with his knee. "I know," he whispered, his eyes bright and bit into his toast piled high with eggs and bacon. He turned to Gully. "When did Roberts buy those supplies?"

"April?" Gully said, passing back the manifest.

Tarek flipped through the journal he was reading. "Kyra, you thought this may be Helena Robert's journal, right?"

Kyra nodded. She'd mentioned it last night.

"The author wrote she sent William a letter telling him about Liam's favorite books. Ones about nature and drawing. Listen to this." Tarek cleared his throat and read.

"'Father has secured a marriage for me to a business acquaintance. Mr. Gloaming is respected and considered a good match for someone like me and Liam. I am distraught. My husband-to-be is old and his reputation cruel. Liam will remain in Gloucester with Mother and Father to begin his education. I am expected to act the ever-devoted wife to Mr. Gloaming in Rhode Island. Father and Mr. Gloaming have set the wedding for September. I will be sent for in July and shall remain in Newport for the summer season. My poor dear Liam will be left alone with no one to love and protect him.

'I've written my William in Jamaica one last time, begging him to come for us. And if his love for me has waned, I begged for our son. I sent him a list of what we will need for the voyage back to the Isle of Man. I told him how Liam loves to paint and read about animals. I reminded William of our dream—our little family in a house by the sea. I pray the letter reaches him. That he still cherishes our dream as I do. I cannot bear to be separated from our son. My heart would break.'

It's from 1712."

Creases formed between Gully's eyes, and he sucked in his cheeks. "I think I saw something in here." His fingers danced through the folder he'd been parsing through. "The legends say the Wraith was coming for them. Here it is." He pulled out a sheet of paper.

Kyra thought it looked like a microfiche printout.

"It's a marriage banns." He read, "'Let it be known that on the twentieth of September in the year of our great Lord 1712, Mister Edward Gloaming of Newport in the Colony of Rhode Island shall wed Mistress Betty Ann Talbot of Lexington of the Massachusetts Bay Colony. Any objections shall be decreed within fifteen days' time by law.'"

"When was that?" Tarek asked at the same time Kyra said, "Who is Betty Ann Talbot?"

"Someone wrote on the bottom *early September*." He passed the page to Tarek.

"He didn't marry Helena?" Kyra frowned. They were missing something. "Maybe my grandfather explains it in his book." She licked the butter from her fingers and pulled the folder containing Aaron Hart's manuscript into her lap. She scanned through the table of contents, looking for the correct time period, and flipped toward the end. "Ugh, how did people research before computers?" She scanned each page and set it aside. No mention of Helena or Liam, but he described in detail the clothing William Roberts chose, the types of silks and muslins. "That's weird. He doesn't mention Helena at all." She flipped to the front. "As far as I've been able to tell, his book is about cargo."

"That makes sense," Gully said without looking up from the pages he was reading. "I looked him up. Hart's specialty was naval finance and trade economics."

Kyra eyed the manuscript with disdain.

"What's the date of the last entry in Helena's journal?" Gully asked, and Tarek passed him the book. Gully opened it at the back, then paged to the middle. "Hmm."

"When was it?" Tarek asked.

"May. She talks about the May Day parade the day before and attending a tea with a person named Mrs. Frances. No mention of William or *The Keres*. That's the last entry."

Kyra cleared their plates. She thought through everything they knew about Helena and William Roberts as she loaded the dishwasher. She worried her lip and poured herself another cup of coffee. She leaned against the counter, thinking. *What happened to Helena? Did the Wraith get her letters?*

Tarek was lying on the couch, feet propped on the arm, reading Aaron Hart's manuscript. Gully was flipping through the folders, making notes in his binder.

"Gull, does the manifest mention Spanish gold?" Tarek asked from behind the pages he was reading.

Gully pulled the ship's log across the table and flipped

through it. "I don't think so." His lips disappeared behind his beard, and he made a smacking noise. "He has records of everything else, but he didn't inventory money. Were coins considered cargo?"

"Are we sure it was in coins?" Kyra asked, and Gully's eyebrows shot up. Maybe they weren't looking for the right thing. He pulled his binder closer.

A phone buzzed. Tarek pulled his from his pocket and checked it. Kyra watched his expression change, harden. He swiped his thumb across the screen, ignoring the call. It buzzed again, somehow sounding more insistent. Kyra couldn't help it. She crept closer, curious. He declined the call again and placed it face down on the coffee table. From across the room, Kyra saw Gully too was watching him. The landline rang.

"Don't answer it."

"Tarek, what's going on?" Both men ignored her.

Gully stood to grab the cordless phone. He looked at the caller ID, and silenced the call. It rang again. Tarek swore. "Don't," he warned.

"Hello?" Gully's voice came out rough and sharp, a tone Kyra had never heard him use before.

"Fucking hell, Gull." Tarek tossed the manuscript on the table and sat up.

Kyra looked between them. *What the hell is going on? The police? Gully's lawyer?*

"No, I don't think that's a good idea," Gully said into the phone, and Tarek made an exasperated noise. "I don't know. What email?" Kyra watched Gully's expression sour. He leveled a glare at Tarek. "Rachel, I really don't think...

You're where? Fine," he snapped. "I'll let him know."

"I told you not to answer."

"How often has she been calling you?"

Tarek glanced at Kyra, then back at the floor. "I've been busy."

"Busy. Right." Gully stroked his beard. "Well," he drawled. "We're gonna hear whatever she's got to say." Tarek's eyes widened in alarm. Gully shrugged. "She'll be here in ten minutes."

"I should go," Kyra said, breaking a long silence.

Gully huffed. "Don't see how, London. Rachel's not comin' to see me, and I'm not supposed to leave without police *supervision*."

Kyra fidgeted. She glanced longingly at the back door. The last place she wanted to be was witnessing another reunion between Tarek and his ex-wife. *I can sit outside? Call a taxi?*

"No, stay, please." Tarek said. "I emailed her last night." Gully made a harsh noise. Tarek sighed and ran his hands through his hair. "After I got back. I asked about her and Hammond's charters. This morning, she emailed me asking to set up a time to meet. She called earlier when I was at the Edgartown police station. Please, Kyra, just come sit." Kyra nodded and returned to the living room. "Rachel can be…" He trailed off as if searching for the right word.

"Tenacious?" Gully offered, and Tarek scowled.

Kyra tugged the hem of her cutoffs. She was annoyed. Tarek had promised they'd speak to Rachel together. If Rachel hadn't tracked him down, would he have even told her that he'd been in contact with her? Kyra shifted in her seat and picked up her grandfather's manuscript. She flipped through the pages too fast, not seeing the print. She heard the rhythmic ticking of a clock in the background.

"London?" Kyra looked up.

Gully was standing over her holding a beer bottle by the neck. He offered it to her and winked. "My experience with Rachel is she's easier to stomach with alcohol. Lots of it, but it's early, so we'll do what we can."

Kyra peeked at Tarek. An open bottle sat on the table in front of him.

"Thanks, Gully," she mumbled, taking the beer.

Tarek was staring at the floor, his hands clasped between his knees.

"What was going on at the Edgartown police station earlier?" It was a test. Would he tell her?

Tarek reached for his beer. He spun the bottle on its coaster. His eyes met Gully's. Gully shrugged.

"I went to speak with Albie Erikson." *The asshole policeman?* "He wasn't particularly happy to see me."

"No, I expect not," Gully snorted.

Tarek's eyes met hers. "After you left last April, I filed a complaint against him with the force. He was reprimanded. Not that it did much, but it's on record. Needless to say, I'm not his favorite person."

Kyra sipped her drink. Was this how he'd burned bridges here? By complaining about the police officers who'd insulted her?

"And, well, now he likes me even less. He wasn't too pleased when I asked him where he was the night of the dive. Home. Alone. His son was at a sleepover." Tarek sipped his beer. "I also asked about his feud with Gully. He said that he was upset when he didn't get the bar. But when his wife got sick, they relied on his police benefits. He wouldn't have been able to afford the medical bills as a small business owner. After she died, he'd have struggled to run it as a single parent."

"I told you talking to him was a waste of time," Gully grumbled. "Albie Erikson had nothing to do with it."

"It's called reasonable doubt." Tarek's bottle hit the table with force.

Kyra flinched.

"Don't you get it, Gully? They're going to arrest you and charge you with murder. All we have now is a defense strategy. It doesn't matter who killed Matty Gray and Jaycee. It just matters that it's plausible it *wasn't you.*" Tarek let out a breath. "But you were right. Albie was a dead end. And he's already filed an official complaint against me."

"Are you serious?" Gully's beard shifted like he was grinding his teeth.

Tarek shrugged. "Yeah, I received an email an hour ago from my captain notifying me I'll be summoned before the disciplinary committee. But he has no alibi, and a known vendetta. It was worth it to check it out."

Someone knocked on the door. Kyra thought Tarek looked almost relieved.

"She's always had impeccable timing," Gully said and pushed himself out of his chair to open the door.

Rachel stood in the doorway, dressed in a figure-hugging sheath dress, the color of poppy flowers. Her long braids were swept away from her face and fell loose down her back.

She'd painted her lips the same orange red color as her dress. She stepped into the room and pulled off her oversized sunglasses. Kyra hadn't hallucinated at the council meeting. Rachel Collins was gorgeous. Striking. Kyra's thousand calorie breakfast congealed in her stomach.

"Rachel," Gully said with a resigned sigh.

"Andre." She annunciated the syllables of his name like they were unpleasant to form. Her mouth spread into a menacing smile, showing all her white teeth. "It's lovely to see you again."

"Rachel," Tarek said from his seat, his ankle crossed over his knee. "What's so important?" His eyes flicked back to the pages in his hand. He'd staged himself in a pantomime of disinterest.

Gully gestured for her to come in. Rachel sat on the couch and arranged her legs, one ankle behind the other, knees angled toward her ex-husband. Her gaze lingered on Kyra for a beat too long before sliding to the bottles on the table.

"It's a bit early, isn't it, Rick?" she *tsked*. "Your idea?" She leveled an icy glare at Gully.

"It's the island. It's always five o'clock." Gully raised his beer in a salute and took a long swig.

Rachel sucked on a tooth, and with a sharp smack, turned to Tarek. "You tell me, Rick. You sent me that *email* asking about seeing the wreckage." The way her mouth formed over the word made Kyra think that she'd found the form of communication insulting. "You said it was important." She studied her poppy painted nails. "I paid enough attention when we were married to know that's not procedure. I also know anything I say in that email can be used as evidence against him. And this is all for him, isn't it? Him and his treasure hunt."

Rachel turned to Gully. "We've never been friends, Andre, but I've no desire to see you in prison." By her tone, Kyra wasn't sure if Rachel was being sincere.

Rachel's gaze flicked to Tarek before returning to Gully. "I think it's better to hear what I have to say before creating an evidentiary record. Don't you?" Rachel tilted her head to the side, her braids shifted.

Kyra glanced at Tarek. His expression was flat, annoyed, but Rachel was right. Tarek should have arranged to speak to her in person.

Tarek stood up and slid his hands in his pockets. "Alright, then. When did you get on the island?"

Rachel huffed and her lips twisted in an unamused smirk. "Ah, I see how it is. Fine." She crossed her arms over her chest. "Three nights ago. I came from a conference in DC. I took a direct from there. I can send you the flight information."

"I appreciate it. How about Hammond?"

"Seth?" Rachel pressed her lips together in a pout. "He flew in the day before me. From Florida. He was at a demonstration there."

"Did you and Seth charter a boat to see the wreck?"

Her perfectly sculpted eyebrow arched. "You know we did, Rick."

"Why?" Kyra asked.

Rachel's eyes snapped to Kyra. "The rigs and the people operating them present a danger to the environment. Raising the wreck will disrupt the sea life. We … I wanted to see what equipment Rose and Kapowski had available to them, so I can better assess the expected damage and include accurate information in our press releases. Seth took some photos. We came back, and we prepared the paperwork to file a TRO to stop the excavation."

"Did you file it? Was it successful?" Gully asked.

Rachel uncrossed her arms. "Andre, you really need to reassess your priorities. You can't spend your treasure from prison." She paused, studying him. "But no, we never filed. Just the threat was enough to get their attention. I've worked with Frank and Terry before. They're better than other marine salvagers. Always respectful. They want to work with the locals and environmental groups. After we raised our concerns, they put together a new proposal. The effort will be more expensive, but it mitigates the risk of damage to the seabed and fishing to a reasonable recoverable level. If it's accepted by the council, I don't believe any further involvement from the Oceanic Conservation is necessary. The project will net long-term benefits to the island and academic communities, and the negative impact to the sound will be contained. Ms. Ames submitted the proposal with her approval to the voting board this morning. As far as I'm concerned, provided the proposal is accepted, we have achieved our goal here." She shrugged.

"Did you see anything suspicious on the salvage boats?" Tarek asked.

Her eyebrows hitched together. "No. They were outfitting some smaller cranes on the Blue Stream rig. Nothing unusual, though."

"Did you know Matty Gray or Jaycee?" Kyra asked, leaning forward.

"Who?"

"The divers," Gully said.

"No, I didn't know them. We may have crossed paths, but I'm not normally on site for these types of things. I could have handled this from Michigan, but since I was already in DC, it made sense to come." She looked at Tarek. Her expression softened. "And I suppose some part of me thought you'd be here, and I thought…" She shook her head slowly. "Well, I'm not sure what I thought, actually."

"Are you waiting on confirmation that the proposal has been accepted before heading back to Ann Arbor?" Tarek asked.

"If the proposal isn't accepted this afternoon, I'll file the TRO. Either way, my flight back is tomorrow."

"And Hammond?"

"I think he's flying back a day or two after me. He thinks there is a nesting pair of dark storm petrels in the Gay Head cliffs. If we can get a photo of them, it would be good for publicity. Their return to the island is evidence the conservation efforts are effective."

Kyra, Tarek, and Gully's phones all buzzed at the same time.

She pulled hers from her pocket. A group message from Chase.

"*Get to Menemsha. The Shack. ASAP.*"

Tarek shot a look at Gully. "Rachel, something's come up. We've got to go."

Kyra picked up the bottles and took them to the kitchen.

She glanced at Gully, who hadn't moved from his seat. He was staring at his phone.

"Rick, please. Wait." Rachel stood.

She placed a hand on his arm. Tarek went still and looked at his ex-wife, his expression wary. With her high heels, they were nearly the same height. Her eyes glided to Kyra, then back.

Something that looked a little like regret ghosted over her beautiful features. "Take care of yourself." She turned to Gully. "Take care of him, Andre."

Gully acknowledged her with a stiff nod.

She unfolded her sunglasses and slid them on. "Goodbye, Rick," she said softly before slipping out the front door.

Chapter Nineteen

KYRA CHECKED HER phone. She'd sent Chase three texts asking what was going on, but he hadn't responded. Tarek was in the driver's seat. The late afternoon sun cast shadows across his face, making his steely expression appear more severe. Periodically, the muscle in his jaw twitched, or his grip on the steering wheel tightened. Tells. Ones Kyra had come to recognize. He was upset, but she didn't know whether he was reacting to the exchange with Rachel or because they'd had to leave Gully home alone.

Tarek's requests for a police escort so they could bring him along had been denied. Kyra suspected Gully had been mere seconds away from tossing Tarek out on his ass.

"I'm a goddamned grown man! I don't need a babysitter!" Gully had bellowed at Tarek when he had declared he was staying home with him. Gully said he was going to continue reading through Hart's research and would call them if he had any news.

She wondered how much of Gully's tantrum was an attempt to pull Tarek out of the broody mood that had settled on him since Rachel's phone call. It hadn't worked.

Kyra reached out and placed her hand over his on the gearshift. Tarek startled and glanced her way. He held her gaze for half a second before turning back to the road. He stroked the side of her finger with his thumb.

Tarek turned onto Basin Road and rounded the curve that would bring them to Menemsha Harbor.

"What the hell?" Tarek mumbled, dipping forward to peer out the windshield.

The tiny village was swarming with emergency response vehicles and personnel.

Tarek pulled off the road and parked on the side in the brush. "Go find Chase." He pointed to a little grouping of buildings just off the town's main commercial row, on a side street. "I'm going to see if I can find out what's going on."

Kyra made her way to the small cluster of buildings. One was some sort of office, another a gallery. Above the third door was a sign. THE SHACK was painted on a piece of driftwood, in jagged white letters like knife slashes. Kyra pushed open the door, and a bell tinkled, announcing her presence. She found herself in a tiny, pristine takeaway fish fry. Chase was leaning forward, elbows on the counter, talking with a man.

When Chase saw her, his eyes lit up with relief, but his expression remained grim. "You made it. Took you long enough. Meet Jimmy. Jimmy, this is Kyra. Kyra, Jimmy."

Jimmy's cool gaze swept over her, then bounced back to Chase, an eyebrow raised in a question.

"She's a friend. And a friend of Gully's."

"Nice to meet ya." Jimmy leaned against the back counter. He wiped his hands on a towel and crossed one ankle over the other.

"You too," she said. "What's going on out there?"

"They found a body on one of the salvage rigs," Jimmy said and jerked his chin toward the marina.

"A body?" Her heart skipped.

Jimmy chewed on the end of a straw, studying her. His gaze flicked back to Chase. "On the big one, the *Discovery IV*."

"That's Blue Stream. Frank Kapowski's vessel." Chase looked at the door. "Where's Tarek?"

"Out there. He's gone to see what he can find out." She waved in the direction of the commotion.

Chase frowned but nodded to Jimmy. "You can tell her what you told me." At Kyra's questioning frown, Chase pointed to a silver comms system behind the counter. "Jimmy hears everything that happens on the docks here."

Jimmy shrugged. "My dad was an admiral in the guard." He tossed the straw he was chewing in the trash, and he stepped forward, closer to Chase and Kyra. He leaned down, so he was eye-to-eye with her. His brown eyes glinted with excitement, and Kyra leaned forward to meet him. "It's Andy Mackey."

Kyra reared back. Chase gripped her shoulder, stabilizing her.

"What? What is?" But she knew.

"The distress call that came in said that someone had killed Andy Mackey. He'd been strung up in the rigging. Gutted." Jimmy's lazy grin widened into something sinister, and Kyra suddenly felt cold. The hairs on her arms stood on end. She glanced up at Chase, uneasy. "They took Kapowski to the station in a wagon and I heard no one's seen Joe."

Kyra frowned. *The fisherman brothers?* She remembered

the awkward interaction she'd had with Lisa and Andy in the Chamberses' kitchen, and Andy's fight with Gully at the meeting the other night. The Mackey family had openly opposed the *Keres* recovery efforts.

"Could it have been an accident?" she asked, allowing herself to hope.

"Doesn't sound like it."

Chase narrowed his eyes. "Jimmy."

Jimmy grinned. "Hey, you didn't hear it from me, but everyone knows the Mackey brothers fought like dogs over a bone. They're always shouting at each other on the docks. Finding one dead and the other conveniently missing shouldn't surprise anyone." Jimmy paused as if for effect. "And then there's the whole deal with Joe's wife."

"Joe's wife?" Kyra repeated. "You mean Lisa?"

"The bone."

"What are you saying, Jimmy?" Chase snapped.

"Lisa Mackey. She was with Andy when they were young. Now she's with Joe, but did Andy ever give up on her? They've always seemed real close."

"You think they were having an affair?" Chase asked, beating Kyra to the question. "And Joe committed fratricide on Frank's boat?" Chase scoffed and shook his head. "This isn't Shakespeare, Jimmy. That shit doesn't happen."

"Maybe I got it wrong." Jimmy shrugged, but his slow grin and gleaming eyes betrayed him.

He wants it to be true.

"We should find Tarek," Chase said. "He'll want to know what Jimmy told us. Thanks, Jim. Text me if you hear anything else."

"You got it." Jimmy shot finger pistols at him.

Chase guided Kyra outside.

"What was all that?" She asked, waving toward The Shack, once they were a few yards away.

Chase pushed his hair out of his face. "Don't mind Jimmy. He makes a shitty first impression. But he's a decent enough guy. And he knows everything that's happening in the harbor, but don't tell him anything. If he knows, everyone else will know it, too, enhanced with Jimmy's own brand of sensationalism."

"He'd spread rumors like that? About Lisa?" Kyra asked.

"Like Margot says, the truth isn't nearly as important as what people want to believe." Chase's tone was bitter.

"And people would want that to be true?" Chase didn't answer. He didn't need to. She'd represented enough tabloids to know everyone loved a scandal.

Kyra had to work to keep up with Chase. His legs were so much longer than hers, but once they reached the crowd, he slowed. People nodded or raised their hand in recognition. A few approached him and he took the time to make small talk, even introducing Kyra. He plastered on his playboy smile and charmed each person. After a minute or two, he would politely but firmly excuse himself, offer to speak with his father on their behalf, or to schedule a time to catch up soon. Always the senator's son.

The tiny creases at the corners of his mouth became more pronounced with each constituent, and her heart wrenched with sadness for him. *He hates this.* Finally, they made it through the crowd, and they found Tarek. He was standing in the parking lot, talking to a uniformed police officer. Kyra recognized him. He was the state police officer Tarek assigned to watch her house last spring. The policeman noticed them coming before Tarek, and he gave her a shy but genuine smile from under his floppy hair.

"Hello, *Miss* Gibson," he said, bobbing his head for emphasis. "Lt. Mark Evans." He introduced himself to Chase.

"Chase Hawthorn." Chase shook his hand.

"Yes, sir. I know," Officer Evans said formally.

Chase side-eyed Kyra and mouthed *sir*? Kyra pressed her fingertips to her lips to hide her smile.

"It's nice to see you again, Officer Evans. What's going on?" she asked.

"Evans was called in from the mainland to assist." Tarek waved toward the crowd.

"That's right, mostly crowd control, sir."

"Do you know what happened?" Kyra asked.

Officer Evans paused and rolled his lips. He glanced at Tarek; his expression wary. "Yes, ma'am. I mean, miss. Yes, miss. A body has been found on the salvage vessel *Blue Stream Discovery IV*."

"Have you been briefed? Did they get an ID on the vic? Do we have time and cause of death?" Tarek asked.

Officer Evans shuffled his feet. "I'm sorry, sir." He shook his head. "I can't share that information with you now."

Tarek made an irritated noise in his throat but nodded. "Yeah, you're right." He stuffed his hands in his pockets. "I'm sorry."

Evans shifted closer and his voice dropped. "I can't share it with you *now*, sir." Evans gave Tarek a meaningful look and made a show of checking his watch. "Oh, my shift ends in an hour. I suspect I'll be hungry then." His comms system beeped. "I'd better get back. Sirs. Ma-... *Miss* Gibson." He bowed his head and walked away.

Chase watched him with a bewildered expression, then turned to Tarek. "What does he mean he'll be hungry? What's that about?"

"Nothing, yet," Tarek said, his eyes tracking Officer Evans.

"Jimmy said it's Andy Mackey."

Tarek nodded. "I ran into Terry. That's about all he said. That the Mackey brothers are involved. He didn't want to get caught here by reporters. Said he's going back to his hotel. He's staying at the Lady Slipper. We'll find him at the bar."

"Do you think he has more information?" Kyra asked.

"I don't know, but at least he'll talk to us. Can you go with Chase? I need to call Gully, give him and his lawyer a heads-up. Evans mentioned that Chief Erikson wants to question Gully about this."

"We'll meet you there," Chase said.

Chapter Twenty

CHASE HELD THE door to the Lady Slipper open and nodded toward the bar in the back. They walked through the lobby. The soles of Kyra's flip-flops *slapped* the herringbone floorboards. She ran her hands down her bare thighs. She felt underdressed in her cutoffs and tank top in the elegant surroundings. Terry Rose was already there, sitting at the shiny oak bar, his eyes fixated on the Red Sox game playing on the television hanging on the wall. Kyra slid onto the stool beside him, and Chase took the one next to her.

"Mr. Hawthorn, Ms. Gibson." Terry raised his empty glass in a salute, and then his gaze drifted behind them. "I figured you two would be with the detective."

"Tarek is checking in with Gully, but he should be here soon," Chase said, raising a hand to the bartender. He flashed a smile intended to charm and leaned over the bar into the man's space. Chase whispered something Kyra couldn't hear, but she saw the bartender's expression change from flirty to serious.

"Of course, Mr. Hawthorn," he said formally, before pouring two seltzer waters and stepping away. He hovered near the entrance, leaning against the bar, out of hearing.

"A friend?" Rose asked.

Chase's smirk didn't reach his eyes. "Something like that." He sat back on his stool and slung an arm across the back of Kyra's chair. Chase turned to Terry and said, his voice low, "Tarek said the police plan to question Gully."

"Those bastards." Terry spat out through his teeth. "I told them a thousand times. Gully didn't do any of this. He knows shit about diving. The man can barely swim. He wouldn't know how to mess with the equipment, even if he wanted to." He clenched his jaw. "They're so sure they got the right man. They aren't looking at anyone else."

Kyra glanced at Chase. He was staring at a spot on the wall, above the television, his shoulders tense. A muscle in his cheek jumped. The allegations being made against Gully must be picking at Chase's barely healed wounds, reminding him when he was on the receiving end of a murder accusation. She laced her pinky finger with his. His shoulder blades slid down his back, and she felt the slightest return of pressure.

Kyra took a long drink of her seltzer water. The bubbles made it hard to swallow.

"That fancy Boston lawyer Collins got him had better be worth it." Terry rolled his lips.

"Do you know when it happened, Terry?" Chase asked.

"The police didn't tell me, exactly." Terry rubbed at his jaw. "They wanted to know where I was between nine p.m. and six a.m. Here, obviously." He waved to the ceiling, where Kyra assumed the guestrooms were. "I came down for breakfast around seven. Good thing Collins has been clinging to Gully like plastic wrap. If the police want to question him, Gully needs a foolproof alibi."

Kyra's stomach dropped. *Oh no.* Tarek was with her until late last night. Gully had been alone. Guilt rose in her throat like bile.

"Gully was alone. At least for part of it," she said, her voice shaky. "After talking to Rene Ramos, the charter company captain," she explained for Terry's benefit. "Tarek came back to my place for a while. He left after midnight." Kyra bit her lip. *It'll be my fault if Gully doesn't have an alibi.*

Chase squeezed her finger, still laced with his. "Don't beat yourself up. Even if Tarek was home, the defense may not consider him a reliable witness." Chase linked another finger with hers. "The police definitely won't."

"What do you mean?" Kyra asked.

"You don't think he'd lie to protect the people he cares about? Like Gully?"

Kyra pressed her lips together. *He would.*

Tarek appeared over Terry's shoulder, with Officer Evans right behind him. Chase unlaced their fingers and turned around to shake Evans's hand.

"Hey," Tarek said. His hand landed on her shoulder. "Let's move over there." He pointed to a table beneath a window where Evans was already pulling over a fifth chair. The bartender materialized at the table with glasses of water and menus. Evans spoke to him, and with a nod, the bartender disappeared. Kyra grabbed her water glass and took a seat between the window and Chase.

"I just got off the phone with Gully. When Connors had suggested that Gully commit to voluntary house arrest this morning, he didn't know there'd been another murder. The prosecutor had called him to discuss the case. She'd implied they expected the judge would sign the arrest warrant today. Now, he thinks it was a strategy to ensure Gully didn't run." Tarek swallowed and ran a hand through his hair.

"You don't think they'll arrest him?" Chase asked.

"Oh, I do. It's imminent, but I don't like how it's being handled."

"What are the charges?" Kyra asked.

"I don't know." Tarek's jaw clenched, and he glanced at Evans. "Do you?"

"I haven't seen the paperwork. Technically, this isn't state jurisdiction." Officer Evans went quiet when the bartender returned with more drinks. When he left, he said in hushed tones, "Erikson was pushing the DA for first degree with a hope to plea down to second, but we'll be speculating until the arraignment."

Kyra's breath caught.

"Just Gray and Jaycee, right?" Chase asked.

Evans nodded. "For now. They won't bring charges for this crime until the victim is officially IDed and cause of death certified by the ME, but Erikson is already pointing to Mr. Gould. He says it's all connected to the wreck."

Terry's mouth screwed up to the side, his jaw sliding back and forth. "That's it then? They're sticking to their insane theory?"

"What is their theory?" Chase asked.

"The newest one? Since they gave up on trying to pin it on me?" Terry huffed, and his nostrils flared. His frown twisted, sharpened. "That Jaycee, Matty Gray, and Gully were working together behind my back to salvage the *Keres*.

They intended to raise the wreck that night, cutting me out. But Gully got greedy and cut them out, too."

"How plausible is their theory?" Kyra asked.

"It's absurd." Terry grunted. He let out a long breath. "Occasionally, I'll sanction a covert dive to get an idea of what we're fishin' out before it's official, but I warned my crew that we needed to do this one by the book. The wreck is too close to the shoal, too high profile to not draw attention. If it really is the *Keres*, this could be the biggest find since the *Endurance*."

"But they went anyway?" Tarek asked. Terry glanced at Evans. "He's okay."

"They did. I was surprised as anyone. I've known Matty these past eighteen years. Best diver I've ever worked with." Terry sucked in his cheeks. His eyes misted just the tiniest bit. He grimaced. "He was meticulous when it came to safety protocols. Jaycee, she's another story. She is, *was* a thrill seeker. Reckless as all hell. I wouldn't be surprised if the entire thing had been her idea." Terry looked at Tarek. "You know there's no way Gully would pass up an opportunity to see the *Keres*. And once Gully and Jaycee got the idea in their heads, Matty Gray wouldn't have been able to talk them out of it. He'd never let Jace do a solo dive. He'd have gone to keep her safe. But he wouldn't have dived with faulty equipment. I know for a fact he inspected it that afternoon. I signed off on the inspection myself. The equipment was dive-ready when we met you all at Gully's place."

"But even if none of that were true, and they were trying to cut me out, which they were not, one shipman and two divers couldn't raise that wreck on their own. Nevermind one man. It's a big job. It's taken days just to plan and it'll take weeks to organize pulling her up without destroying her. I'll testify and say the same thing if it comes to it." Terry's shoulders rounded, and he rubbed at his temples.

Kyra sneaked a glance at Tarek. He was spinning his water glass on the coaster, his jaw set.

If Gully and Terry's team went behind his back to see the Keres, *the prosecutor has persuasive evidence that they aren't as loyal as Terry thinks but if Gully couldn't raise the wreck by himself, what would be the benefit in killing Matty Gray and Jaycee?*

"What about just the treasure?" Kyra asked. "Could they have tried to take that and leave the wreck?"

Terry's eyes focused somewhere above Kyra's head, thinking. "The *Keres* is still mostly buried. We'll have to excavate her to get inside her hull. No," Terry said, shaking his head. "If there *is* a treasure, pulling it up that night would have been impossible."

"Officer Evans, were you able to get more information about what happened on the Blue Stream ship?" Kyra asked.

Officer Evans threw a glance at Tarek, who gave him a curt nod. "This didn't come from me. It's not official or public information, but they have preliminarily identified the body as Andy Mackey."

"Oh, it's Andy." Terry said, now staring at the tabletop.

Kyra thought his voice tremored.

"The police showed me photographs when they questioned me. I recognized him right away, even with the blood. I've been sitting in meetings with him for the past two days. They said he'd been stabbed."

"That's right," Evans said, glancing around the table. He lowered his voice further. "The Coast Guard medic on scene said he thought the wound could have been caused by a harpoon. Mr. Mackey was likely speared through a lung. He drowned in his own blood."

Terry swore loudly, drawing attention from the bartender at the far end of the room. He glanced over, then returned his attention to the baseball game.

"What about the rumors that he was strung up in the winch system?" Chase asked.

Evans nodded. "We want to keep it quiet. We don't want to alarm the public, but it's true," Evans said in a low voice. "The assailant wrapped the winch system around Mr. Mackey's chest and hoisted him up. Contusions suggest he was still alive when he was displayed."

Terry closed his eyes. He took a shuddering breath. Kyra bet he could see the images of Andy Mackey behind his eyelids. When his eyes opened, she could see the strain and horror written on his face.

"Officer Evans?" She patted his shoulder. His skin had taken on a waxen sheen. "Are you okay?"

"I'm sorry, ma'am. No, not really, to be honest. Violent crimes isn't my normal assignment." He looked over at Tarek with a weak smile. "Can't say I like it much."

Tarek clasped him on the shoulder. "I know. Thank you."

Kyra realized he was here for Tarek. *Just like last spring.* When he'd come to the island at Tarek's request, to protect her.

"Who found him?" Kyra asked, unable to imagine seeing

something so horrible.

"Mr. Kapowski's morning crew. They arrived on the rig just before seven. They called Mr. Kapowski, then made a distress call to the Coast Guard," Evans said. "Chief Erikson's team received the call from the guard and were deployed to the scene. A request was made to my HQ for support. I volunteered. I got on island just after nine to assist with crowd control."

"What about Frank? It's his boat. Could he have had anything to do with it?" Chase asked.

"He has the same alibi as me." Terry said. "He was here this morning. Came downstairs just before I did. He was sitting in the dining room, hadn't even had his coffee when they called."

"Do they know what time Frank got in last night?" Tarek asked. Terry shook his head. "Evans?"

"No, sir. I wasn't there when Mr. Kapowski or Mr. Rose were questioned."

Tarek ran his hands through his hair. "I've got to get back to Gully. Prep him for questions about Andy Mackey."

"I don't understand why the police would be looking at Gully for Andy's death," Kyra said. "The council was going to agree to the new plan. All the objections were addressed. The salvage is happening, isn't it? What motive could Gully have to hurt Andy Mackey?"

"It is," Terry said. "It's been scheduled for October. After the summer season. After the derby."

"The derby?" Kyra repeated.

"It's an annual month-long fishing competition," Terry answered. "It's a decades-old tradition on the island. Ida was adamant the salvage wouldn't interfere. The Mackeys wanted it pushed to February." He shook his head. "But raising a wreck in the winter is too dangerous and expensive."

"But if the salvage was approved, why would the police think Gully had anything to do with Andy's death?" Chase repeated Kyra's question.

"Based on the information I've seen, sir, Mr. Gould is a person of interest because..." Evans held up his hand and counted on his fingers. *One.* "He and Mr. Mackey were seen having a disagreement earlier this week at an island council meeting." *Two.* "Mr. Mackey had vowed not to agree to the salvage efforts if they occurred before the New Year. And three, Mr. Gould could stand to lose quite a bit of money with the delay of the salvage." Evans put his hand down.

"I thought Gully's interest in the *Keres* was academic. What money?" Kyra asked. She chanced a glance at Tarek, but he was staring at Rose with a steely expression.

"Well, that's not entirely accurate, Ms. Gibson." Rose cleared his throat. "My company does contract salvage. We're paid for the job, not on the value of the haul." Terry pressed his lips together and shifted his eyes like he was uncomfortable. "Gully is paying for the *Keres* haul himself."

Tarek stiffened.

Terry raised his hand, palm out facing Tarek. "Don't start, Collins. Gully and I made this deal years ago. He's backed by investors and everything. If he ever located the *Keres*, I'd come. I'd help bring it up. By Gully's estimates, if the hold is still full, we're looking at around a hundred million. If it's not, the historic find alone is worth about half that." He rubbed at his jaw with his knuckles. "A few storms, further exposing her to the elements? She could be destroyed or whatever is down there could be spread all throughout the sound. It's a risk not to pull her up immediately. So yeah, he could lose a lot of money." Terry shrugged and stared into his empty glass.

"Shit," Chase whispered.

Tarek pushed away from the table, the screech of his chair jarring in the quiet bar. "I'd better get back to him."

Kyra's phone buzzed. Terry said something Kyra didn't catch while she fumbled in her bag for it.

Grace.

"Excuse me," she said, standing up. She walked to the other side of the room and the bartender gave her space for privacy. "Grace?"

"Hello, dear," Grace greeted her in a flat tone, lacking her normal enthusiasm. "I'm glad we've caught you. Have you heard the terrible news about Andy and Joe Mackey?"

"I have. We only just heard. I'm so sorry. Is Charlie okay?"

"It's all so terrible."

"Is there anything I can do?" Grace was quiet for so long Kyra thought the call had dropped. "Grace?"

"Yes, I'm here. I'm sorry. You're not free now, are you, dear?"

"I can be. Did you need me to pick something up for you?"

"Oh no, nothing like that. Julia has us well taken care of. But if you and Detective Collins are available to come by the house, we could use your help." Grace must have been upset. She referred to Tarek by name, not by any of her normal teasing labels for him.

"Oh." Kyra shot a glance at Tarek. He was still seated at the table listening to Officer Evans. "I'm with him now. I can ask."

"Thank you, dear. Thank you. As soon as you can." Grace hung up without saying goodbye.

She returned to the table and slid her phone back into her purse. She worried her lip.

"Everything okay?" Tarek asked.

"That was Grace. She said she and Charlie need help with something at home. They asked for you."

"For me?" His forehead creased.

"It's okay. I can handle it by myself," she said, knowing Tarek wanted to get back to Gully. He already had so much to worry about. Whatever this was, she could handle it herself.

"Sir, I've asked to be assigned as Mr. Gould's chaperone. I can stay with him. I'll also get word when … *if* … the arresting officers are coming."

"The captain agreed to that?"

"She didn't disagree, sir, and I don't see why I'd give her a reason to."

Tarek clasped the younger man on the shoulder. "Thank you, Evans. You have no idea. I owe you. Big."

Evans ducked his head and Kyra noticed the tips of his ears had turned pink under Tarek's gratitude.

Tarek turned to Kyra. "Let's go."

Chapter Twenty-One

"HOW DO YOU know we're even on the path?" Tarek said under his breath and shifted closer to Kyra.

It had taken a while to get back to South Beach from up island. With all the traffic coming in and out of Menemsha, the police had closed down roads. They'd been forced to take a detour through Tisbury and had arrived in Vineyard Haven just as two ferries unloaded, further delaying their return. When Gully called with news that his lawyer wanted to schedule a call for the morning, Tarek's mood only worsened. Kyra had half a mind to tell him to just go back to Gully's house.

Tarek was right, though. It was hard to see. A cold front was coming in, and ominous clouds dampened the feeble light of the setting sun. The lengthened shadows camouflaged the path that connected her property with the Chamberses.

"I know where I'm going. I've done it a hundred times." *Seven? A hundred? Who's counting?* "It's just this way." Kyra's toe caught a branch or rock, and she hurtled forward.

Tarek caught her around the waist and yanked her back, keeping her on her feet. "A hundred times, huh?"

Kyra whirled around to face him and caught his amused

expression. He'd been teasing her. "I got us here, didn't I?" she said, and slipped through the trimmed-back hydrangeas and onto the Chamberses' lawn.

She raised her hand to knock on the door, but before her knuckles came into contact with the fiberglass, it was thrown open and Grace pulled her into a hug. Kyra sputtered and patted the older woman's shoulder.

"Hi, Grace. Everything okay?" Kyra shared a concerned look with Tarek.

"Thanks goodness, you're finally here." Grace pulled back, her hands still on Kyra's arms. Kyra noticed smudges of mascara underneath Grace's left eye and was a little taken aback. She had never seen Grace anything but perfectly put together. Grace released her, her eyes on Tarek.

"Grace?"

But Grace didn't respond to her. She'd already latched onto Tarek's forearm and was pulling him toward the living room.

"This way. Thank you for coming, Detective."

"Of course."

Kyra followed them, shutting and locking the door.

"Char and Lisa are in the living room."

Charlie was curled up in a corner of their big sectional. Her untamed curls sprung in all directions, an erratic, dark halo around her head. Another woman sat in the armchair across from her. She was sitting, almost folded over herself, her blonde hair hiding her face. She was wringing something in her hands, a tissue. Lisa Mackey sucked in a ragged breath and looked up.

Her eyes were rimmed red. Tears streaked her cheeks.

Kyra's heart went out to the poor woman. Regardless of who Andy Mackey had been to her, it was clear she was beyond distraught.

"Lisa," Grace murmured. "Do you remember our neighbor Kyra? Ed's daughter? You met at the party. This is her friend, Detective Collins. They're here to help."

Kyra shot an alarmed glance at Tarek. She wasn't clear what help they could offer, but his focus was on Lisa.

"Please, call me Tarek." He squatted down in front of her. "Mrs. Mackey?" His voice was warm, his tone comforting.

Lisa's hands shot out and clamped around his. Her body shook as she sobbed. He repositioned himself so he could console her, running his thumb across the top of her shoulder with one hand and holding both of hers with his other. He let her cry.

Kyra realized he'd probably comforted many people who'd lost someone over the years. How many times was he the one to deliver the news of deceased loved ones? A soft noise came from behind her, and she turned around. Grace was pouring tea from an antique pot. The earthy floral smell of chamomile rose with the steam.

"Would you like some?" she asked.

"Yes, please, thank you." Kyra didn't, but it'd give her something to do with her hands. She took a seat next to Charlie. Charlie's dark eyes were red and raw, too. *Right, Andy was her childhood friend.* Kyra gave Charlie's hand a gentle squeeze.

"Thank you for coming," Charlie whispered.

Kyra nodded and shifted in her seat. Grace handed her a

delicate teacup atop a matching saucer before retreating to her own seat on Charlie's other side. Kyra stirred her tea, a subconscious reflexive movement. The tiny spoon made the softest hum against the porcelain.

"Grace?" Charlie prompted.

Grace cleared her throat. "We thought you and the detective could help, dear." She turned to Lisa. "Lisa, our Kyra saved Char. She helped the police solve those murders last year." Kyra stiffened.

"That wasn't quite how it happened," Kyra muttered into her teacup. The memories of being assaulted, hauled onto a sailboat, and set adrift didn't make her feel like a successful investigator. "I didn't *solve* anything. I … we were… We were very lucky."

Tarek caught her eye, his eyes darkening, like he was also remembering that day last spring. Remembering rescuing her and Charlie from the *Neamhnaid.*

"You kept us alive." Charlie turned to Lisa. "She saved us."

Kyra chewed her bottom lip. The praise made her uncomfortable. The real heroes of that day were Tarek and Chase. Kyra couldn't lay claim to that.

"Lisa, tell them what you told us. They can help." Grace gave Lisa an encouraging smile.

Lisa sucked another ragged breath in through her teeth. "I can't believe this is happening."

"Mrs. Mackey?" Tarek moved to sit on the coffee table directly in front of her. "I'm right here. You can tell me." Lisa's knuckles turned white as her grip on Tarek tightened. "It's okay," he coaxed in a gentle tone Kyra had never heard him use before.

A single tear slid down Lisa's cheek. She brushed it away and nodded. "I can't find Joe. My husband. He's missing and the police won't help me." Lisa sniffled.

Kyra peeked at Charlie, who made a motion with her hand. Kyra's eyes widened. *What?* Charlie gave her another *do something* motion. Her gaze flicked to Lisa and back.

"Lisa." Kyra leaned forward, giving a side-eye to Charlie. "Please, can you start at the beginning? What do you mean, Joe is missing?"

"I can't find him. I tried calling him and texting him. His phone is off. It goes straight to voicemail. I tried at the office, and his mother's, but no one knows where he is. The police said he's not a missing person until he's been gone over twenty-four hours."

"When was the last time you saw him?" Tarek asked.

Lisa swallowed. "This morning, I think."

"You think?" he prompted.

"He went out last night. He came home late, after I was asleep, and left before I got up."

"So, you didn't actually see him?"

"Umm, no." Lisa turned wide eyes on Tarek and blanched. "But he always comes home." Lisa swallowed and looked uncomfortable.

"Lees," Charlie said. "They need to know the truth."

Lisa's gaze met Charlie's and her mouth stretched down. "It's only happened a few times," her voice was soft.

Kyra leaned forward. "What's only happened a few times?"

"Sometimes he needs more time to get his head on

straight. He'll take a day or two."

"Mrs. Mackey, your husband disappears for a day or two randomly?"

Lisa snatched her hands away. "It's not random. And he answers his phone! Checks his messages." Lisa's voice rose.

"Okay, Mrs. Mackey," Tarek said, his tone placating. "Why don't you walk us through it. What happened last night? Why did he leave?"

Lisa didn't respond. Her eyes were wide, her hands flexed against her thighs.

"Lees, you need to tell them what you told us. They can help," Charlie pushed. "They can't help you unless you tell them."

Kyra placed her teacup down and scooted to the edge of her seat. "Please, Lisa."

Lisa wiped at her eyes. She sagged back in her chair and wrung her hands together. She swallowed and sucked in a deep breath.

"Last night, after dinner, Joe took a call. He was on the back porch. I wasn't trying to listen, but he was shouting. He was speaking with Andy. His brother. They were arguing. Again." Lisa looked up and Charlie gave her an encouraging nod.

"Again?" Tarek asked.

"They've always had a tumultuous relationship, but recently they've been at each other's throats. They argued all the time. Last night, after he hung up, Joe was upset. He said he was going for a drive. To clear his head, you know? He normally just drives around. He hadn't come home yet when I went to bed. That was around eleven."

"Does he do that often? Take drives?" Kyra asked.

Lisa looked at the ceiling, her lips stretched into a frown. When she looked back at Kyra, her words were halting. "Yes. Often enough. When he's upset. But he's only left the island twice, and both times he texted me, telling me he was staying on the mainland."

Kyra bit into her bottom lip. She scanned Tarek's face, but his attention was on Lisa, his expression unreadable.

"And this morning?" Tarek prompted.

"I didn't have any texts or calls from him. And he wasn't there when I woke up. I assumed he'd already left for work. It's not unusual. He often leaves at four or five in the morning while the fluke or stripers are running."

"When did you realize something was wrong, Mrs. Mackey?"

"The police came to the house looking for Joe. That was around eleven this morning. They wouldn't tell me what they wanted him for. I told them Joe had left for work." Lisa swallowed a sob and continued. "Then just after they left, Sophia called. She was hysterical. Screaming and crying. She said Andy was dead. Murdered. She said Joe killed him." Her voice shook.

Joe? Kyra's mind whirled. *But the police think Gully did it.*

"I called Joe, but it went straight to voicemail. If he'd gone out this morning, he could have lost cell service. I thought I could use the radio at the office. I drove over, but it was empty. Everyone was out on the pier. Where … where they'd found Andy."

"Could he still be out on the water?" Kyra asked.

"I don't think so. All our boats were docked. The crew

had never gone out. They'd been waiting for Joe, but then Andy was..." Her voice trailed off and tears streamed down her cheeks. "I tried to tell the police that Joe was missing, but they said that he'd turn up and to keep trying his phone. But I know. I know something is wrong."

Kyra drummed her fingers against her thigh. Tarek probably thought the same thing. She wasn't convinced Joe Mackey had returned home last night. "Lisa, what about his car?"

"His car?" Lisa pressed her lips together. "I don't know."

"Is it home? At the office in Menemsha?"

Lisa shook her head. "It's not in the driveway at home. I didn't notice it in Menemsha."

"You didn't look for it?" She tried not to sound accusatory, but Lisa still winced.

"No. The parking lot was already full when I got there. The police had cordoned it off, but I didn't think to look for Joe's car. I was looking for Joe."

"What about Andy's car?"

Lisa blinked. Twice. Kyra watched her throat bob as she swallowed. "I saw it. In his usual spot."

"Are you sure?"

Lisa shook her head, but said, "I think so."

"What were they arguing about, Mrs. Mackey?" Tarek asked.

"The business." Lisa picked at the hem of her T-shirt. "Andy and Sophia, his wife, want to sell the fishing business. They hate it here. Hate the fishing industry. But Mackey's is Joe's whole life. Joe wants to expand, build a restaurant and a fish store, another location in Edgartown or Nantucket. He has so many ideas. Good ones."

"They were arguing about expansion?" Kyra asked.

"Not exactly. Joe and I, we had plans to buy out Andy's share. It was the deal when Andy moved back to help. We've been saving for years. We should have been able to afford it at the end of the season. But then they found that wreck."

"The *Keres*," Kyra offered.

"I don't know the name." Lisa shook her head. "I don't know much about the wreck itself, just that they plan to salvage it. That the ships are there now, doing preliminary work, scaring away the fish. Our recent hauls have been disappointing. Joe and Andy think it will only get worse."

"We're aware," Tarek said grimly. "There has been a lot of opposition from the local community, but I understand the two sides have come to a compromise?"

"Yes," Lisa nodded. "Mr. Kapowski and Terry Rose proposed a new plan after the council meeting. They agreed to delay the salvage until after the season and would take precautions to protect our oyster beds. They also promised to commit a large amount of money to the island."

Kyra snuck a glance at Grace, who nodded, confirming Lisa's statements.

"Our losses would have been minimized, but not zero. Not close. Even with the concessions, we'll take some financial hits, especially with the oysters. We spoke with the accountant yesterday. We won't have enough money to buy out Andy and Sophia this year. If the mitigation efforts are effective, and we have no other surprise expenses, we might be able to afford it next year." Lisa raised her eyes to Kyra's, then looked over at Tarek. She let out a sigh. "Sophia and

Andy wanted Joe to object, vote against the new plan, encourage others to vote against it, too. They want the salvage delayed until the winter, after we've bought them out."

"Was that a possibility?" Kyra asked.

"No, probably not." Lisa sighed. "If they wait, the island won't receive as big of a financial incentive from the salvagers. There's no way Ida Ames and the council would agree to take such a loss just for us. I heard Joe going over the numbers again with Andy on the phone last night. Joe was trying to convince him the sacrifice of another year or two was worth it for the good of the island."

Charlie made an irritated noise, and Kyra caught the warning glance from Grace, the subtle shake of her head.

"I don't think it worked. Joe was just so upset when he hung up."

"Mrs. Mackey, do you have any idea where Joe would have gone?"

"No." Lisa shook her head. "After this morning, I called everyone I know. Friends, family, even the staff." Fat tears rolled down her cheeks.

"Where has he gone in the past?" Kyra asked.

She shared a look with Tarek. She suspected he was thinking the same thing she was. The same thing Jimmy had implied earlier today. *Could Joe have killed Andy and run off?* Kyra bit her lip. *If it's possible, why aren't the police looking for him?* She remembered what Tarek said, how he thought the case against Gully was personal. Maybe the police didn't want another suspect.

"Sometimes, he'd be at the office. Or his mom's house.

He had some buddies here and on the mainland. I called them too, but no one's seen him."

"Lisa, we have to ask." Kyra tried to sound sympathetic. "Could Joe have been involved with Andy's death? Could he have hurt him and run?"

Lisa blanched. "No! Never. Joe isn't violent. He'd never hurt anyone." Lisa's words tumbled out. She lowered her gaze to the floor. Her eyes shifted back and forth like she was searching for an answer in the Chamberses' rug. "They fought, but he's family. He loves his brother." Lisa said almost to herself.

"Okay, Mrs. Mackey." Tarek reached out to pat her clasped hands. "Thank you for telling us." He slid forward on the table, shifted his weight, like he was going to stand, when Lisa's gaze shot up.

"Can you help?" she begged. "Can you find him for me? Please?"

"Find him?" Kyra repeated, her mind going blank.

Lisa's eyes widened, and she blinked twice before throwing an accusing look at Grace.

"We'll do what we can, Mrs. Mackey." Tarek said and stood. Kyra thought he sounded strangely formal, all of a sudden. "He couldn't have gotten far. I agree with the local authorities. I'm sure he'll turn up, but we'll see what we can do."

"Thank you, Detective. Thank you." Lisa looked up at him, gratitude shining in her eyes.

"Can I see your phone?"

Lisa frowned, but dug it out of her handbag and unlocked it for him. "Why?"

Tarek ignored her. His thumbs flew over the screen.

"Lisa, what was he wearing last night?" Kyra asked.

Lisa focused on Kyra; her expression confused. "I don't remember exactly. One of our logo T-shirts? He wears them most days. Jeans?"

"Anything else?"

"His Mackey's jacket wasn't on the hook this morning. That's why I thought he was at work."

"Thanks," Tarek said, handing the phone back to Lisa. "The police were right. Keep trying to contact him." Lisa nodded and hiccupped.

Charlie motioned to Grace, who went to Lisa, took her hand in hers.

"I need to get back," Lisa whispered, her voice hoarse. "What if he comes home? And I'm not there?"

"You'll stay here with us tonight," Charlie said.

"We should go. Try and get some rest, Mrs. Mackey. Joe will turn up."

"Thank you, dear, Detective. Please, if you hear anything."

"We'll let you know."

Kyra gave Grace's shoulder a squeeze and followed Charlie and Tarek to the foyer.

At the door, Kyra stopped and turned to Charlie. She placed her hand on her friend's arm. "I'm not sure we can do anything."

"I know." Charlie's voice was strained, and she placed her hand over Kyra's. "I feel helpless just sitting here. I need to feel like we're helping, doing something. Joe and I are all that Lisa has left. She has no other family. Just Joe and Andy, and now Andy's..." Charlie's voice trailed off. "We need to know he's okay. Please."

Kyra nodded. She understood. She'd been in much the same position last spring.

"Charlie, do you think Joe could have hurt Andy?"

"No." Charlie's response was immediate and vehement. "Never."

"We'll do what we can." Tarek said, standing off to the side of the door. "If Lisa hears from him, let me know right away."

Charlie nodded.

"One more thing. Do you think Grace has a list of attendees at the council meeting the other night?" Kyra asked.

"I don't know, but if not, she can get one from Ida. I'll ask?"

"If you don't mind."

Charlie promised to get the list from Grace and wished them goodnight. They stepped out onto the dark lawn. Their motion tripped the floodlights.

"Do you have a flashlight app?" she asked. Her phone had one, but it was on its last dregs of power, the battery icon red.

Tarek turned his on, and Kyra followed him to the path.

"Why did you check Lisa's phone?"

"Families normally have a tracker on each other. I checked the find my phone feature." He stopped and turned around.

Kyra blinked in the light of his phone before he lowered it to the ground.

"The phone was turned off at eleven forty-seven last

night. He was in Menemsha."

She stopped walking. "What are you thinking?"

Tarek shook his head and turned back around. She scrambled to keep up with him. *Could he have gone to the office? Seen Andy? Argued?* She remembered what Officer Evans had said about Andy's body. How it had been displayed. It was so violent. Kyra shuddered.

She stepped onto the first step of her porch and turned around to face him. "Do you think Joe killed Andy?"

Tarek sucked in a breath and looked up at the house, avoiding eye contact. *He thinks it's possible.* Kyra blinked. *Reasonable doubt.*

"You're going to tell Gully's lawyer."

He slid his hands into his pockets. He nodded.

"Are you going to find Joe?"

Tarek looked at her, and she saw the desperation in all the shadows on his face.

"They're going to charge him, Kyra. They're going to accuse him of murdering his friends, and probably Andy Mackey. He needs a strong defense, and his lawyer needs a story that someone else killed those people. He needs a story he can sell to a judge and jury. As long as Joe is missing, I have one. For all we know, Joe could have killed Matty Gray and Jaycee. Or maybe Andy did, and something happened between him and Joe. The truth doesn't matter." Tarek shook his head. "But if it could have been one of the Mackey brothers, I have reasonable doubt."

Tarek pushed his hands through his hair. "So, no, Kyra, I'm not going to look for Joe Mackey. I'm going to try to find as much evidence as I can that proves Gully isn't guilty.

That he is being maliciously targeted. And if that means I have to offer up the Mackey brothers, I will."

Kyra turned away. She climbed up the rest of the stairs. Her hand dragged on the rail. She understood Tarek's position. His priority was protecting Gully, and she didn't begrudge him that. But not looking for Joe felt like she'd be betraying Charlie, and the memories of Matty Gray and Jaycee. She wasn't sure protecting Gully was enough. She wanted to find the monster who hurt these people, who hurt Gully and Tarek and Charlie, the people she cared about.

Kyra punched the code into the keypad to unlock the door and pushed it open. She stepped inside and turned around. Tarek still stood at the bottom of the steps, looking up at her.

"Kyra." The way he said her name, it said more than any words. It was a plea for permission to choose his friend, for her to understand, and for her to forgive him.

"I understand, Tarek, I do. But I want to find out the truth."

"I know you do." Tarek gave her a wan smile. "I'd expect nothing less."

Kyra waited in the doorway until she saw the red from his taillights disappear.

Chapter Twenty-Two

THE SOFT *PAT-A-TAT-TAT* of rain against the glass pulled Kyra's attention from her laptop. She squinted at the wall of windows from her place on the couch. It had begun raining, not hard, but with those big sloppy raindrops of a moving weather system. She pressed her lips together in a line. The weather matched her foul mood.

She had tossed and turned throughout the night. She'd stared at the ceiling fan going over everything she'd learned—the *Keres*, Jaycee, Matty Gray, Andy and Joe Mackey, Gully's financial interest, Tarek's nonaction.

It was the last one that had her stomach tied in knots. She'd contemplated what Tarek had said, what he'd been saying since the day after the night dive. He'd never claimed he wanted to solve the murders or prove Gully's innocence. He'd been building a defense.

But it wasn't enough. Kyra wanted to know what happened to Matty and Jaycee. She wanted to know what happened to the Mackey brothers. Hell, she even wanted to know what happened to William and Helena Roberts.

In the middle of the night, she'd sat up in bed, feeling like a Tom Cruise cosplay, because she wanted the truth. So, she'd made a decision at a time when all good decisions are made—three a.m. She was going to find Joe Mackey. She was going to find who killed Matty Gray, Jaycee, and Andrew.

This morning, sitting on her couch, she didn't know where to start. She was out of her element and felt helpless and a little foolish. *How am I supposed to find a man I've barely met?* Her horrible mood was only made worse by the twenty-some-odd messages from her boss. Apparently, Assaf had decided her holiday was over and she was officially back at work and the demands kept coming in.

"Gibs review attached. Prep risk strategy for Project Omicron."

"Loriann's merger with the US company is proceeding. Need diligence report ASAP."

"Bleeding wanker," Kyra hissed and rubbed her forehead.

She was so not in the mood to deal with him today. Kyra sighed. To his credit, Assaf had mostly left her alone for the week, only checking in periodically with updates. She supposed she should be grateful he'd demonstrated some restraint.

She pulled out her phone to text Chase.

"Do you know anyone at the Steamship Authority? Can someone check if Joe Mackey's car was taken off island?"

She waited for his response; her phone clenched in her hand.

"I can ask Jimmy. If Joe's car was seen on a ferry, he'd know about it."

Kyra frowned. She didn't like Jimmy knowing their business, but if Tarek wasn't going to help, she didn't see what other choice she had.

"Ask him."

Chase responded with a thumbs-up emoji.

She slipped the phone into her pocket and walked into the kitchen to make herself another cup of coffee. Cronkite wove between her ankles. His hangry yowls bordered on screeches.

"Shut up, cat. I fed you. You're not dying." Cronkite sat down on his haunches and gave her a look that she could only describe as blistering. "How can you exude so much disdain without eyebrows? Fine, you win." She added a few kibbles to Cronkite's bowl. He didn't so much as twitch. "What? What do you want?" She reached out to scratch his ear, but he dodged her touch. He glanced over his shoulder before sauntering from the room with a certain tail flick. One, she'd begun to think, was cat language for *fuck off.*

Her phone buzzed. Grace. She had half a mind to ignore the call. Her thumb hovered over the silence button. *But maybe Grace has news from Lisa?*

"Hello?"

"Good morning, dear. How did you sleep?" Grace sounded tired.

"Fine, you?" Kyra was sure she sounded just as weary.

"Char was up most of the night with Lisa, so I didn't get much sleep. But I'm not complaining," Grace rushed. "I'm glad you're able to help her. It means so much to Char, and to Lisa." Kyra shifted the phone to her other ear. "But that's not why I'm calling. Char told me about the list you requested. I had Ida send it over this morning. We've just dropped Lisa off, and Char wants to go to Café Joy. Would you like to meet us? Char, when will we be there?" Kyra heard Charlie in the background. "In half an hour?"

"Love to. I'll see you soon."

Kyra was soon backing the Range Rover out of the driveway. Her car cut through the thick fog swirling just above the road. It clung to the grass and shrubs shrouding them in strange viscous shadows. The temperature was high, the air thick with heat and moisture, nature's steam room.

In sharp contrast to the gloom outside, Café Joy embodied its cheerful name. Packed full of patrons, the air conditioning whirred with exertion, and condensation clung to the windows. Nina gave Kyra a jaunty wave and pointed to the back of the room. Kyra's eyes followed the proprietress's finger to a table in the back. There, tucked under a window, Grace and Charlie were studying menus, giant steaming mugs already set in front of them.

"Hi, ladies," Kyra greeted them as she stepped up to the table.

"Morning." Charlie looked up from behind her menu. Kyra noticed the dark circles under her eyes. Charlie covered her yawn with one hand and waved to the seat across from her with the other. "Sit, sit."

Grace set her menu down and straightened her silverware. "So glad you made it. How was the rest of your evening?" A server materialized to take Kyra's coffee order.

"Uneventful." Kyra turned to Charlie. "How's Lisa?"

Charlie deflated. "As good as you'd expect, but she's putting on a brave face." Charlie added cream to her coffee and stirred it with a spoon. "We just took her home. She wants to wait there in case Joe returns. Ida has people checking in on her periodically and I'll stay with her there tonight."

It continued to amaze Kyra how tight-knit the island community was. Their hostility for the off islanders was countered only by their fierce protectiveness of each other.

"She hasn't heard from him then?"

"No. She tried calling him every hour throughout the night, but nothing. This morning, she called everyone in her contacts list, to see if anyone had spoken to Joe." Charlie shook her head. Grace took Charlie's hand.

"I'm checking in with Tarek later. I'll let you know if I learn anything."

"Have you decided on breakfast?" The server interrupted them, setting down Kyra's americano. They ordered. Grace made a disapproving frown when Charlie didn't decline the cream cheese frosting with her French toast.

"Did you and Tarek come up with anything last night?" Charlie asked when the waitress had left.

Kyra snaked her fingers through the mug's handle. She debated telling them what Tarek learned about Joe's phone, but decided against it. It would only frighten them. It was still possible he'd turned the phone off last night, but Kyra was having serious doubts they would be so lucky. She was purposely avoiding thinking that something terrible had happened to Joe Mackey. She shifted in her seat and took a sip of coffee.

"No. I'm looking into whether his car was seen on the ferry to Woods Hole." Kyra worried her lip. "I can't help thinking that Joe going missing the night Andy died isn't a coincidence."

Charlie sucked in a sharp breath. "What do you mean? Do you think something's happened to him?"

"I don't know." Kyra shook her head. "We're missing something. And I think it's connected to the *Keres*." Kyra drummed her nails against the ceramic of her coffee mug. "I just don't know what it is. That's why I asked for that list of attendees." She turned to Grace. "I'd like to know who else is interested in the *Keres*. Do you have it with you?"

"Oh, right." Grace dug into her pristine St. Laurent tote bag and retrieved a few sheets of printer paper folded in half. "Here. Ida emailed it over this morning. I went through it and also added people I remember being there and crossed off people who didn't attend. We don't have a sign in or anything formal for those meetings, but we do have a list of contacts we notify." She slid the pages across the table.

Kyra spread them out side-by-side, so they could all see the names. Her stomach sank. There were at least two hundred names on the list.

"This many?"

"It's what I could confirm." Grace frowned, misinterpreting Kyra's dismay. "Do you need the list of all members? Really, that's everyone with a mailbox on the island." Grace rubbed her knuckles. "I can probably get you that. Would it help?"

"Let me see?" Charlie reached for the pages. "The salvage won't impact the vacationers and the summer people who get bent out of shape about their views. They won't see it." Charlie ran a finger down the list. "Do you have a pen, love?" Grace rummaged through her bag and finally emerged with one. "I think we can cross off some of these people." Charlie crossed off name after name. She stopped at one, tapping it with the tip of her pen. "Ugh, Elise is such a pain in the ass."

"Elise?" Kyra asked, trying to make sense of the upside-down list.

"Elise Elmer. She runs a bunch of social events for the old biddies' club. She takes it upon herself to speak for thirty or forty people, none of whom spend more than a week or two on the island each year. Most of the houses in her area are summer homes and rentals." Charlie rolled her eyes. "Elise would be opposed to the salvage, though."

"Why?"

Charlie circled Elise Elmer's name. "Because she's a difficult old hag."

"Char!" Grace pressed her hand to her heart. Then she dropped it to her lap and shrugged. "Don't say I said anything, dear, but it's true. She's horrible. But, Char, there's no way she could have hurt Andy Mackey or those other young people."

"No," Charlie agreed, and drew a strike through the name.

"Why?" Kyra asked.

"Elise is in her seventies and walks with a cane," Charlie answered, still looking at the list. "I don't recognize these people. Do you, Grace?" Charlie passed the list back to Grace, who slipped on her reading glasses.

"Oh yes, these are the mainlanders. Press, the salvage companies, a representative from some insurer, and the protesters."

"Protesters? Do you mean the conservationists?" Kyra peered at the list.

"Well, yes, some of them are here on behalf of environmental groups, like, er, Ms. Collins." Grace stumbled over Rachel's name. "These other people are concerned citizens.

Activists." She circled a selection of four names. "They filed for permits to stage a protest against the salvage efforts yesterday."

"Really?" Kyra scanned the list and noticed Dr. Seth Hammond among the names. She frowned and pointed. "Rachel, umm, Ms. Collins told us yesterday that the Oceanic Conservation was dropping its objection, pending approval of the new salvage plan."

"Yes, that's true." Grace nodded. "Could they have filed preemptively? The council was scheduled to vote to approve the new plan yesterday. Ida postponed the vote in respect for the Mackey family, but without Andy or Joe's dissents, we expect it to be unanimous."

"They didn't hold the vote?" Kyra asked. "You mean the salvage is still stalled?"

"Officially, yes." Grace turned to Charlie. "Char, do you remember when Ida said they would hold the new voting session?" Charlie pursed her lips, thinking, but before she could answer, Grace pulled up the calendar on her phone. "Next week is our regular monthly meeting. Probably then. Ida won't want to delay the voting long. She wants to get the funds contribution in writing as soon as possible, but we have no reason to believe it won't pass."

"What about the protests? Will those proceed?" Kyra asked.

"I'm not sure." Grace frowned. "I know we're planning to make a public statement and issue a press release detailing the new plan and its approval by the council. They invited representatives from all the environmentalist groups to comment. But we won't release that until the contracts are signed. We have the OC's statement pending a passing of the vote." Grace paused and her brow creased. "You know, I think Ida may have said Dr. Hammond declined to comment."

Kyra tapped her fingers against her coffee mug. *That's odd.* She wanted to ask why Grace thought he'd declined, but the waitress stopped at their table with their breakfast. She set their plates down. Kyra eyed Grace's tofu and vegetable scramble doubtfully, then looked at Charlie's plate and bit back her laugh. Charlie's plate was piled with a three-inch-thick slab of challah French toast covered in berries and frosting. Charlie's eyes were round as moons, taking in her breakfast, a kid let loose in a candy store.

"Don't worry, love, I'll share." Charlie nudged Grace's shoulder.

"Thank you, Char." Grace heaved a sigh, her lips turned down. Grace gave her wife a withering look but accepted the bite Charlie offered her on her fork. "Gracious, that's delicious." She licked the frosting from her lips.

Charlie hooted and clapped her hands together.

They didn't linger after finishing their meals. Kyra promised to catch up with the Chamberses later, but right now, she needed to talk to Tarek. She wanted to ask him if Rachel really had dropped the Ocean Conservation's objections.

By the time she pulled into her garage, the rain had given way to continuous mist and the temperature had dropped into the near bearable range. She texted Tarek photos of the pages Grace had given her, asked him to confirm that the OC had dropped their objections, and asked how Gully's meeting with the lawyers had gone. Her fingers hovered over the touch screen. She typed out a question asking about Joe, but deleted it. She tried twice more before giving up and tossing the phone aside with a harrumph.

Kyra searched the internet for everything she could find about the Mackey brothers, hoping to discover something that might give her a clue where to search for Joe. They seemed like ordinary people. Andy had run a successful real estate brokerage firm in Southern California before returning to Martha's Vineyard. Sophia had an out-of-date IMDB page listing a few acting credits. Joe and Lisa Mackey were prominent figures supporting the local community.

She remembered what Jimmy had alluded to yesterday—that Lisa might have been having an affair with Andy. Kyra had thought they'd acted strange when she'd come upon them in the Chamberses' kitchen, but Lisa seemed truly distraught by her husband's disappearance, and she'd been adamant that Joe wouldn't hurt his brother. Kyra tapped her nail against the laptop casing. *Who would kill Andy, and why? Why was he even on that boat? What was gained by such a violent display?*

Her phone buzzed. Tarek on the group chat.

"Meeting went about as well as expected. We are refusing to cooperate and have declined to be questioned about Andy Mackey. Connors expects this will accelerate Gully's arrest. Gully and I are going through the list now. Also sent it to Rose and Kapowski."

Kyra read his text through twice more. According to Terry Rose, Frank Kapowski was the first person his crew called when they found Andy. He had been on the scene. She typed back.

"Do you think Frank would talk to us?"

"I'll ask."

Kyra slipped her phone into her pocket. She paced the house, waiting impatiently for Tarek's response. She found herself at the doorway to her father's office. The room reminded her so much of him. It felt wrong to change it, but at the same time, she'd always be trespassing on his space if she left it the same. As usual, it was darker in here than in the rest of the house. And cold. She shivered and flicked on a table lamp. The light did little to diffuse the shadows that clung to the room's corners.

Cronkite sauntered in, his little paws announcing his arrival with a soft *pfft, pfft.* He rubbed past her, his fluffy body sliding along her calf, and hopped up onto the big antique desk. Kyra followed him. He flopped down, shuffling a pile of mail. Kyra stared at it. *Oh right.*

She fanned out the envelopes. Her other hand stroked Cronk's velvety ears. Most of it was junk mail addressed to her dad. Some had her name as the homeowner of record, but something caught her eye. A newsletter. From June.

Kyra unfolded it, opening it up to the front page. It was the Martha's Vineyard free quarterly newsletter. It contained a calendar of events and local announcements, and a few advertisements. The headline article was accompanied by a half page-spread of a photograph of the clay cliffs and a man holding a camera with a massive lens. The headline read, *Birdwatchers, Storm Riders Return to Martha's Vineyard.*

Kyra scanned the article. It announced the return of a rare breed of bird to the island, the dark storm petrel. A male and female had been seen nesting in the cliffs. She read further.

The storm petrel was a strange bird, preferring to fly during storms. There hadn't been recorded sightings of the bird on the island for nearly eighty years and their return is attributed to conservation efforts on the cliffs, protecting their nesting grounds, and the cleanness of the Vineyard Sound.

"This must be the bird Rachel was talking about," she murmured to the cat. He ducked his head and rolled onto his back.

Kyra's phone buzzed with a message from Tarek on the group chat.

"Gully got in touch with Frank. He's agreed to talk to us."

"Meet at my place?" Chase responded. *"Is Gully still a free man?"*

Tarek: *"For now."*

Kyra watched the little dots fade in and out. She was relieved that Gully hadn't been arrested yet, but she knew it was only a matter of time.

"Cool. Bring the babysitter cop."

Chapter Twenty-Three

KYRA TURNED ONTO the curving driveway of Mander Lane Farm. She drove past the public parking area, and the sign warning off trespassers, that read in big block letters PRIVATE PROPERTY NO ADMITTANCE, up to the Hawthorn's mansion. She stared up at the behemoth building. It struck a striking figure against the sky, even more so with the swirling gray clouds throwing shadows on the Victorian turrets and contemporary glass and metal additions. She made a face. She hated this house almost as much as Chase did. Letting loose a sigh, Kyra grabbed the bags of snacks she'd picked up from the market and climbed the steps to the big wraparound porch. She rang the bell.

The door cracked open, and a single alpine-blue eye peered at her. Chase threw it open.

"You brought food. You're my favorite." He pulled the bags from her arms. "Come on, we're in the family room." Chase led her to the back of the house, through the massive kitchen to a living area just beyond.

Kyra had never been to this part of the house. It gave her pause. This room, so unlike the smothering formality of the rest of it, was warm and welcoming. A large sectional sofa sat in front of a cold fieldstone hearth. The too large television, suspended above the mantel, played a baseball game.

Tarek, Gully, and Frank were already there. Gully sat on the couch; his socked feet propped up on the coffee table. His hands were on his stomach, his eyes closed. Frank was standing, his back to the room, looking out the window toward the old barn site. He turned when he heard them enter. Tarek stood up from the couch, his hands sliding into his pockets. She noticed he'd gone back to his unofficial detective uniform of dark jeans and rumpled oxford.

"Miss Gibson!" a cheerful voice greeted her from behind, and she whirled around. Officer Evans. "How are you today, Miss Gibson?" He bobbed his head and stepped around her.

Chase quirked an eyebrow at her and pushed past him to access the wet bar counter, taking up the length of the room. "What d'ya bring me?" He dropped the bags on the counter and tore into them.

"Chase," she scolded, but he just threw her a mocking grin and nodded above her shoulder. Kyra turned around.

"Hey," Tarek said, keeping his voice soft. He attempted a cautious smile that didn't reach his eyes. He looked like he was trying to hide behind his detective persona and not quite accomplishing it. The strain and worry were visible in the lines of his face, the set of his shoulders. "I'll introduce you." He reached out to her, his fingers brushing the base of her spine.

"Frank, this is Kyra Gibson."

"The pleasure is mine, Ms. Gibson," Frank said, stepping forward. He shook her hand over the coffee table.

"Kyra's helping with…" Tarek paused. "The investigation."

Kyra internally winced at the resignation in his tone. "Please call me Kyra. It's nice to meet you. Hey, Gully."

"London." Gully raised his giant paw in a salute without opening his eyes, then let it drop.

"How are you feeling?" she asked, knowing the question was as stupid as it sounded.

Gully grunted, a defeated, hopeless sound, and said, "Fucking swell."

"I'm coming with the snacks." Chase brought over a tray laden with the food and drinks Kyra brought. He slid it onto the coffee table with a flourish, then flopped on the couch next to Gully, and kicked up his feet.

"Did you just get up?" She swept a critical eye over his basketball shorts and worn prep-school t-shirt. His messy hair was even more disheveled than usual. Chase met her eyes over a handful of cheese puffs. He shrugged and flashed a lazy grin, but she took in his bloodshot eyes and peaky pallor. He hadn't called her last night. He hadn't called her in a few days, now. She'd thought he'd been sleeping. Something in her chest cracked.

Frank cleared his throat, drawing their attention. Kyra wondered what he made of them—political playboy, a murder suspect, a few cops out of their jurisdiction, and her, a random Englishwoman here for the summer playing detective.

Frank directed his question to Tarek. "Gully says you have some questions for me?" He flicked his shrewd gaze to Gully, then back to Tarek. "I'm not going to lie to you, Detective Collins. Had Terry not asked me as a personal favor, I'd have declined this interview. Do I need my lawyer here?"

Kyra stiffened.

"Don't be an asshole, Frank." Gully grumbled. "Tarek isn't with the department on this one, you know that."

"I'm here in the capacity of a concerned citizen. Everything said here is strictly off the record, if that makes you feel better," Tarek said through gritted teeth.

Frank nodded, satisfied with the answer. He sat in one of the armchairs and crossed an ankle over his knee. "And what about him?" Frank nodded toward Officer Evans.

"He's my babysitter."

"Yeah," Evans sighed and stood up. "I'll go." He reached for a can of soda.

"Through there is the media room." Chase pointed. "Remote's on the table. Take a cookie." Evans took the cookie Chase handed to him and shuffled down the hall.

"I reserve the right to decline to answer." Frank raised an eyebrow at Tarek, who nodded. "Alright then. What do you want to know?"

Tarek inclined his head toward Kyra. She pushed down the small swell of pride at being allowed to take the lead. He'd deferred to her twice now.

"Yes," she said, turning to Frank. "Thank you for agreeing to speak with us." Kyra pushed her hair behind her ear and sat down across from him. "Yesterday, when Andy Mackey's body was discovered, can you tell us what you told the police?"

Frank's face slackened in surprise. "I'm not supposed to say anything. I can't confirm that it was Andrew Mackey."

"Frank." Tarek's tone held an unsaid warning.

Frank glanced at Gully, who popped open a can of soda and raised his hand, palm to the ceiling. "Fine," Frank said, turning back to Kyra. "But this doesn't get back to me."

"No, of course not," Kyra agreed. The couch cushions dipped as Tarek sat down next to her, perhaps a smidge closer than appropriate for colleagues.

"Yesterday, we were scheduled to do some scans of the wreckage. I wanted to get a rough idea of our approach. Get some more images for the marketing. Routine stuff. My crew arrived on board to start their rounds. My master diver Anders, he found the body." Frank leaned forward and grabbed a soda. He picked at the tab. His hand trembled. "They called me first. I'd just come down for breakfast at the hotel. I told them to call the Coast Guard and the harbormaster. My guys are trained in basic first aid, but they were too late. There was nothing they could do. I ran down to the rig. Got there just as the emergency response crews were arriving." Frank sucked in a deep breath and focused somewhere behind Kyra. He set the can down and sat back in his seat. His hands gripped his knees tight enough that his knuckles paled. Kyra guessed he was picturing whatever horror he'd witnessed that morning. "I got on the boat. I wish I hadn't. Mackey had been strung up. On the crane. Ropes wrapped around his middle, pulled tight by the winch. There was so much blood. I've never seen anything like it." Frank swallowed and leaned forward like he was going to reach for his soda, but stopped and sat back again. He ran a hand over his face. "I spent the rest of the morning at the station answering questions."

"Can just anyone operate the winch system?" Kyra asked.

Frank tilted his head, considering before he shook his head. "It's complex machinery. A person would need to be familiar with it to use it properly." He rolled his lips. "But to do what they did? That took no finesse. They just tightened the winch. The controls are labeled. Anyone could have figured it out. The firefighters had to cut the body down. The cables had cut too far into him." Frank's face blanched. "He was strung up with incredible force."

Kyra thought that over. *It was so gruesome. To stab someone, wrap them in cables, then suspend them.*

"Tar?" she asked, her voice soft. "Is that normal? To mutilate a loved one like that?"

Tarek sucked in a sharp breath, and he stiffened. Gully's eyes narrowed and his beard shifted. *Tarek had shared his strategy with Gully.*

After a long moment, Tarek shook his head. "No, it's not. Not without a history of other concerning behavior."

Gully seemed to get smaller, somehow, his shoulders curling in.

"Did you know the Mackeys?" she asked Frank.

"Mmhmm. I've known Joe a few years now. I only met Andrew for the first time after that council meeting."

"Ida said that you'd come to a consensus on a new salvage plan. Were the Mackeys on board?"

"Yes, ma'am."

Kyra grimaced and caught the slightest amused twitch in Tarek's cheek.

"They weren't thrilled. Joe was more receptive than his brother. But they knew there was no way that wreck wasn't coming up. Andy's wife was pushing to delay it further into the winter." Frank shook his head. "Thing is, Rose and I don't need their permission under maritime law. If it's not us, it'll be someone else. Someone who doesn't have the ties to the island and its community like Gully and Terry. No one else would make the concessions we're making. No other salvager would give a damn about a few hundred oyster beds, or the locals' interests. For fuck's sake, we're planning to bring her up during hurricane season. If a storm hits at the wrong time, we could lose her." He rubbed his forehead and his chest puffed up.

"And you? Why did you agree?" Chase asked around a mouth of cheese puffs.

"Terry's a good friend." He glanced at Gully, who nodded. "My equipment is state-of-the-art. We'd cut the salvage timeline in half with my help. So, we've agreed to go in together on the haul. Even if she isn't worth much, the media attention for pulling up a three-hundred-year-old pirate ship and one with such a great story is priceless."

"We've been talking to Ida," Gully said. "There's interest in a museum either on the island or the mainland for the pieces we retrieve, like the masthead and whatever other things we find. Part of the financial contribution we're making to the island may go toward the museum idea. It will bring in tourist and research money. Frank and Terry would be recognized for the discovery."

"Hi."

As one, their heads all turned toward the entryway.

A handsome man dressed in rumpled trousers with embroidered turtles and a half-done up shirt raised a hand and gave them a sheepish smile. "I called a cab. I can see myself out."

Kyra's gaze pinged from the visitor to Chase. The skin around his eyes looked thinner, the creases there more pronounced. She should have known he'd been hurting, but she'd been too wrapped up in her own drama to reach out to him, and he'd sought solace elsewhere. Her stomach hollowed out. She tried to catch his eye, but Chase's playboy mask was now firmly in place.

"See you later, Ger." He raised his hand in a lazy salute.

With a shy wave, Gryphon-Gerry slipped from the room.

"So, Frank, why was Andy Mackey on your ship?" Chase asked and grabbed another handful of cheese puffs. Tarek slumped further in his seat, annoyed. Chase held his gaze and slowly licked the cheese dust off his fingers.

"No idea." Frank shook his head. "We'd been meeting at their offices or at the council offices. There was no reason for him to be on my rig. Another thing. We don't have harpoons."

"You don't?" Kyra sat up straighter.

"No, ma'am. So, whoever killed him brought it with them, and took it when they left, or threw it overboard. Last I heard, the police hadn't located it."

"Any idea where it came from?" Kyra asked.

"Not really." Frank pressed his lips together.

"Nearly all the fishing boats carry them," Chase said. "And spearfishing is pretty popular. Many of the boathouses keep them. The murderer could have gotten it anywhere."

"Do you think it could have been Joe?" she asked.

Frank paused, considering. "I don't know. I don't know Joe all that well."

"When was the last time you saw him?"

"Why?" Frank's eyebrows rose and he glared at Tarek. "What's this about, Collins?"

"He's missing. I promised his wife I'd try to help find him," Kyra said.

Frank's eyebrows crashed down in a scowl. "Same time I last saw Andrew Mackey alive. Day before yesterday. We worked out the new salvage plan at the council offices in Tisbury, then handled the details over email and phone calls." Frank pulled out his phone and tapped on the screen. "This was the last communication from him." He handed her his phone.

A text from Joe to Frank: *Andy is planning to vote against. I'll talk to him.*

Joe had sent it just before seven the night Andy was killed. She passed the phone to Tarek, who returned it to Frank after reading the exchange.

"I don't get it." Chase leaned forward, his elbows on his knees. "Even if Andy was going to object, if Ida, the environmentalists, and the islanders were on board with the new plan, the vote would have passed. They didn't need either of the Mackeys' votes. So why would Joe kill him?" He paused, thinking. He grabbed another handful of cheese puffs. "Unless it wasn't about the vote? In which case, what is it about? The wife? Some sort of message?"

A message. A display. A piece of the puzzle fell into place. Andy Mackey's death was meant to send a message. She just didn't know what it was or who it was intended for.

"Well," Frank hedged, and everyone looked at him. "Yeah, *most* of the environmentalists agreed to the concessions, but the Oceanic Conservation was still making noise. About some bird. They're claiming that the salvage in October, during hurricane season, is going to impact the bird's preferred hunting and migrating schedule." Frank made an annoyed huffing sound. "We can't do the summer because of the fishermen. We can't do the spring when the fish run, and the birds migrate. The winter has its own set of issues for marine salvage, and now this guy is going on about two birds." Frank rubbed his jaw. "It's not even a rare or endangered bird. There are millions of 'em up in Canada."

"Did Rachel confirm that the Oceanic Conservation dropped their claims?" Kyra asked Tarek.

"Mmhhmm." He nodded, turning toward her. "I called her after I got your text. She was already at Logan, waiting for her connection. She said she'd sent over her approval on the press release congratulating the council on a well-developed conservationist approach to the salvage. The OC had dropped their objections. The vote now is really just a formality."

"No, that can't be right." Frank pulled his phone out. "I got an email from them this morning saying they were going to file a lawsuit unless we agreed to postpone." Frank studied his screen, his forehead creased. "Yeah, right here. Dr. Seth Hammond signed it."

Kyra frowned and took the phone from Frank. She read the email.

"Why don't they think *you* did it?" Chase asked, tossing a cheese puff up and catching it in his mouth.

Frank glared at Chase. "I didn't kill anybody, if that's what you're asking," Frank snapped. "I'm surprised you, of all people, would make false accusations."

"I didn't accuse you. I just asked why you're not a suspect." Chase shrugged.

"Security cameras. The police checked them. I was in the bar at the Lady Slipper with Terry, and then I went up to my room." Frank held out his hand for his phone, his mouth twisted into a grimace. He stood up. "Is that all?"

Kyra handed it to him. "Yes, thank you."

Tarek stood and reached over to shake Frank's hand. "Thank you, Frank. If you think of anything, let us know."

"I'll show you out." Gully lumbered to his feet.

Before exiting the kitchen, Frank turned around. "There is one more thing," he said, sliding his hands into his pockets. "The police told me not to say anything. Keep it out of the press. But fuck them, right?" He glanced at Gully. "Whoever was on the rig tossed the bridge. Tore it to pieces. There isn't much to steal. Most of it's bolted down. But I keep a pistol and some ammo with the emergency supplies. It's gone." Frank nodded to Kyra and followed Gully to the door.

Gone?

Kyra's fingers drummed the coffee table. Whoever stole the gun must have found it after killing Andy. *Shooting someone is easier than stabbing them with a harpoon. But then, what were they looking for?* She reached for a cookie from the plate on the table. She munched on it, barely tasting its sweetness. Chase was right. It didn't make sense for Joe to have killed his brother, if this was about the salvage. If it was about Lisa, why kill him on Frank's boat? *No, this has to be about the* Keres. Kyra's eyes landed on Gully just as he reentered the room. Fear slicked down her spine. *If this is a scheme to sabotage the salvage efforts, the next logical victim would be Gully.*

Chase spoke, "Well, that was *enlightening.*" He huffed and tore open another bag of chips, emptying it into the bowl.

"Detective?" Officer Evans appeared in the doorway on the other side of the room. He shifted on his feet. He was gripping his cellphone in one hand. His other hand was raised like he'd forgotten to put it down. "That was Chief Erikson. Gully needs to turn himself in. Now."

Chapter Twenty-Four

GULLY DIDN'T SAY a word. He just collapsed in on himself. It was the same expression she'd seen on Chase's face last spring. Despair.

Tarek dragged Gully into the bathroom to wash his face, change his shirt. All the while, he was on the phone. He called Gully's lawyer, demanding he meet them, then Terry Rose, and finally, to her surprise, a woman that might have been Gully's mother. Tarek's voice had gone soft, the same tone he'd used with Lisa last night. He spoke in soothing tones, promising he'd take care of his friend.

Kyra was a helpless observer. In their rush, they didn't say goodbye. Kyra watched Tarek push Gully into his car and follow Officer Evans down the drive and off the farm.

When she returned, Chase was back on the couch, his head back, eyes closed.

"Chase?" His head snapped up, and he blinked. Again. "Are you okay?" Chase didn't respond, and that said volumes. Kyra took a seat next to him and his hand grasped hers.

"Jimmy texted."

"And?"

"No one saw Joe's truck on any of the late night or early

morning ferries." *Shit.* Kyra slumped back in her seat. "But one of the guys who works at the filling station said he saw it parked in the Menemsha lot. He noticed it when he took a smoke break around eight p.m., and it was still there when he locked up at midnight. Frank's rig was docked next to the station." Chase's chin dipped down so they were eye level. "Joe was there."

"Is the car still there?" Chase shook his head. "Has Jimmy told anyone else?"

"No one else has asked him, but if they do, he can't keep a secret."

Kyra thought that over. "Do you know what happens to Gully next?"

"You don't?" He raised an eyebrow.

She shook her head and gave him a sheepish shrug. "Not that kind of lawyer."

"They'll go to the station first, for processing. Then to the courthouse in Edgartown," Chase said. "Once he's been charged, there will be a statement." Chase let her hand go and pushed his hair off his forehead. "Kay," he said in a serious tone. "The sooner Gully can present evidence the police are targeting the wrong guy, the better. Once he's been charged, and the press has the story, it'll be more difficult. The DA doesn't like to back down in high-profile cases, and a false arrest will make Erikson look like an idiot. They'll push this to save face."

Kyra knew he was speaking from experience. "We don't have any evidence, Chase."

Chase made a frustrated noise and sat back.

"Except..." Kyra swallowed.

"Except what?"

She stared at the coffee table. "What about Dr. Hammond?" Chase frowned. "The environmentalist. Gerry's friend took him out to photograph the Rose boat that afternoon. The boat captain said he didn't see anything unusual. But what if Hammond caught something on his camera? They were out there when we were all at Gully's pub. He could have seen someone or something that would lead us to who sabotaged the equipment." Kyra broke eye contact. "I think it's worth at least trying. I can't sit here and do nothing." She stared at her hands knotted together in her lap. She felt Chase watching her.

"Okay." He stood up and hauled her up beside him. "Let's find this Dr. Hammond."

Chapter Twenty-Five

"I'M REALLY SORRY, Mr. Hawthorn. It's against hotel policy for me to share information about our guests." The woman behind the reception desk at the Lady Slipper Inn batted her thick eyelashes at Chase.

"It's okay." His eyes flicked to her name tag. "Emma. I understand. I was hoping to catch him and his colleague Ms. Collins before they checked out. We're big supporters of the work they do, you know." Without saying it, his words were heavy with the implication of political ties. Chase leaned forward to whisper in Emma's ear, his eyes half closed. She let out a breathy giggle and started typing on the keyboard. Kyra gritted her teeth to keep from rolling her eyes.

"Mr. Haw—Chase," Emma tittered.

Kyra scoffed. Chase gently stepped on her toe, a warning.

"Ms. Collins checked out already, but Dr. Hammond has extended his stay. I can try his room for you?"

"I'd *appreciate* that, Emma." He gave her his hundred-watt smile. Kyra almost felt bad for the girl. Emma dialed the room and waited on the line as it rang through. After six rings, she hung up.

"I'm afraid he's not answering, but you can leave a message for him. Did you want to leave your number?" Emma's eyes grew hungry.

"Wonderful, thank you, *Emma*. We'll leave him mine." Kyra wrote her phone number and passed it over the desk.

Emma's expression darkened; her pouty lips pulled down.

She turned back to Chase, placing a hand on his arm. "I really shouldn't do this, but Dr. Hammond was here about an hour ago. He was asking about parking at Aquinnah to see the cliffs at Gay Head."

"He did?" Chase stepped back and turned to Kyra. "Do we want to try him there?"

Kyra nodded. "Thanks, Emma!" she said with a wave, unable to hide her mocking tone.

Chase yelled a hasty, yet more sincere, thanks over his shoulder as he followed her out the door.

Once Chase was behind the wheel of his Bronco, Kyra gave him a wry grin.

"What?" Chase demanded, scowling.

"What did you say to her?"

"I said that the color of her blouse brought out her eyes." Kyra's mouth dropped open. What took her aback was that he meant it. *Bollocks, that's sweet.* Another little piece of Chase revealed itself. *He sees people how they want to be seen.*

"It worked, didn't it?" Chase raised an eyebrow in a challenge.

"It did, indeed."

Chase pulled out onto North Road. "Maybe a little too well." His lips pulled to the side in an exaggerated grimace. "Thanks for leaving your number."

"Any time." That poor girl was probably already half in love with him.

The weather had kept most of the tourists at home and the streets were empty as they climbed the curving road up to Aquinnah. The rain had stopped, but the wind had picked up and it howled around the Bronco. They pulled into a parking spot below the Gay Head lighthouse, next to the only other car in the lot, a battered Prius with rental plates. Chase turned the car off and ducked down to peer up at the sky through the windshield. Clouds swirled, illuminated from behind by a sun fighting to come out.

"Do you think this is a good idea?" he asked.

"Probably not." Her answer made Chase grin. "We're only asking if he saw anything while on the charter. I'm sure it'll be fine."

She sounded more confident than she felt. A thin band of apprehension tightened around her chest. They should have waited for Tarek, but who knew when he'd be available with Gully at the station.

Steeling her resolve, Kyra reached for the door handle. "We'll take a quick look around, and, if we can't find him, we can wait for him at the inn. I'm sure Emma wouldn't mind."

Chase leveled her with a look and she laughed.

Kyra stepped out of the car. Wind whipped her hair back and goosebumps erupted over her bare skin.

"Here, take this." Chase handed her a semi-clean windbreaker and pulled a long sleeve T-shirt over his head.

Kyra slipped her arms into the jacket. The nylon clung to her skin. "Any idea where he'd be?" she asked, looking around the empty preserve while she rolled up the too-long sleeves.

"Probably down by the cliffs?" He pointed past the cylindrical brick structure.

They made their way past the lighthouse and around the original foundation. The landscape sloped down a steep hill before the cliff's edge.

"Probably that way." Chase pointed to an overgrown but discernible path; the entrance barred with a single chain.

"Are we allowed to walk on these trails?" Kyra whispered.

"They're not open to the public, but maybe he doesn't count?" Chase stage whispered back.

"And us?"

"I won't tell if you don't." Chase held the chain up so she could crouch underneath. "I've always wanted to hike these cliffs and see the mud pools. But they were closed before I was born." Chase eyed the gray skies. "Probably would have chosen a nicer day, though."

Kyra didn't disagree.

She followed Chase down the path, much steeper than it looked from the top. It wove down the side of the cliff, just wide enough to walk single file. Kyra strained her neck to peer over the edge without getting too close. It was a drop to the rocky beach below. The cliffs weren't too high. Falling probably wouldn't kill her. Landing though, on the rocks or in the surf … that might. She stepped closer to the crumbly clay wall behind her.

Chase reached for her hand to help her over a fallen branch. She was glad she'd had the foresight to wear sneakers, but wished she'd worn pants. The bramble and reeds scratched her legs, leaving angry red marks on her shins and calves.

"That must be him." Chase pointed.

Below them, about a third of the way down, a man with

a safari hat and camera equipment was squatting in the brush off the path. Kyra inhaled to call down, but Chase shushed her and pointed. About two yards from her sneaker, camouflaged by its coloring, sat a small mottled brown bird.

"Is that the storm bird?" she whispered.

Chase gave her a look. "It's *a* bird," he deadpanned. "Come on."

The path hadn't been maintained, and the climb down was hazardous. The morning's rain had only made it worse.

"I think he's just around there." Chase pointed.

The path twisted around a tree and disappeared. Using the tree to help her balance, Kyra stepped around it and found herself on the cliff edge, a sheer drop to the beach below. Her heart leaped. Chase yanked her back by her jacket. With a garbled cry her hands flew to the neckline to keep it from choking her.

She coughed.

"Fucking hell. No wonder they closed these trails. Stay to the inside and in front of me. Be careful." Chase needn't have told her.

Puddles had formed in the center of the path, and Kyra tried to keep to the inside, taking care with each step. She stepped over a branch, and her sneaker slid in the wet clay, throwing off her balance. Her scream was cut off when she was hauled back by her arm, right before she dove off the edge.

"Shit. Are you okay?" Chase asked, his eyes sweeping her.

"I … ah … yes. Thank you." She pried her fingers from his forearms and swallowed back the pressure in her chest. *I could have gone over.* She took a few deep breaths and rolled her shoulder back, the old injury twinging. "This was a fucking terrible idea."

Chase raised his eyebrows. "You think?"

They continued along the cliff edge, his hand gripping hers almost painfully. At another hairpin turn, Chase pushed her forward, his hand on her waist. "I'm right behind you."

"Where is he?" Kyra couldn't see over the scrub pine.

"Right there, about forty more feet. He's squatting. Next to that bush." It took ten more minutes to climb down. Kyra could feel the mud caked on the backs of her legs.

"Dr. Hammond?" she called out, raising her voice to fight the wind.

The man stood up, his hat flapping. He pushed it off his head, and it swayed from the string around his neck. He spotted them, and his brows knitted together.

"Yes?" He wiped his glasses on his shirt. "Can I help you?"

Kyra stumbled down the hill closer to him.

"Kyra," Chase murmured.

"Oh, yes. We're sorry to disturb you. The hotel said we could find you here."

Seth Hammond took a step back, taking them in. He glanced at Chase, and something flickered behind his eyes. "Who are you?" he asked, his tone suspicious. "Are you reporters?"

"No, not at all. We're, uh, we're supporters." Kyra pointed at herself and Chase.

Chase's eyebrows flew up, but he recovered quickly and schooled his expression, turning on the charm.

"Oh." Hammond held a camera in one hand and cradled the large telephoto lens with the other.

"I'm Kyra, and this is my friend…"

"Chase." He raised his hand in a wave. His other hand tugged her back a step by her belt loop.

"Pleasure to meet you. We're big supporters of what you're doing." Chase gestured to the cliffs and sucked on his bottom lip. "Uh … here."

Kyra glared at him.

Hammond frowned.

"So, Dr. Hammond, Chase and I, we … we're working with some members of the island community who are…" *I really should have thought up a story before rushing down here.* She cursed under her breath and met Chase's eyes, a silent plea to help her.

He huffed his annoyance. "What my esteemed colleague is trying to say, Doctor, is we're with a group of concerned citizens who aren't convinced the marine salvage efforts on the Devil's Bridge by those mainlanders were properly scoped. And we wanted to hear your opinion. The concierge at your hotel said you were here doing some research, and as *concerned citizens*, we thought we'd come by to speak to you ourselves. I hope we're not disturbing you."

Kyra gaped at him. *Really?* Chase just barely lifted one shoulder in response.

Hammond frowned and shook his head. He scuffed his boot in the sand. "I was under the impression that the island's population blindly followed that Ida Ames woman." Dr. Hammond's lips turned down in a sneer.

"Ms. Ames has her supporters," Chase said. "And detractors."

"You live on the island, then?" Dr. Hammond asked.

"Yes, I have a house in Edgartown, and Chase runs a farm near here."

"Which one?"

"Mander Lane. It's a family business."

"Senator Hawthorn's farm?" Hammond's eyes gleamed. "You're that Chase, then? Chase Hawthorn."

"The same."

Kyra didn't like the way Hammond looked at Chase. It was predatory. The hairs on the back of her neck rose. *We should leave.*

"I've been trying to arrange a meeting with the senator since I arrived."

"I'm afraid my parents are remaining in Washington this summer, but as you can imagine, we are very interested in the island's conservation efforts." Chase shifted behind her.

"And you're interested in the petrels?"

"Yes." Kyra said, figuring it was the answer Hammond was looking for. She nodded to his camera. "Were you able to photograph them?"

"Not yet." He held up his camera. "They're nocturnal, except during storms, when they fly. I thought I could get some images, but it doesn't look like it's going to storm today." He pressed his thin lips together. "Their other name is storm riders. They're very rare. One hasn't been seen on Cape Cod in decades, but now we have a nesting pair."

"We heard. Very exciting. Your colleague said their return was because of the successful conservation efforts," Kyra said.

Hammond's expression darkened, and he refocused on Chase. Kyra resisted the urge to step in front of him, to shield him from view.

"That's why I've filed the lawsuit to halt the salvage efforts." Hammond squatted back down. He pulled a camera bag out from underneath a bush. "They're most active in the fall, you know, during hurricane season. They need to hunt before their southern migration." His words were measured and calm as he unclasped the camera lens and covered his camera, packing away his equipment. "The salvage could scare them. Keep them from hunting. They won't have the energy reserves for the migration. Or worse, scare them from leaving entirely and they'll die over the winter." He raised a fist to his mouth. "It's unacceptable to interfere with their migratory patterns. And I haven't even mentioned the impact to the seabed in the ravine and the shoal." He finished packing his bag and stood up. "The sediment being disrupted could kill the algae and other plants that sustain the fragile ecosystem." Hammond spoke fast. The words tumbling from his lips. He breathed in through his teeth in a long hiss and fixed his gaze on Chase. "With the backing of Senator Hawthorn, the judge would be a fool not to grant my injunction. I can count on your father's support?"

"Sure." Chase raised a shoulder in a halfhearted shrug. "I've got a call with my father tonight. I'll mention it, and he'll take it up with the judge. In return, though, I was hoping you could help me." Hammond's jaw set and he waited for Chase to continue. "You chartered a boat to see the salvage rigs a few times. Did you see anything unusual?"

"Unusual? Like what?"

"The first time you took the charter out—the afternoon before the accident when the divers drowned—did you happen to see anyone or anything in Menemsha that seemed out of place? See someone on the Rose Marine ship that afternoon?"

Hammond frowned. Then he nodded. "Yeah, I did. I

saw that local man. The one with the beard from the council meeting. The one obsessed with pirate treasure."

Kyra froze. *That's impossible. Gully was with us at the pub.* Chase's fist at her waist band tightened.

"I saw him in a motorboat, in the harbor. Near the Rose Marine boat. I didn't think anything of it, but he could have been coming from the Rose ship. Probably caught him right after he disabled the poppet valves."

Chase stiffened behind her.

The poppet valves? Tarek said the police were not releasing how the equipment was sabotaged. How would Hammond know?

It was so specific. Her brain slid the pieces into place. Hammond on her flight. Hammond's diving magazine. Hammond in Menemsha while Matty Gray and Jaycee were at Gully's pub. Hammond, who opposed the salvage efforts. Hammond meeting with the salvagers and the Mackeys.

Shit. Her heart banged against her sternum and her body broke out in a cold sweat. *We have to get out of here.*

"Chase," she whispered, taking a step back to stand beside him. She suppressed the urge to look at the path up. *How long will it take to climb back up? Get help?* Aquinnah was far from everything.

"Ah, yes. Good. That's all we wanted to know." Chase's voice was strained. He took a step backward, tugging Kyra with him. "We won't keep you from your storm birds any longer, Doctor."

Hammond grimaced. His eyes flashed behind his glasses. "Well, shit."

"Chase," Kyra croaked, but Chase didn't respond. He'd gone utterly still.

Chapter Twenty-Six

IT WAS LIKE her consciousness left her body. From above, almost in slow motion, she saw herself turning to face Seth Hammond, seeing the black barrel of the gun pointed at them. No, pointed at Chase. She blinked and shuddered as her perspective collided with reality, her vision tunneling in on Hammond's sneer as it deepened and twisted into something terrible.

"I didn't plan for this, but it couldn't have worked out better." He unlatched the safety with a click that sent a jolt of electricity through her. "The body of a senator's son will send a much louder message than some local fishermen. A message that can't be ignored this time."

Kyra's ears roared. Her brain was scrambling to process what her eyes were seeing.

"You give me too much credit. No one will care. I'm not exactly respectable," Chase said, sounding bored.

Hammond's forehead creased, and his hand lowered a fraction.

Chase's fingers spasmed at her back. Then she was airborne, propelled to the side. She fell. Kyra screamed as she slid down the cliff face.

"Run!" A broken scream.

Kyra tried to scramble to her feet, but she couldn't find purchase in the wet clay and bramble. She slid further, grasping at the bushes, roots. Anything.

Her hip slammed into a rock, and the air flew from her lungs. She lay there for a moment, stunned.

"Fucking *run!*" Chase screamed again.

He crashed through the brush above her. She tried to stand. Then she heard it. Three sharp claps. Like stone hitting stone. She flattened back to the ground. Chase slammed down, covering her body with his.

"Are you hurt?" But he didn't wait for her answer. He hauled her to her feet. His hand gripped her wrist and Chase dragged her down the cliff.

Down, down, down. Chase pulled her. They didn't bother with the path, they slid down the banks, only staying on their feet by pure luck and Chase's will. Someone screamed from above and Kyra's heart nearly stopped. She prayed Seth Hammond hadn't come across someone else. Chase yanked her forward, momentum holding her up when she tripped.

"Don't stop!"

They broke out onto a familiar secluded beach and Kyra fell to her knees. Her breath came in short, wheezing gasps. Her hands and knees sank in the saturated sand. *Wait.* She looked up. Lost Beach was nearly gone. Covered by the rising tide.

"The caves! Come on." Chase wrenched her up. They sprinted toward the sea caves, running in the water to hide their footprints. Kyra stumbled after him into the second cave opening.

Inside, the floors were wet with sludgy sand and pools of stagnant water. She slipped and her hand gripped the wall covered in kelpy grime. She remembered what Tarek had said about the tides at Lost Beach.

"Are you hurt?" Chase wheezed. He was doubled over, his hands on his knees. He sucked in a few breaths, then looked up and scanned her body for injuries.

She shook her head. Her brain still reeling. *He shot at us. He. Shot. At. Us.*

"You?" she asked, her voice shaking.

He shook his head.

"Chase, we can't stay here."

"We can't go back out there." He spoke between attempts to catch his breath. "The tide is coming in. We can't go up. There's a lunatic up there." Chase spat at the ground. He ran his hands through his hair and yanked his phone from his pocket. "Do you have yours? We need to call the Coast Guard. Tarek. The police. Fuck. Anyone."

There was a splash.

"Shit," Chase wheezed. "Go! Further back. Now!"

They slinked back into the caves. Kyra ran her hand along the wall. The sand floor turned to wet clay. The mud sucked at the soles of her shoes, releasing them with soft *spluts*. She prayed their steps couldn't be heard over the waves. The further they moved from the entrance, the darker it became. Shadows crept closer and closer, pushing in on all sides. The tunnel veered sharply to the left, dumping them into total darkness. Chase swore and turned on his cellphone flashlight. He shined it around the space.

"Try Tarek," he whispered.

With shaking fingers, Kyra dialed. Chase motioned for her to follow deeper into the caves. The call went to voicemail. She tried again. He answered on the third ring.

"Hello?"

"Tarek. We're in trouble. Seth Hammond chased us into the sea caves at Lost Beach." She was babbling. "He has a gun. He killed Jaycee and Matty Gray. Andy Mackey, too. He's following us."

"What?" Tarek's voice was thick, confused.

Kyra sucked in a breath to say it all again, slower, calmer, needing him to understand her. But his voice came over the line, muffled, but harsh, like he was snapping at someone. Then rustling. She pressed the phone closer to her ear.

"This is Sergeant Hernandez with the Menemsha Police Department." A gruff voice took over the call. "You need to get above the tide line. Some of the tunnels go up. Look for the high ground."

Kyra heard someone in the background. Tarek.

"Do not try to swim for the beach." Kyra glanced up at Chase. *Had he heard?*

His lips were pressed together in a thin, tight line, his jaw clenched. He nodded.

"Mr. Haw-thorn! Come on out. We can discuss this. I'm not going to hurt you or your treasure hunter friend. This is all just a misunderstanding."

Chase's eyes widened in the dim light of his cellphone. He put a finger to his lips. He flipped off the light and grabbed her hand. Kyra ended the call and slipped her phone back into her pocket. She molded her back against the slimy wall.

BANG! The shot echoed in the cavern. Kyra ducked and threw her arms over her head.

"Move!" Chase pulled her into the dark.

Chase led them further into the depths of the cave. He walked fast, one hand gripping hers. It was so dark Kyra couldn't see him in front of her. She kept stumbling over the uneven ground.

Chase tripped and Kyra went sprawling to the muddy floor, her hand slipped from his. She pushed herself up into a sitting position. She could see nothing. Just black. Some rational part of her brain knew Chase was only a few feet away, but she couldn't see him. She couldn't see anything. *Alone.* Her brain seized in terror. Her heart banged in her ears, against her ribs and her breaths came in pants. *Calm down. Calm the fuck down.* Her hands moved to her lips. She mouthed the words against the pads of her fingers. Calm Down.

"Kyra." Chase's voice was a whisper, but in the emptiness, it blared.

"I'm here," she whispered back.

Chase's phone illuminated his face. She swallowed back a relieved whimper and scrambled to her feet.

"I'll keep the light on. Listen for Hammond." He swept the light around the space. They'd entered a sort of cavern, with low ceilings. The floor was covered in sludge and water. Chase's flashlight reflected off a pool. It pulsed. Kyra stilled. *Chase's torch is playing tricks.* The puddle moved again. The water was pulsating, overflowing the sides in gentle ripples.

"Fuck. We have to go back."

Chase didn't need to tell her what the pools were. Kyra

knew. Blowholes. Ready to fill the cavity with sea water when the tide came in. The evidence was on the walls. The ceiling. Seaweed caught in the ridges in the rock. She swallowed back a wave of nausea.

She followed Chase as they backtracked until he stopped. They were at a fork she hadn't noticed passing in the dark. He peered down each one, keeping the light's beam on the ground. "I think we came from that one." He pointed to the one on the left.

"Are you sure? How can you tell?"

His face was blank.

She could see the fear in his eyes. "Okay, we'll try that one." Each time they made a choice, they gambled with their lives. Eventually, they would run out of time to backtrack.

Chase led them into the tunnel. They walked in silence. She had her ears trained behind her, listening for boot steps on the clay, but then a thought crossed her mind. She let out a shaky breath.

"Chase, could he have come this way?"

Chase tilted his head to listen. He shook his head and raised a shoulder in a helpless gesture. *So yes.*

"Try Tarek again."

Kyra dialed. The call spun, trying to connect. CALL FAILED.

"No service. You?"

"No, not since we entered the caves. We keep going. Turn yours off. We need to conserve the battery."

Kyra held her breath while she shut her phone down. "We'll find a way out," she said, wincing at the shakiness in her voice.

Chase studied his watch. "High tide is in about ninety minutes. We keep going up for at least that long."

She took his hand, cold in her own, and gave it a squeeze. He squeezed it back and took a deep breath, like he was trying to steady himself before leading them deeper into the cave.

They walked in silence, stopping and listening at every fork. More than once, they chose a tunnel that appeared to go up, before sloping back down toward sea level, the roar of the ocean forcing them to go back. Each time, she held her breath, convinced Seth Hammond would be waiting for them when they emerged.

"Where is he?" she whispered when she couldn't contain it anymore.

"I don't know. He could have run back up the cliffs. If we drown in here, or get lost and die, we'd accomplish his goal. My parents, Margot anyway, would stop the salvage to find me. A dead son would do wonders for their approval rating."

"Chase." Kyra swallowed back a sob. Coming to see Hammond, not waiting for Tarek. This was all her fault. Her chest ached. He could die. Chase could die, because of her and her stupid impulsiveness. "I'm so, so sorry." She was so frightened for him, she barely had room to be afraid for herself.

Chase stopped short. He swung around, grabbing her shoulders. He stooped down so they were eye level. "No fucking way," he seethed.

Kyra froze.

His fingers bit into her shoulder blades. "You don't get

to do that. This isn't on you. This is on that zealot outside. You hear me?"

Before Kyra could respond, he crushed her against him. His heart beat strong and wild under her cheek, and she hugged him back. She gave herself permission to spiral until he released her.

When he did, he stepped back. His eyes burned into hers. "And we don't let that asshole win."

She steeled herself and nodded. "Okay. We find a way."

They trudged on and on. And on. It could have been minutes or hours. One step after the other. Despite the underground chill, sweat slicked down her spine. Chase's windbreaker clung to her clammy skin.

The incline was gradual. Kyra barely noticed when the mud hardened to dry clay. It wasn't until her breathing became labored that she realized they were climbing. That she wasn't slipping in mud, but loose sand on stone.

"Chase." Kyra tugged on his hand. "I think we're clear of the tide. Let me see your light." Chase passed his phone to her. She pointed it at the ground and the walls. There were no water lines. No dried seaweed clinging to the granite. Chase pressed his hand against the cavern wall.

"It's dry." Chase's eyes lit up; his cracked lips moved in a ghost of a relieved smile. "Come on, let's keep going."

"Would it be better to stay here? Try to make our way down during low tide?" The relief of knowing they wouldn't drown had been too short lived. *Can we even find our way back to the beach?* No, she wouldn't let herself think that.

"I think it's better to keep going. We don't know what's behind us." He didn't give her time to consider. He reached for her hand.

The tunnels were unpredictable. Sometimes it rose in a steep incline and just as often it leveled out. It twisted and turned until Kyra lost all sense of direction. Even the heights of the caverns changed. Sometimes the ceiling dipped so low she had to crouch, her hand gripping the waistband of Chase's shorts so she wouldn't lose him in the darkness. Other times, it was just tall enough for her to stand. Chase had been in a near continuous stoop since entering the sea caves.

They wound their way deeper into the cliff-side underneath Aquinnah, away from the beach. The air became stale. The briny sulfurous smell of rotting sargassum was replaced by the scents of dust and decay. Death.

Even when the climbs leveled out, Kyra's breathing remained labored. Her lungs worked hard to pull oxygen from air that hadn't been fresh in eons. She stopped walking and pressed a hand to the cavern wall. Her breaths came in gasps. *How long have we been down here?* It couldn't have been very long, but it felt like hours or days. They were lost.

"Chase." It came out like a wheeze.

He stopped and turned around, his light bouncing off the gray stone and then on her face. She recoiled, her dark-acclimated eyes overreacting.

He slid down to the ground. A soft sigh escaped his lips as his spine finally straightened. Chase reached for her hand and pulled her to sit beside him. "We'll rest."

"How are you okay?" Her head dropped to her knees.

"Believe me, I'm anything but okay." He made a dry, brittle sound. "I've had a lot of practice hiding how un-okay

I am, though." Even through the haze of adrenaline and panic, Chase kept up his forced good spirits.

She tucked herself against his side. She hated herself for how glad she was that he was with her. If she'd told him to stay home, he'd be safe right now. She'd probably be dead, or worse, stuck wandering these caves in the dark alone.

She hiccupped. "Chase."

"We're going to get out of here. We just need to keep going."

Kyra nodded and inhaled a shaky breath. She pulled away so she could see his face. "I am sorry."

"You can apologize later. Over drinks. And steaks. And lobster." They sat a few minutes more in the silence, only disturbed by their breathing. He nudged her with his shoulder. "Should we continue?"

"Yes, I'm ready, now." Kyra lurched to her feet as Chase did the same. They were both unsteady. His face twisted in discomfort as he forced himself back into a crouch. He shined the light down the tunnel. It held the shadows just at bay. He passed his hand back. She placed hers in his and she followed him into the gloom.

Chapter Twenty-Seven

CHASE PAUSED AT another fork. He shined the light down each tunnel. The left tunnel sloped down and curved away from the light. The right fork rose in a steep incline. He took long enough, studying each tunnel, shining his light back the way they'd come, that Kyra felt compelled to say something.

"We can split up. Each go for a few minutes, then turn back."

Chase slid his eyes to her and shook his head. "No. Together." He nodded toward the tunnel on the right. "This one," he said, but she caught the waver in his voice.

It was so steep Kyra's crouch became neutral. Pushing into the climb, Kyra focused on the ascent. Her sneakers slipped on the uneven ground, and she had to use both her hands to keep steady. Without the physical connection to Chase, her anxiety ratcheted up. She gritted her teeth, willed herself not to blink, to keep him in her sights. Her fingers trailed the rough-hewn walls, so different from the bottom of the cave system. The sharp ridges scratched the pads of her fingers and palms.

Chase stopped, and Kyra ran into him with an *oomph.* He stumbled a few steps and Kyra grabbed him. "What?

Why'd you stop?"

"Look." Chase shined the light around the tunnel. Although it wasn't a tunnel. It was a cavern, with ceilings high enough even Chase could stand upright. Chase stepped to the side and stretched to his full height, rolling his shoulders. Kyra stepped beside him, copying his movements. Her back pinched from the prolonged stoop.

"What is this place?"

"I don't know." Chase shined his light along the stone walls covered in even striations. "I think it's manmade, though." He ran a finger against the markings on the wall. Kyra looked closer. The walls were rough. The floor, too, was more uneven, jagged under her shoes. This wasn't eroded by the sea, or whatever dug out the cave system. It was created by something else. It was possible it had been carved or blasted.

"But why?"

"It could have been a cache. Or maybe the Wampanoag people used it? I don't know the stories."

Kyra's eyes followed the beam from Chase's phone. Old beer cans, cigarette butts, piles of garbage and cloth littered the floor, pushed against the walls. Plastic milk crates had been arranged in a circle around a rusty camping lantern sitting on the floor.

"It looks like someone else knew about this place. Kids probably." He toed a can that once held cheap beer. "Here, hold this for me." Chase handed her his phone and reached for the lantern. He turned the knobs and inspected the fuel chamber. "It's empty. No fuel or wick," he said, dropping it to the floor with a clang that reverberated through the room.

Kyra jumped, causing the light to ricochet around the space. "What's that?" Chase pointed and Kyra brought the light back.

She shined it over what she'd originally thought was more wall but was actually a stack of debris pushed up against it, kitty-corner to the room's only entrance.

Kyra crept closer. "It looks like a doorway behind there." Kyra poked at the pile, and it tottered.

"What is that stuff? Think there's another lantern? Something we can burn?" Chase asked.

Examining the pile, she poked it with her toe, and it jostled.

"Take this." She handed the light back to Chase. Kyra yanked the sleeves of her jacket over her hands and pushed the pile. It collapsed in a dusty heap, toppling to the floor.

Chase jumped back with a curse. Kyra coughed, put her sleeve over her nose and mouth. But there, hidden behind the rubbish, was an opening. Not high, Kyra had to stoop to enter.

"No, absolutely fucking not." Chase pulled her back. He pointed. "It's collapsed. We need to get out of here. It's not safe."

"I just want to see. I won't go in. Lend me the torch." She reached back and felt him slide his phone into her hand.

He was right. It had caved in. Just beyond the opening, the ground was littered with rubble. The sides were slopes of dirt and rock. It might have once been another room. It was hard to tell. She shined the light around the space. First the walls, then the ceiling, and then the back where the light diffused, swallowed by the dark. *It's deep.*

"It could be a tunnel," she breathed. "I can't see the back." She extended her hand, pointing the light into the blackness, and stepped forward into the cavern.

She was yanked back by her jacket, throwing her off balance. Her heel slid, and she fell to her ass with a *harrumph*. She looked up to see Chase glaring at her.

"Fucking hell, Kyra!" Chase snatched his phone from her hand. "Are you insane?"

Kyra's fingers landed on something smooth. *What? Did I slide on it?* It was a disk of some sort, cool to the touch, like metal. She held it up, but it was covered in grime.

"What's that?" he snapped. His breathing was too fast.

"Nothing." She stood and slid it into her pocket.

"We need to backtrack to that other tunnel." His words came short and clipped.

"Someone brought all this stuff here," she said and pointed to the milk crate circle. Chase's jaw ticked. "Do you think they brought them through the caves? From the beach?"

Chase's expression changed. *Rumors say the tunnels connect to the lighthouse.* Kyra's eyes slid to the collapsed cavern. *Is that the way out?*

Chase tracked where she looked. "Fuck no." Chase checked his phone and even in the dim light, Kyra saw his jaw clench. "We gotta move. We keep going up. That's what the policeman said, right?"

At the top, they'd walked past the original foundation. It'd been filled in. Even if they reached it, would they be able to get out?

"Yeah, keep going." Kyra bit into her bottom lip hard

enough to draw blood. Chase watched her, his features creased with worry.

Kyra let Chase lead her back out of the cavern and through the tunnel. This time they took the left fork, the one that sloped down. The ceiling became lower and lower. The sides closed in on them, so Kyra had to walk directly behind Chase. She walked stooped low over her knees. Her back and thighs protested each step. She couldn't fathom how Chase could stand it. He was stooped so low his hands could touch the ground.

The light went out, pitching them into darkness. Kyra gasped and ran into him. She fell to her knees. She yelped at the impact. Then she froze. Blind. She gasped and reached for him. Her hands flailing.

"Kay!" he yelled, but his voice sounded so far away.

Empty.

"Chase! I'm here. I'm here," she wheezed.

Kyra had never experienced darkness like this. It closed in, suffocating her. She couldn't breathe. She was drowning.

Hands patted at her chest, her shoulders, her face. She bit back a scream. Hands gripped her jacket.

"The phone died." Chase's voice rang out in the dark. He pressed his forehead to hers and she gripped his arms.

She heard his breathing. Deep ragged inhales, slow exhales. Like they did during his panic attacks. He was trying to stay calm.

"We need yours." He pulled away.

Ever so slowly she released him. She reached back into her pocket, fumbling for her phone. She squeezed her eyes shut and pulled it out, gripping it tight with both hands. *If I drop it...* She didn't let herself finish the thought.

She turned it on, holding her breath while it booted up. The stillness in the air made her think Chase did the same. The phone blinked on and the dim light from the home screen hurt her eyes in the black. Her breath came gushing out, and she bit back a sob. She passed him the phone. Chase turned on the flashlight.

"Kyra." His voice was barely a whisper. He grabbed her arm so tight she winced. "Kay, you have service!" His fingers shook as he typed in her passcode and called Tarek.

"Kyra!" Tarek answered on one ring.

"It's Chase."

"Is she with you? Is she okay? Where are you?" Then an afterthought, "Are you okay?"

"We're still in the caves. I don't know where." Kyra heard Tarek curse. "Tar, listen. We're trying to find the lighthouse access tunnel."

"I'm on my way to Aquinnah. The Coast Guard is at Lost Beach, but they can't access the tunnels until the tide recedes. Keep going up. How much battery do you have on your phone?" Chase checked it, and he went white in the feeble light.

"Seventeen percent."

"Fuck," Tarek hissed. "Put it in battery saver mode. Don't call unless it's an emergency. I'm coming to you from the top." He hung up.

Chase just looked at Kyra.

She swallowed. "Lead the way."

Chase let out a long breath. He unfolded himself and climbed to his feet. Kyra gripped his waistband, her nails biting into her palm through the nylon.

They walked on. Kyra's ears filled with her labored breathing. In and out. In and out. The stale air clung to her insides.

Eventually, the floor leveled out, but the ceiling remained low. The tunnel weaved and curved. She could be walking into the bowels of hell itself and she wouldn't know.

Then she felt it. The change. The smooth granite floor was gone, replaced by rough striations under the thin soles of her shoes. Kyra put a tentative finger to the wall. Like that other room and the tunnel that led there, these walls seemed carved.

"Chase." She tugged on his waistband. "The walls."

He tried to turn around, but he was too wide crouched over in the narrow space. He fell to his knees with a grunt and ran his fingers along the floor. His eyes met hers.

"Like that room?"

"Manmade," he murmured to himself. "Come on." He stood, leading her onward, but he moved faster now.

The tunnel inclined, and Kyra swallowed back the relief that they were once again climbing. But the relief was short-lived. The ascent became uneven, crude steps hewn into the stone. The stairs were in a state of ruin, crumbling underfoot. They had to slow their pace to keep from falling. With a bite of fear, Kyra pulled her hand from Chase to use the wall to stabilize her climb.

They turned a corner and Chase stopped.

"What?" she asked, steadying herself against the wall. She looked past him. They were in another cavern, this one smaller and dirtier. Chase shined his flashlight all over the space, carefully surveying the walls and floors. Like the other room, the walls and floors were rough, evidence of being carved out of the stone. It was wet in here too. Kyra avoided a large puddle of water and stepped out from behind him.

"What is this place?" she asked. The darkness muffled her words. Swallowed them whole.

"There's no way out." His tone had changed, triggering her memory of when she'd met him last spring.

"Chase?"

He stepped back against the wall and slid down. He took a big breath and sighed it out. The light from the phone cast shadows across his face, darkening his normally bright eyes.

"Chase," she whispered again, sliding down beside him.

The floor was wet. Cold water seeped into the denim fabric of her shorts.

"We can't go back," he said and he showed her the phone. The battery signal was an angry red. Seven Percent. "I can't get us back." His head dropped back against the wall. "I'm sorry."

"It's not your fault. It's my fault. I should be sorry."

"You're not?" She detected the hint of humor in his voice.

"I'm sorry I didn't tell you not to come today. If I'd said no..."

"Don't be an idiot." Chase shifted his head, so it rested against hers. She scooted closer, and he wrapped his arm around her shoulder.

"I love you." She hadn't said those words to anyone but her aunt in years. It felt true and wasn't it a shame she was only saying them now, when they were probably going to die. The smile that played at her lips was grim.

"Love you." He gave her a gentle squeeze. "Kay, if we're not using the phone, we should turn it off."

"No." *The darkness.* Terror gripped her heart, and she couldn't breathe. "We can't."

"We need to conserve power."

"No!" She yanked herself away and fell into a puddle, water splashing up, soaking her shirt and shorts.

"Ugh." Chase grunted and scooted back.

But Kyra froze. She touched the water again. It was cool. She raised her wet fingers to her nose and sniffed.

"What are you doing?" he said in disgust. Even in the face of death, Chase was a prima donna.

"The water. It's not stale," she said. "It's fresh. It smells like…" She paused, inhaling it in again. *What does it smell like?* "It smells like nothing, not even dirt. Oh, my god." She jumped to her feet, looking about the room wildly. "Chase, the phone. Now." He handed it to her and scrambled up.

"What are you looking for?"

"It's rainwater." She shined the light up and down the walls. "There must be a leak. A big one. There's so much water here." She waved to the ground. Chase stumbled to where the light hit the wall and ran his hands along the stone.

"Shine the light on the ceiling."

Kyra moved the light above her and gasped. "Chase! Look."

Chase's eyes traveled to the ceiling. It wasn't rock, but wood.

The ceiling was wood. They were in a subbasement. Kyra's breath came fast and shallow. Her hands started shaking.

"We're in a cellar."

"Call Tarek."

Her fingers fumbled on the touchscreen.

"Kyra!" Tarek's voice crackled.

Chase yanked the phone from her hand. "Tar, I think we're underneath the old lighthouse foundation."

"Keep the phone on." The line went dead, and Chase grabbed Kyra's hand. He pulled her against the wall to wait. The phone's screen shut off, blanketing them in suffocating darkness.

Chase slid down to sit on the wet floor, and she followed. The wait was torture. Each moment an eternity.

She checked the phone. Five percent. She dropped her head to his shoulder and he wrapped his arm around her, tugging her closer.

They sat in darkness.

Three percent.

She couldn't see Chase, but felt his chest move with each inhale.

She wanted to check the phone, but if it had died, she'd fall apart.

Bang!

Kyra started. "Chase! Chase!" she screamed.

"I'm here," he said, his arm around her tightening. "What the fuck was that?"

Did Hammond find them?

The loud bang that had startled her came again, and she screamed. Chase threw his arms around her head as dirt and rubble showered down on them.

"Chase! Kyra!" a voice called from above.

"Tarek!" Chase was on his feet in a second and Kyra lost him in the dark. She froze.

"Chase, we're going to break open the floor. Stand against the wall." The voice sounded so far. Everything sounded so far.

"Kay, stay where you are," Chase commanded. "I'm coming to you." She heard him move. "Say something."

"Something," she said without thinking, her voice cracking.

Chase snorted a laugh and muttered something about a snarky bitch.

"Gah, careful!" she yelled when he trampled on her.

"How was I supposed to know you were there? I can't see shit! Give me your hand."

Kyra flailed until she hit something and grabbed.

Chase made a surprised choking sound and bit out, "Hand. My hand." His hand closed on her wrist. He pulled her up next to him and held her close.

"What's going on?" she asked in the darkness.

"No fucking idea." Before Chase could say anything more though another bang hit the ceiling followed by another. "Sledgehammers, I think."

Mortar, bits of wood and dirt rained down on them with every bang of the hammer. Then she heard a creaking noise. A snap and a crash. Chase covered her with his body, shielding her from whatever was happening above them. She took in a breath and started coughing. Her ears rang.

"Chase," she choked, but he couldn't respond between his own coughs.

"Chase!" a voice called from above. Kyra tried to look beyond him, and she flinched from the brightness streaming in.

"Down here!" Chase yelled; his voice hoarse.

"The fire department is coming down! Stand back!"

Kyra blinked through tears as three men lowered down through the hole in the ceiling. Their headlamps illuminated the room. The first man to land moved toward them, and the second lit an emergency lantern.

"Are you hurt?" he asked.

"No." Chase coughed.

"Ma'am?"

"No, I'm okay. I'm not hurt."

The fireman gave them a quick once over and nodded. "Stay here. We'll get you out." He moved to speak to the other firefighters and spoke into a communications device on his shoulder. "We're lowering a ladder. Can you climb it?"

"Yes," Chase said while Kyra nodded.

A ladder was lowered down from the ceiling.

"You go first. I'll be right behind you."

"Ma'am, do you need assistance?" When she shook her head, the fireman stood back and motioned for her to climb. Kyra grabbed the rungs and stepped onto the ladder. It was longer than she expected, but once her head crested over the edge, hands grabbed her, hauled her up. Suddenly she was in Tarek's arms.

"Are you hurt?" He pushed her back roughly, his hands digging into her biceps. His gaze roved over her face, her body. When she didn't answer right away, he ran his hands over her, searching for injuries.

"No, Tar, I'm fine." She covered his hands with hers, stilling them. He stopped, and their eyes met. His eyes were wide, crazed.

He looks terrified.

"We're fine," she repeated, her voice soft. "Thank you." He helped her to her feet and guided her out of the way, just as Chase came over the edge and collapsed on his back. His chest heaved, and he rubbed his eyes.

When Chase had caught his breath, convinced the paramedics and Tarek that he wasn't injured, Kyra asked, "What about Seth Hammond?"

Tarek shared a glance with another man. *Officer Evans.*

"No, Miss. Gibson. We found his rental car, but we haven't located him."

Chapter Twenty-Eight

KYRA AND CHASE sat in uncomfortable chairs in an interrogation room at the tiny Gay Head Police Station. The room hummed from the overworked air conditioner, and Kyra shivered. Her wet clothes clung to her, chafing her skin. Her legs were covered in bruises and scratches … and mud. Chase had lowered his head to rest on his crisscrossed arms. His eyes were closed. She knew he wasn't asleep, only by his intermittent huffs of annoyance.

The door creaked open, and Tarek stepped in, carrying three large takeaway coffees and bottles of water. "I thought you could use something to warm you up. And rehydrate."

"Thank you." She reached for the cup. It burned her icy fingers.

"I want whisky with mine," Chase mumbled, sitting up. He accepted the coffee and water with a nearly unintelligible, "Thanks."

"They're still looking for Hammond. They're searching the caves, but they'll have to give up soon. The tide will come back in."

Kyra did the math in her head. She and Chase had been lost for five hours. It had felt like days. Weeks.

Tarek spun his coffee cup on the stainless-steel table, his

lips pressed into a line. "They searched his car. You said he had the gun when he chased you, so I didn't expect them to find it." He shook his head. "But they did find a box of 9mm bullets, and a harpoon."

Chase made a sputtering noise. "A harpoon?"

"It's being sent for testing." Tarek sat back in his chair.

"But why would he keep it?" Chase asked.

"To dispose of later? Frame Joe? I don't know. I doubt he had thought through the killings." Tarek swallowed. "We found a set of keys matching the make and model of Joe's truck in Hammond's car. The truck was found hidden in the woods near Menemsha. Security footage at the Lady Slipper shows him exiting the building before the crimes were committed and re-entering shortly after wearing a blue and aqua striped jacket." *Mackey colors.* He took the water bottle from Kyra's hands and opened it for her. "My guess is he planned to take the truck to the mainland, dispose of the weapons, abandon the truck, return to the island, and go back to Michigan. The Coast Guard is searching the harbor for Joe's body now."

"What about Gully?" she asked.

"With your statements, the security footage, a DNA match for Andy Mackey on the harpoon, and Hammond's history of violence, Erikson has agreed to drop the charges against him."

"History of violence?" Chase repeated. "What history of violence?"

"He's a person of interest in an investigation in Miami after a protest turned violent last week. A man was stabbed. He's been in the hospital since. Doctors aren't confident he'll regain consciousness. I pulled Hammond's record. He has assault charges." Tarek sounded tired. He looked at Kyra and took her hand in his. "I should have listened to you. I was so obsessed with protecting Gully and his defense; I didn't try to solve this case. The Mackey brothers..." his voice trailed off.

"It's not your fault." But the regret in his eyes told her he thought it was.

The door to the interrogation room opened, and Officer Evans stepped inside. "Hello there, *Miss* Gibson. Mr. Hawthorn. I just got word. You're free to go."

"Evans can take you up to your car, Chase, or we can get it to your house."

Chase pushed back from the table. "Just take me home. I'll get the car tomorrow." He turned to Kyra and pressed a kiss to the crown of her head. "Text me when you're home. And shower. You stink." He nodded to Tarek. "Officer Evans, after you." He waved to the door and followed the officer out.

"Tosser," she muttered, after he left. He was right, though. She could feel the grimy stench on her skin.

"I'll take you home." Tarek pushed back from the table. Kyra stood and pulled Chase's ruined jacket tighter around her shoulders. Something slipped from her pocket and fell to the floor. She bent down to pick it up. The metal disk she'd picked up in the cavern. "What's that?" Tarek stepped closer.

"I'm not sure." Kyra's fingers ran over the corroded metal. She poured some water on it and used the hem of her jacket to clean it, removing some of the dirt to uncover oxidized brass. "There's an engraving." She scrubbed harder.

"Helena Roberts," she read aloud and sucked in a breath.

Tarek reached for it. "Where'd you find this?" he asked, turning it over in his hands.

She told him about the room in the caves. "Do you think?" She left the rest of the question unvoiced.

"Maybe," he said, running his finger over the metal. "But that's a mystery for another day."

Epilogue

17 August 1712

A MAN STOOD on the beach watching the black schooner drift out to sea. Her sails hung limp and loose, and she lilted port-side, taking on water through the holes they'd cut in her hull. His heart twisted, the pain a reminder that he still held on to a remnant of his soul. His men were stacking trunks and crates into four longboats that would bear them into town under the cover of night. From there, he'd secure passage back to the Isle of Man for himself, his wife, and his son. *His wife and son.* William looked at her, his wife Helena, standing mere feet from him watching the *Keres* meet her fate. She gripped Liam's tiny hand in her own. William's first mate whispered in his ear. The native island people had agreed to help them make their way to town, for a price. They were shrewd negotiators. Too many of the trunks would remain behind, hidden in the caves.

He helped his family into the longboat. His crew prepared for launch. He looked to the south; the sky already dark with the coming storm. The *Keres* disappeared over the horizon, making her final sail to hell. The captain gave the order, and with a heave, the longboats shoved off the shore.

Fin.

Thank you for reading ***The Wraith's Return***. I hope you enjoyed summer on the island with Kyra and the gang. Next up is a Thanksgiving-themed thriller, ***Widow's Walk*** coming November 2024. ***The Wraith's Return*** was my second book and I'm still learning. I'd love to hear what you thought, what you liked, loved, or even hated. You can write to me at raemi.ray@gmail.com and find me on my website at www.raemiray.com. Finally, I've a giant-to-me favor to ask. Please consider leaving a review. Reviews positive and negative are how readers find writers. You have my deepest gratitude.

Until the next ferry over ~ Raemi.

If you enjoyed *The Wraith's Return*,
you'll love the other books in…

Martha's Vineyard Murders series

Book 1: *A Chain of Pearls*

Book 2: *The Wraith's Return*

Book 3: *Widow's Walk*

Available now at your favorite online retailer!

Acknowledgments

When I embarked on the journey to write a book in 2021, it was a lark. I had never expected it to go anywhere, and I especially never thought I'd one day be writing a series. Book Two in the Martha's Vineyard Murders series will always hold a special place in my heart. It made the experience real. I wasn't just a bookish girl, with a time-consuming hobby, but I was an author. That said, I could not have done this alone. An army of incredibly talented and supportive people held my hand every step of the way, and to each and every one of you, I owe my deepest gratitude.

To my ride or dies, the girls who stood by me, encouraged me, and never once made me feel bad for all the canceled plans, my hermit tendencies and crippling self-doubt, or the endless jabbering about my fictional characters. This book is as much your achievement as mine. Thank you.

To the supportive community at Tule Publishing. You are truly a family. A special thanks to Hannah, Heidi, Lee, Mia, and Monti for all your hard work on the book and its beautiful cover. And of course, no thanks would be complete without acknowledging my editor, Sinclair Sawhney who pushes my boundaries, forcing me to address my weaknesses to become a better writer and storyteller, and without whom this series would not exist. Thank you for believing in me. I can't wait to see where we go next.

About the Author

Raemi A. Ray is the author of the Martha's Vineyard Murders series. Her travels to the island and around the world inspire her stories. She lives with her family in Boston.

Thank you for reading

The Wraith's Return

If you enjoyed this book, you can find more from all our great authors at TulePublishing.com, or from your favorite online retailer.

Made in United States
Orlando, FL
25 August 2024